WIL

WHEN KAMBIA ELAINE FLEW IN FROM NEPTUNE

WHEN KAMBIA ELAINE

FLEW IN FROM NEPTUNE

Lori Aurelia Williams

Simon & Schuster

SIMON & SCHUSTER BOOKS FOR YOUNG READERS

An imprint of Simon & Schuster Children's Publishing Division

1230 Avenue of the Americas, New York, New York 10020

Copyright © 2000 by Lori Aurelia Williams

SIMON & SCHUSTER BOOKS FOR YOUNG READERS

is a trademark of Simon & Schuster.

Book design by Paul Zakris

The text for this book is set in 11.5-point Goudy.

Printed and bound in the United States of America

10 9 8 7 6 5 4 3 2 1

Library of Congress Catalog Card Number: 99-65154

ISBN 0-689-82468-8

FIRST
EDITION

This book is dedicated to my mother, who lived only long enough to catch a glimpse of the kind of woman that I was to become, and to my sister Lydia who has held my hand through many a storm.

Much appreciation goes to Laura Furman, a very special friend and mentor, and to Robert Tatum, who never lets me down.

Special thanks to the University of Texas Department of English and the James A. Michener Center for Writers.

WHEN KAMBIA ELAINE FLEW IN FROM NEPTUNE

Chapter 1

Mama and Tia got into a fight this morning. Mama found a package of red condoms in the back of Tia's drawer. Mama was really pissed off. She held the condoms up and shouted at Tia so loud the dead folks at Peaceful Rest Cemetery down the street could hear her.

"Tia, what are you doing with this mess?" Mama asked, slamming the drawer of the rickety dresser. She pressed her face real close to Tia's. You could barely see where Tia's began and hers ended. Tia didn't say nothing. She just stood there in her blue jeans miniskirt, with her slanted eyes blazing fire, and her hands on her hips.

"Did you hear me, girl?" Mama asked, looking like she was about to explode; the little veins in her forehead had popped out so far they looked like huge earthworms underneath her coffee skin.

"I'm waiting, girl," Mama said. "You tell me what this mess is for!"

"Ain't nothing to tell!" Tia yelled. She brushed past Mama with her black ponytail whipping behind her back, stomped over to our bed, and flopped down in the middle of the sagging mattress. Then she folded her arms across her chest and glared at Mama like Mama had stolen her favorite tube of lipstick. Mama rushed over to the bed and pointed a finger at Tia's face.

"Didn't I tell you to come to me about this, Tia?" Mama asked. "I always told you to come to me. You know damn well that we talked about this."

Tia rolled her eyes.

"Let me tell you something, little girl!" Mama yelled. "You just better keep your dress down and your drawers up. Don't you be bringing home no babies for me to feed. Do you understand me, little girl?" Tia crossed her legs and stared out of the window over the bookshelf, like she wasn't particularly interested in what Mama had to say. Mama drew her hand back like she was going to slap her, like she was going to knock her all the way back to the middle of June. And Mama could do it too. She was a big woman, strong and solid-built. She stocked groceries at Miller's One-Stop weeknights. She could send Tia flying across the room with just one lick. But she didn't. She just shoved the condoms into the pocket of her blue terry robe, shook her head, and stormed out of our room, dropping pink curlers out of her slick black hair as she hurried through the doorway. After Mama left, Tia got up from the bed and ran into the bathroom. I heard her turn the rusty door lock and break into sobs, as if she had actually caught a whipping.

I sat down in her place on the bed and listened to her cry. Guys had been sniffing around Tia since she was my age, twelve. Unlike me, she was sort of a looker. She wasn't really pretty. Her forehead was a bit high, and her lips were just a little too thin for her broad nose. Her face was average, with only a touch here and there to give it a spark, and her cheekbones were just a little high.

To be honest, it was really Tia's body that kept the guys coming around. Below, everything fell into place with a lot extra on top. It was the "on top" that made the boys act all stupid and stuff. Grandma Augustine had always said that she didn't think Tia would last more than three winter seasons past her first period. She said that Tia would hear her womanhood calling her with a vengeance, and she would answer long before Mama was ready for her to stop wearing bows in her hair and lace dresses. She said that there was no way to keep it from happening, because Mama had done the same thing at her age. Mama had gotten pregnant with Tia when she was only fifteen. "Mistakes made in the dark always come to the light through your children," Grandma Augustine said.

I wasn't sure if Grandma was right, but I was sure that Tia was hurting. I wanted to knock on the bathroom door and tell her that it was all right, but I couldn't. I was a reader and a writer, but not much of a talker, at least when it came to feelings and stuff. I got up from the bed, pulled open the top dresser drawer, and took out my blue notebook and a pen. *Everything's a mess,* I scrawled. *Anger is covering our house like pitch on a rooftop, and I'm gonna be late for school.*

After things finally died down at the house, I ate a quick breakfast of Froot Loops and ran three blocks to the bus stop. When I arrived, there was the new girl standing in the street next to the black-and-white bus sign. I had seen her once or twice from my bedroom window. She and her mother had moved next door to us a couple days ago. She was about my age, but she was thin where I was fat, and short in the places that I was long. She was lighter than me too, kinda butter-colored, like the shortbread cookies Mama cooked every Easter. Her hair was coarse like mine, but it wasn't black. It was reddish tan, and in the early morning sunlight it looked almost blond. Her eyes weren't brown, either. They were olive. She wore a dingy white dress that had two deep clip marks on the shoulders, as if she had just yanked it off of the clothesline. There wasn't any traffic on the narrow neighborhood street, but she was just standing there staring into the filthy rain gutter, staring into the blackness, as if she expected something to crawl out. I was curious, so I hopped off the curb and stared into the gutter too.

"Whatcha looking at?" I asked in a friendly voice. She just kept staring into the gutter, as if she didn't even know I was there. I hunched my shoulders. Maybe she hadn't heard me. It was windy out. A hot breeze was rustling through the tall pecan trees in the vacant lot behind the bus stop, and a Naughty By Nature tune was blaring from the open window of Perry's 24-and-7 beer joint across the street. The small aluminum-sided building was vibrating from the beat.

"Whatcha looking at?" I asked, even friendlier than the first time.

"My bracelet," the girl said in a soft voice. "My bracelet, it slipped off and fell down there." I leaned in closely and peered into the rectangular-shaped hole, but all I could make out in the darkness was a white plastic cup and some pages of a crumpled old newspaper.

"I don't see nothing," I said.

"It's in there," she said. "I gotta have it. We gotta get it out."

I wasn't really sure who she meant by "we." It wasn't *my* bracelet that was down there. I looked in the hole again. I thought I saw something moving around. *It's a rat,* I told myself, *a big, hairy rat with red eyes and yellow teeth.* There were plenty of them in the Bottom—big, shaggy monsters that lived in the walls of our tiny rent shacks, underneath our porches, and, of course, in the rain gutters that lined our littered streets. "I ain't sticking my hands down in there, girl. You must be crazy!" I yelled.

The girl didn't even look my way. She got down on all fours and shoved her thin hand into the drain. As she leaned into the hole her dress hiked up, exposing her underwear. Her yellow panties were shabby and ripped in several places. The elastic was loose and hanging halfway down her bony thighs. She was wearing worse than hand-me-downs. She was wearing worn-outs.

"Let me get your bracelet," I said. "My arms are longer than yours."

I got down on all fours and she stood up. I stuck my hand into the gutter and fished around in the trash until I felt something round. It had to be the bracelet. I pulled it out and stood up. It was plastic, transparent, and purple. You could buy a dozen like it for a buck in any dime store on Main in downtown Houston. I handed it to her with a scowl on my face. She snatched it and held it up to her breast, like it was a new dress or something.

"Thanks," she said, with a big grin. "I woulda been really upset if I couldn't of got it."

"It's just an old plastic bracelet," I snapped. "You can buy 'em for nothing downtown."

"No! You can't buy this anywhere. It's a magic bracelet," the girl said. "When I hold it up in the moonlight, I become so tiny that only the ants can see me. When the wind blows real hard, I blow away like dust until I find a wonderful, beautiful place to land." With that, the girl slipped the bracelet over her wrist and stepped up on the curb.

"I gotta go. I'm gonna be late for school," she said, fingering the bracelet and starting to walk off quickly.

"You go to my school, Martin Middle, don't you?" I asked.

"Yeah," she said. "But my mama didn't give me money to ride the bus."

"I'm Shayla. What's your name?" I called after her.

"Kambia," her voice trailed. "I'm Kambia."

I stood there in the street and watched her skinny body stepping lightly over the dirty sidewalks. There was something that bothered me about that girl and her silly magic bracelet. I just couldn't imagine anybody showing underwear like that for a ten-cent toy. It was way too weird. She was way too weird. I stepped up on the curb to wait for my bus.

For the past three weeks there had been nothing but rain, buckets of it pouring out of the gray sky, overflowing our gutters, and flooding our streets. But last night the rain stopped, and this morning the sun was shining bright over our houses, reclaiming its place among the clouds. It looked like it was gonna be a nice day. That is, until Mama got a visit from Miss Earlene Jackson.

Miss Earlene lives in a large two-story shack a few blocks up the street. She is a mean-spirited, sour-faced woman with pop eyes and a huge belly that hangs over her thin legs like an oversized water balloon. The children in the neighborhood call her Frog.

Frog came raging up our porch steps around noon. She had a look that would have turned the devil into a Christian, and she was throwing hell all over the place with each step. Mama stopped sweeping the living-room floor. She opened the screen door and stepped outside with her broom in her hand. I followed her out so that I could check out what was going on.

"Can I help you, Miss Earlene?" Mama asked, tugging the front of her flowered dress with her free hand. Mama had been doing housework all morning, and her dress was drenched with sweat and clinging to her huge frame.

"You sho can!" Frog yelled, throwing bits of spit in all directions. "You can tell that fast-tail mare of yours to stay away from my Doo-witty!"

"Excuse me?" Mama said. She opened her eyes real wide, like she didn't believe what Frog had said.

"You heard me!" Frog yelled. "You keep that little fast-tail mare of yours away from my Doo-witty!"

Mama's eyes narrowed.

"What fast-tail mare of mine is you talking about?" she asked. Her voice was real calm and controlled, but you could see just a hint of red pushing up through the ebony of her cheekbones.

"That little butt-wiggling, leg-spreading gal of yours, Tia, that's who I'm talking about," Frog spat. "You keep that little heifer from slipping 'round my house with my Doo-witty."

"With Doo-witty? With Doo-witty? With Doo-witty?" Mama repeated over and over, like she was in some kind of trance. Tia with Doo-witty, the thought of it made you want to throw up. Doo-witty, whose real name was Donald Dwight, was Frog's only son. He was twenty-three. He was a slow, drop-jawed, long-headed dope. When the boys in the neighborhood played The Dozens, they always said that he was so stupid that he was once fired from the M&M's factory for throwing away all the Ws. Tia with Doo-witty, it wasn't possible. Tia was fine, and she made great grades in school, like me. She could choose.

"Tia fooling with Doo-witty," Mama said. "What would my Tia want with Doo-witty? Doo-witty so stupid he had to repeat the eighth grade three times. He wouldn't even know when his own birthday is if you didn't bake him a cake. What would my baby be doing messing 'round with that thing?"

"Well, how do you explain this?" Frog yelled. She pulled a lacy beige bra out of her pocket and shook it in Mama's face. Mama's jaw nearly fell onto the front porch. On the right cup of the bra, embroidered in gold floss, were the letters *T. M.* Mama had been sewing our initials on our underwear ever since Tia started middle school. In gym it was common for other girls to swipe your undies. Hard times made some kids do the craziest things. I leaned against the porch column and shook my head.

"I guess you can believe your own eyes, cain't you?" Frog said with a smirk on her bloated face. "Ain't you gal named Tia Marie?"

Mama didn't answer. She just kept staring at the right cup of Tia's bra, like it was gonna do a dance or something.

"Now," Frog continued. "Like I said before, you keep that slut of a gal of yours away from my Doo-witty. I got plans for Doo-witty. It ain't too late for him. I been putting a little aside each week. Pretty soon I'm gone have enough to send Doo-witty to a decent college. I don't want no little gal throwing her legs over her head and messing up his chances."

Mama took a deep breath and let it out. Her eyes snapped away from Tia's bra and fixed on Frog. They were now just little slits in her face, and right in the middle of those slits you could see Mr. Anger jumping up and down in his red anger suit. Mama's hands started to tremble, then that tremble traveled on up her arms until her whole body was shaking.

"Ain't no college in they right mind gone let in Doo-witty," Mama said through clenched teeth. "And even if they did, the only thing that he could major in is Fool, and he already passed that course."

Mama lifted her broom up and pointed the handle at Frog.

"Now, I ain't no fighting woman," Mama said. "But if you don't get yo' frog-looking behind off my porch, I truly believe that I can make an exception in your case. You got two seconds to get outta my face, or I'm gone swat your fat ass with this broom, like you was a fly at a church picnic."

Frog got off our porch—and fast. She ran down the steps and rushed out of the wooden gate. She hit the pavement and sprinted off down the street with that big double-size belly jiggling left and right over her skinny legs. Mama ran down to the gate behind her.

"If I catch you or Doo-witty 'round my baby, I'm gone see what the law got to say about it!" Mama yelled. "Do you hear me? I better not catch you or that sorry-ass Doo-witty 'round my Tia." She watched from the gate until Frog disappeared between a row of beat-up old cars lined up in front of the red-brick project down the street; after that she came back up on the porch and swept Tia's bra into the pink rose bushes that were still growing wild on the side of the porch.

Mama sat down in the old wicker rocker beside the screen door and sighed. Her eyes looked heavy, like they were ready to drop tears. But Mama didn't cry. She always said that even from a little girl, she couldn't make water come to her eyes. So she just sat there rocking in the chair while she turned on the shower in her soul and let her tears run all over her insides. I walked over and took one of her hands in mine. While I ran my fingers over her rough skin, I made a note in my head to jot down in my blue notebook later: *Mama is all broken inside, and sorrow is hanging from our ceiling like icicles from Christmas trees.*

After a few moments Mama got up and went in the house. I didn't follow her this time. I knew what she was going to do. She was going to go into the kitchen and fix herself a pan of hot-water corn bread. Mama always fixed the bread when she was upset. She said that there was something about the sound of the cornmeal patties sizzling in the hot grease that calmed her nerves. She said that it was soothing, like listening to the blues or jazz. I decided to leave Mama to her comfort. Besides, I knew that after Mama's nerves calmed a bit she was going to go find Tia and drag her home.

Tia was at her best friend Maxi's house. Maxi was a short, dumpy, chatty girl who lived on Divine Street, three blocks away from Frog. Tia went to Maxi's house every Saturday morning to watch rap videos on the black cable channel. Mama was going to go snatch Tia away from Maxi's house as soon as she had eaten the last crumb of her bread. It wasn't gonna be pleasant in an hour or so. I could see 'em now, fussing and arguing down the street, putting on a real show. That was the way it always was with Mama and Tia. They were like lemonade and hot chocolate. They were good by themselves, but when you put them together all you got was one big mess. This was one fight I figured I could miss. I didn't want any of those sparks that were gonna be flying off of Mama to burn me up along with Tia. I hopped down from the porch.

"Mama, I'm going down the street a bit," I hollered as I strolled up the walkway.

"Don't go too far," Mama hollered back through the screen door. I went through the gate and banged it shut behind me. The neighborhood was in heat shock. It was almost ninety-eight degrees. Here and there a fuzzy-haired kid could be seen throwing a plastic ball against the concrete porch steps, or drawing his name on the sidewalk with buckets of neon-colored chalk, but that was the extent of the activities going on in front of the rows of paintless, run-down houses. Most people were inside sitting next to their window fans. As I passed by the open windows I could see tips of dark heads flashing between the twirling blades, and hear the soft whisper of voices floating over the whir of the fan motors. When it was this hot, it was common for most of the adults to stay inside until the cooler hours of the evening, with two exceptions:

Perry's 24-and-7 was hopping as usual. The stereo was blasting a Marvin Gaye tune, and groups of stylishly dressed, sweaty brothers and sisters were standing in the open double doors gossiping, their dark brown hands wrapped around open cans of Coors beer.

The other group of people out in mass were the women of the Tabernacle of the Blessed Redeemer. On the third Saturday of each month the women put their men out of the church and held a women-only cleansing revival. Arm in arm they filed by twos into the one-story, dome-shaped sanctuary, their shiny hair covered with satin scarves, their smooth black legs sticking out from underneath their knee-length ivory robes. Once inside the church, the ladies would sing spirituals until they felt the spirit hit them. Then they would hop up and dance down the aisles, shaking tambourines and chanting. When this was over, they would hear a sermon on the role of women in and out of the church by their leader, Sister Ashada, the tabernacle's female soul-saving minister. Finally, they would take part in the sprinkling ceremony, where they were sprinkled with sand from Jesus' footprints that was supposed to take away all their sins.

Mama had taken me and Tia there for a service once. It was right after my daddy, Mr. Anderson Fox, took off on her and moved in with another woman. Mama had just been laid off from her job at Walgreens. The bills were stacking up and the food was low. Mama said that we needed the hand of God to help us quick. Even though she wasn't especially religious, she took us to one of the cleansing revivals. She said that Grandma Augustine always told her that God liked a clean soul. When the spirit hit, Mama got up and danced in the aisles like the rest of the ladies, but Tia and I just sat there. The whole thing seemed really odd to me, and I wanted no part of it. I wasn't too big on church, and I hadn't yet made up my mind about how I felt about Grandma Augustine's God. But Tia really liked the revival and the friendly way that the ladies treated us and one another. She said that she would have gladly got up and danced too, if she hadn't had a runner in her panty hose.

Tia is very particular about her looks. It generally takes her more than an hour each morning to fix her face for school.

Since I didn't see any kids my age hanging out in front of the houses, I decided to head on down to the bayou, just a little ways from the house. It was a regular meeting place for the teenagers in my neighborhood. When there was nothing better to do, you could always find a few of them chillin' and knocking back a few sodas along the bank or listening to some tapes. That sounded great to me. Any place was better than home, at least for now.

The roar of the bayou hit me as I stepped through a prickly cluster of blackberry shrubs that guarded the entrance to the dirt path running along both sides of the bayou. The runoff from our streets had drained into the murky green waters, and they were much higher than normal. The current was moving swiftly, rippling and churning as it pushed forward downstream, splashing against the tall weeds growing on the side of the black dirt cliffs.

I walked over to the edge of the cliff, took a deep breath, and let it out. The bayou was the place where the people in the neighborhood dumped all the old stuff from their houses that they didn't want: broken furniture, old clothes, used-up toys, worn-out tires. Mama said that it was filled with little chunks of other people's lives, the parts of their lives that they wanted to forget. I leaned in and listened to the water carry those chunks away. It was peaceful, calming. The bayou was to me like hot-water corn bread was to Mama.

When I was through enjoying the sound of the water, I turned back and continued on up the path. It was nice and cool as I strolled underneath the tall trees that lined the right side of the path, their spacious branches stretching toward the warm blue sky like huge upside-down feather dusters. It was turning fall, and the pecan trees were loaded down with hard green pecans, while the spindly branches of the pine trees were thick with large, scaly cones. The once muddy ground had already started to dry up, etching deep lines into patches of the smooth gray soil, and I took my sandals off so that I could feel the tiny cracks with my bare feet.

I was a few yards up the path when I spotted something, no, someone, lying in the middle of it. I didn't have to get too close to know that it was Kambia. She was lying in the center of the path on her back with her legs together and her arms straight at her sides. I could see that she was wearing the same dingy dress. In fact, I had seen Kambia in that dress at least a half a dozen times.

Kambia and I had the same fourth-period biology class at school, that is, when she came to school. Since she moved here Kambia had missed more than half of the classes. She hardly ever showed up. When she did come, she said the craziest things, and the other children laughed at her. When Mrs. Feely, our teacher, asked Kambia where babies come from, Kambia said that they were born in morning glories. She said that they dropped out of the violet, dew-drenched flowers early in the morning when everyone was asleep and crawled to the homes of their new mothers. She said that sometimes the babies fell out of the morning glories before their time, and that they turned into a sweet-smelling mist and rose high up into the heavens. When it rained, it was God sprinkling the bodies of those babies all over the earth. The other kids all thought that it was the funniest thing they had ever heard. They laughed long and loud, until Mrs. Feely slammed her bio book down on the counter and told Kambia to go stand outside where she couldn't disrupt the rest of the class. Kambia didn't seem to mind at all. She just got up and calmly walked out.

After Kambia was gone, Mrs. Feely told us that she had never heard such foolishness in her life. She told us that we were there to learn science, not fantasize, and that there was no place for clowns in her room.

I hurried over to Kambia. To tell the truth, I was more curious than concerned. Mama had made me go over to her house a couple of times and knock on the door to see if she wanted to do some stuff, but she always came to the door and said no. Kambia's mom didn't let her come out on Saturdays or even after school. Her mother, a tall, light-skinned woman with red eyes and heavy ankles, didn't allow Kambia out much, unless she was sending her to the corner store for cigarettes or wine coolers. Allen's Pick-and-Carry would sell anything to anybody, no matter how young, as long as they had the cash.

I walked up to Kambia and stopped by her head.

"Are you all right?" I asked, looking down at her face. Her eyes were closed, but I could see the soft flutter of her eyeballs underneath the lids, as if she were dreaming.

"Are you all right?" I repeated. She didn't respond. I started to panic. I bent down and tugged her arm.

"Hey, are you okay?" I asked again. She opened her eyes and looked at me with a dreamy expression.

"I'm a piece of driftwood," she said. "I've just floated down from the Mississippi River and washed up here on the bank."

"You're a space cadet," I said, and dropped her arm.

"No. I'm an old, hollow piece of driftwood who has lived its time and come here to rot. I'll turn into rich fertilizer and nourish the earth, then years from now people will grow flowers or vegetables in me and I'll be reborn and made fresh."

"You're a crazo," I said. "I don't have time for baby games. I'm gonna go find some other kids to do something with. Besides, if you were a piece of driftwood, you would be in the water. That's what driftwood means, a piece of wood drifting on the water."

"I am a piece of driftwood," she whined, in a voice that sounded like my three-year-old cousin, Lisa.

"You're too babyish," I said. "I gotta go."

"I tell you I am a piece of driftwood," she repeated. "I just floated down from the Mississippi and washed up here on the bank," she said, pushing her small pink lips into a pout.

"There's no way a piece of driftwood could make it all the way here from Mississippi," I said. "I'm going." I started back up the path, but she grabbed my ankle. She scrambled to her feet and ran over to the edge of the water.

"I'll show you," she said, sitting down on the bank and throwing her skinny legs over the side. "I am a piece of driftwood. Watch how I float on top of the water."

I ran over to her. "Are you crazy or something, girl?" I asked. "That water is really deep. You can't float on it. You'll drown."

She took off one of her white sandals and flung it underneath a pecan tree. "Driftwood don't wear shoes," she said.

"Girl, you are really nuts!" I cried. "I don't want to play this game. I'm leaving." I turned around and walked a piece from the cliff, thinking that she would follow me, but she didn't. She started humming loud, a nursery rhyme, "Three Blind Mice." I turned around. She took off her other sandal and flung it in the direction of the first one. She started sliding on her butt through the thick weeds toward the water, moving up and down with her knees, like an inchworm or something.

"You're gonna drown," I said. "The water is too fast. You can't swim in it." She just kept sliding, sliding and humming, sliding and humming. I didn't know what to do. I ran over and tried to grab her arm, but she was outta my reach. I looked downstream. On the left side of the bank. I could see a group of boys in cut-off jeans dragging on cigarettes and throwing rocks in the water. I thought about running and getting them, but by the time I got down there Kambia would be in that bayou, for sure. What in the world was wrong with her? She had to be a slice short of a full pound cake. I leaned in over the cliff.

"Kambia!" I yelled. "This isn't funny. You can get really hurt. Stop being so stupid." She didn't even turn around.

The water was splashing something fierce against the base of the cliff. She just kept sliding and humming. Should I go down after her? I couldn't really swim. All I could do was dog-paddle, which was usually okay when the bayou water was calm. Everybody knew not to get into the water after a rainstorm. Even the youngest kids in the neighborhood knew that the water was really dangerous after we had had a flash flood. I looked down. She was still sliding, getting nearer to the water. Some of it had splashed up on her white dress, and the tail of it was covered with little pieces of black leaves and twigs.

"I believe you!" I shouted. "You are a piece of driftwood!"

"And where did I come from?" she shouted back, over the roar of the water.

"You just washed up here from the Mississippi!" I yelled. "Where you'll rot and nourish the earth!"

"Fine," she said. She started to inch her way back up the cliff the same way that she had got down, scooting that bony butt of hers backward instead of forward, grasping hunks of weeds to help pull herself up. When she finally reached the top, I grabbed her arm and tugged her up.

"I told you," she said. "Now do you believe me?" she asked with a satisfied look in her olive eyes. I wanted to wring her neck, break her in half like she was a peppermint stick or something, but I just cut her a look that woulda stopped a charging dog and marched back over to the path.

"You make me sick," I said.

"Wait, don't go, hold up," she cried. I kept walking. She ran up beside me.

"Go away," I said. "I don't want to hang out with you."

"Come on," she said. "I just wanted you to play with me."

"I don't like the way you play," I snapped.

She tugged my arm. "If you let me hang out with you, I'll tell you my deepest secret," she said. I stopped.

"What is it?" I asked.

"Wait," she said. "I gotta get my shoes."

By the time Kambia and I returned home I still hadn't quite forgiven her for making me afraid of the bayou for the first time in my life. She was kind of spooky and I wasn't too cool with spooky. But she had, at least, kept her promise to me and told me her secret, though I wasn't sure if it was really a secret or just something that her mother had told her not to tell.

According to Kambia, she and her mother had moved to Houston from Dallas because some woman was after her mother. She said that her mother was stepping out with some guy who owned a fish shack, and his wife found out about it and told her mother that she would slice her up like a sweet potato pie if she caught her on the streets, so Kambia and her mom caught a Greyhound to Houston. Kambia's secret was a little bit believable. Her mother had lots of boyfriends. Tall dudes, short dudes, bearded dudes, there was always some guy coming outta her house, especially at night. I wasn't sure where her mom had found a job, but wherever it was, she sure did meet a lot of guys.

Besides Kambia's secret the only other thing that I learned about her was that she was a reader, like me. Her favorite books were Linda James mystery novels. The one that she liked the best was about Linda James and her family moving one summer into an old house that was built at the turn of the century. The house is filled with trapdoors, secret passageways, and stuff like that. In the book Linda James spends the entire summer exploring all of the magical new things that the house has to offer.

"I wish I could do that," Kambia said as we headed up her walkway. "I wish that I could do nothing but explore all day and all night. I would find all the wonderful things that the world had to hide, then I would take them, put them in an empty mayonnaise jar, and look at them every morning when I woke up," she said, twirling down the brick walkway like a leaf caught in a whirlwind. When she reached the porch steps, she suddenly stopped twirling and ran up them so fast that I barely saw her feet moving.

"I gotta go," she said, standing in the middle of the porch.

"Bye," I said. I turned and started off down the walkway, but something made me turn back. I wasn't sure what.

"If my mama says that it's okay, I can walk to school with you sometimes," a little voice inside me blurted out.

"Cool," she said. "I don't really like walking alone."

"Okay, I'll ask my mama tonight," the voice said. I continued on down the walkway. As I stepped onto the sidewalk I heard the creak of the screen door, then a loud, shrill voice that I knew from experience was her mother's.

"Kambia Elaine. What the hell are you doing outside of this

house? I told you to keep your ass in here, didn't I?" her mother yelled. The screen door slammed.

Tia was sitting on the front porch of our house when I got home. Her eyes were puffy and swollen and her nose was red. She was licking her wounds. Tia's way of doing this was braiding her hair. She was sitting in her plaid short shorts and her demi-top, separating long strands of it with a plastic comb and weaving it into thin twists. I walked up the steps and slid in behind her. Taking the comb, I started to braid her hair in the opposite direction, over where she had gone under.

"What's up, Tia the Chia Pet?" I asked.

"Where you been, Shayla?" she asked.

"As far away from you and Mama as I could get," I said.

"Mama is seriously trippin'," Tia said. "What am I gonna do? Mama treats me like I ain't more than two years outta my diapers. She always going on at me about stuff everybody else is doing. Why cain't she see that I don't eat peanut-butter-and-jelly sandwiches no more?"

"I don't know, Tia Chia," I said, "but if I was you, the next time I went somewhere I wasn't suppose to be, I would make sure that I brought home everything that I took with me."

"I know," Tia said, turning in the direction of the rose bushes. Her bra was still there, blanketing the soft petals. I guess neither she nor Mama was brave enough to claim it.

"I really messed up this time," she said. "I really messed up."

"Messed up" was an understatement of what Tia had done. Mama loved hard, but she didn't forget easy. Tia had drilled a hole in Mama's heart and all Mama's trust of her had run out of it. It was gonna be a long time before Mama forgot what she done. "Stuff everybody else is doing," Tia had said. I couldn't imagine anybody else messing with Doo-witty. But then, after hearing why Kambia said she and her mom had moved from Dallas, I figured Tia wasn't the only one getting herself into trouble over some worthless guy. I decided that I was gonna leave guys alone until I was about forty.

Poor Tia. I stopped combing her hair, put my arms around her neck, and gave her a big hug. I wanted her to tell me what was going on with her and Doo-witty, but I didn't know the words to make her feelings flow. I also wanted to tell her about the stunt that Kambia had pulled, tell her that I thought that Kambia was really spaced-out, and that she mighta jumped into that bayou for sure, but nothing came out of my mouth. So I just made another note to add to my blue notebook later, when the house had cooled off: *Tia's nature is boiling out of her like hot soup out of a pot, and Kambia Elaine just flew in from Neptune.*

Chapter 2

Silence is clinging to our house like vines on a fence. Mama and Tia don't talk anymore. They have carved out little spaces in the house for themselves, like birds on an overcrowded telephone line. Mama's space is in the kitchen. When she isn't at work, you can find her standing at the stove, her heavy, dark hands stirring oversized pots of simmering collard greens or frying thin slices of sweet potatoes in a cast-iron skillet.

Tia's space is on the front porch. When she isn't hanging out with Maxi, she is perched on the side of it, her long legs dangling near the now roseless bushes where her bra is still lying. When I'm at home, I spend most of my time alone in my room, writing in my blue notebook, and wondering who let the butterflies out of our house and replaced them with wasps.

The whole thing is a complete mystery to me. I can understand Tia tossing out her jump rope and putting away her Barbie doll, but for Doo-witty? What does she see in him? Does he take her breath away, like those glamorous ladies always say in those old movies on late-night TV? How could Tia let Doo-witty touch her in places that Grandma Augustine says guys aren't even supposed to see? Once, when I was coming home from Grandma Augustine's house down by the tracks, I peeped into the open door of an empty boxcar of one of the parked trains and saw a guy and a girl pressed up against each other, going at it like crazy. The girl's eyes were closed and her smooth skin was all sweaty. From the expression on her face I wasn't sure if she was liking it or hating it, but she wasn't yelling and trying to get away, so I figured that she didn't mind it too much. But how in the world could Tia be doing that with Doo-witty? I know that I couldn't do it with Doo-witty or anybody else. I didn't even like dressing in front of the other girls in gym. I always shimmied into my gym suit in a stall.

Grandma Augustine says that Tia has just gone plumb crazy. She says that it ain't Doo-witty that's got hold of Tia, it's a Foot Grabber, a little demon that pushes his way outta hell when girls get about Tia's age, grabs 'em by the foot, and makes 'em cut the fool with no-account men when they ought to know better. She says that that's what happened to Mama years ago. "Them ole Foot Grabbers is slick as okra," Grandma Augustine says. "They can make young girls believe it's spring in the dead of winter, make them see apples on a tree when there ain't nothing there but bare-ass branches. I know. I seen 'em at work with your mama."

When Grandma Augustine told Mama about the Foot Grabber, Mama said that it was just plain ole backwater nonsense, superstitious hogwash handed down from the slaves that we descended from, who settled in shacks along the bayou after black folks was turned loose from the plantations. She told Grandma Augustine that she had enough to worry about without having to worry about demons running around in her house. "Mu'dear, I done told you that that ain't nothing but black-folk, 'fraid-of-the-dark foolishness," Mama said.

Grandma Augustine said that it wasn't foolishness, and she was sure of that. In fact, she was so sure that she paid a visit to Madam Vahilia Racine, a so-called voodoo priestess who lives on the other side of the tracks from her house. Grandma Augustine got Madam Racine to mix up a potion that would chase Tia's Foot Grabber away. The potion was in a half-gallon milk jug. It was a thick, egg-yolk-colored liquid that smelled like rotten seafood.

Ignoring Mama's feelings, Grandma let herself into our house with her key Saturday morning, hobbled right into me and Tia's bedroom, and dumped that potion all over Tia's head. Tia was just getting out of bed. Grandma Augustine nearly drowned her with it before she jumped up hollering. Then I got a whiff of it and jumped up hollering too. Mama came running to see if we had set our gowns on fire with the old gas heater in the corner of our room. "What in the world is going on here?" Mama asked, running through the doorway, clutching her blue terry robe. She took one look at Tia and almost fainted. Tia's head and face were covered with the stinky liquid. Huge globs of it were dripping outta her long hair and sliding down her high cheekbones onto her flimsy peach cotton gown. Between the sticky gook Tia's slanted eyes looked like they were ready to run a faucet full of tears.

"Mama, look what Grandma did," she whined.

"Lord have mercy Jesus!" Mama cried, holding her nose. "Mu'dear, what you have done to my baby?"

Grandma hobbled over to Mama on her cane. Grandma is a big woman, even bigger than Mama, stocky-built, with salt-and-pepper hair, piercing dark eyes, and a no-nonsense face.

"Vera, ain't nothing for you to get upset over," Grandma said. "I told you before. All I'm trying to do is get rid of whatever done put that gal on the wrong track." Mama took a deep breath and let it out.

"Mu'dear, now you know that I don't believe in none of that bone-reading, chicken-feet-hanging, card-flipping craziness in my house."

"It ain't craziness, Vera," Grandma Augustine said, shooting Mama a sharp glance that woulda sent Dracula back to his coffin.

"It is craziness. And you of all folks ought to know better. Ain't you been trying to get me to take these girls to church on a regular basis for the past few years?" Mama said. "Mu'dear, this goes against everything that you always been trying to make me believe is true."

"Maybe it goes against it some," Grandma Augustine said. "You know I been a faithful servant of Jesus pretty near from when I was old enough to walk. As I see it, I ain't never had but one strike against me, and that was you coming up with a big belly before I even knew you was starting to look at men in a womanly way. I can't do nothing about that, but I sho can make sure that that gal over there," she said, pointing to Tia, "don't pull her skirt up and run down the same road you took. The Good Book is a strong post to lean on, but sometimes you need support from other places. You don't want that gal to make the same kinda mess you made outta your life, do you? I told you this was coming, didn't I, Vera. All you got in this world is a shack and them kids. Is that what you want for her?"

Mama rolled her eyes at Grandma, then she stared down at the floor, like there was a fancy picture or something woven into the carpet. Tia flopped down on the bed and cut her eyes at Grandma Augustine. Grandma pointed her finger at her.

"Don't you be looking at me like that, little girl!" she yelled. "If you was able to do what's right on your own, none of this would be going on."

"What's right, Grandma? What you think?" Tia snapped. Grandma Augustine glared at her.

"Don't let your mouth start something your behind cain't stand," Grandma Augustine said. Tia got quiet.

"Vera, did you hear how she talked to me?" Grandma Augustine asked. Mama didn't say nothing. She just kept staring at the carpet. In fact, she stared at it for so long I began to think that she really was looking at a picture or something. Finally, after several seconds, she raised her head. For a moment she looked like she had all the life beat outta her, but her dark face soon turned from sad to serious.

"I want everything for that gal that you wanted for me," Mama said, pointing to Tia. "But there's been enough shame in this house. I ain't adding no more to it. Mu'dear, I love you. But you cain't run my house and yours, too. I birthed these babies. What they do or don't do in life ain't got nothing to do with nobody but me. Tia, go wash that mess outta your hair," Mama said.

Tia left for the bathroom, leaving a sticky trail of yellow glop with each step.

"You sho is making a mistake," Grandma Augustine said.

"They mine to make, Mu'dear, and not yours," Mama said. "I done had more than my share of folks coming over here telling me what to do with my child." Mama sighed and let it out. "I'm gonna go start up some breakfast, unless you want to do that, too," she said. Grandma Augustine opened her mouth like she was gonna say something, but she just clamped it shut real quick and got a kinda hurt-puppy look on her wrinkled face. Mama pretended like she didn't see it.

"Shayla," Mama said. "Open the window, then take them wet covers off that bed and put 'em in a pillowcase or something. Tia can drop 'em off at the Washateria when she goes to Maxi's house. Get some soap and water and clean that stuff up before it stinks up the whole house." I moved toward the bed.

"No," Grandma Augustine said softly. "I'll clean that mess up. I made it." Grandma Augustine set the potion bottle down on the floor and hobbled slowly over to our bed. Her shoulders were slumped and her flowered tent dress seemed to droop off of her.

Mama stood in the doorway and watched until Grandma Augustine's withered hands started to yank the yellow-stained patchwork quilt away from Tia's side of the bed, then she left the room.

For a few seconds I remained where I was. I was trying to make sense of what had just happened. Mama had never won a fight with Grandma Augustine before. It was usually Grandma's way or no way at all. If Grandma said that the sky was brown, it was brown. If she said that the grass was blue, it was blue. That's the way it was with her. I had never known Mama to go against her. Tia's relationship with Doo-witty was throwing everything out of whack. I walked over to our rickety old dresser, opened the top drawer, and took out my blue notebook. *The cats are barking and the dogs are meowing,* I scrawled, *and confusion is crawling up our walls like roaches.*

I knew that Tia was going to be in the bathroom for a while, so I decided just to slip on some clothes and start my day without taking a bath. I didn't think that Mama would have too much of a complaint. She had had enough showdowns for the day, but I wasn't too sure that Grandma wouldn't raise a fuss about it. I kept looking at her out of the corner of my eye as I yanked a faded red-and-black plaid skirt and a well-worn turtleneck out of the drawer and threw them on. I adjusted them with a tug or two, then snatched one of Tia's plastic combs out of a straw basket on top of the dresser, grabbed my black sneakers out of a cardboard box that me and Tia used for a shoe bin, and headed for the door before Grandma could ask me about my lack of grooming.

I was safely in the hallway when I remembered my watch. Grandma Augustine had given me a small Timex watch for my birthday last year. I never went anywhere without it. I had this thing about time. I always had to know how long it took me to get somewhere, how much time fell between the cracks while I was doing things like walking or riding the bus. I figured if I knew how much time I was throwing away, I could cut off a little bit here and there and have a lot extra to do the things that I really wanted to do. Grandma Augustine says that this is a stupid idea. "Girl, slow down—take your time. Life slips away quickly, and it's peppered with worries," she always tells me.

I walked swiftly back into the bedroom past Grandma Augustine and knocked on the bathroom door. My watch was in an empty Kleenex box on the back of the toilet, where I left it each night.

After several taps Tia came to the door wrapped in a ragged towel.

"I need my watch," I said, slipping past her into the bathroom.

The smell of Lysol nearly knocked me out as I walked over to the toilet. Tia had wasted no time in trying to get rid of Grandma's potion. Besides perfuming the place with air freshener, she had run the old porcelain tub full of sudsy water. Her cotton gown was wringing wet and lying in a heap in the sink.

"You're gonna have to get a rubbing board to get that smell out," I said, pointing to it and holding my nose.

"I know," she said. "I cain't take it to the Washateria. It'll clear the laundry room quicker than a pile of dead rats." We both started laughing. Tia tucked her towel in across her big breasts. She snatched a plastic bottle of shampoo off of the metal rack over the tub and squeezed some of the clear liquid onto her hair, tossed a handful of tub water onto the liquid, and worked the mixture with her hand until her whole head was covered with a thick, foamy lather.

"You look like a big Q-Tip," I said.

Tia smiled and sat down on the toilet. I reached behind her and grabbed my watch out of the flowered tissue box. Tia looked at me and sighed.

"Grandma Augustine is gone plumb crazy," she said, rolling her eyes. "Her girdle is too damn tight or something."

"Her panty hose, too," I said, giggling and winding my watch.

"What in the world was she thinking?" she asked, shaking her head.

"I don't know," I said, stretching the watchband over my wrist.

Tia shook her head again, dropping a small glob of lather onto the green linoleum. Her face got real sad. She looked at my watch for a second, then turned and stared at the torn tulip wallpaper over the wicker laundry basket in a corner of the bathroom.

"Doo-witty winds my clock, you know," she said. "On the inside. He keeps the stuff moving inside of me. Do you know what I mean?"

I sighed and stuck her comb in my skirt pocket. "I'm not really sure," I said.

"I can't write everything away like you do, Shayla," she said. "Sometimes I look around here and I see where we at, and my whole body just comes to a stop: my mind, my heart, my legs, everything just sort of turns off. Doo-witty starts me back up."

"How does he do that?" I asked, not really sure how to take what she was saying.

"I don't know," she said, turning back to me with a wrinkled brow. "I haven't been able to make that out just yet. He just does. Maybe it's the sound of his voice, the way he sometimes calls me Tia the Chia Pet, like you do, but real tender, and soft-like, you know. I'm not sure. I just know that he does, and for a little while I'm all right again and nothing can turn me off."

I leaned over and patted her arm. "Grandma Augustine always

says, 'Once you're all wound up, you better make sure when that spring pops loose that you're spinning in the right direction.'"

Tia laughed. "I know," she said. "Grandma got a saying for every occasion. She's the one that ought to be trying to write books."

I laughed. "Have a good bath, Tia the Chia Pet," I said, and left the bathroom.

After flopping down on the living-room sofa long enough to rake Tia's comb through my fuzzy hair, I ran into the kitchen. I expected to find Mama standing in front of the oak cabinets with her hands covered with biscuit flour, mixing dough in one of the ceramic mixing bowls, but she wasn't there. Her large frame was squeezed between the refrigerator and the stove. She had her hands on her hips and her face pressed up against the tiny window over the canned goods shelf, staring out through the foggy glass. I walked up and pushed in beside her.

"What's up, Mama?" I asked.

"That gal," Mama said. "That little gal next door that you been walking to school with. She out there in that same dingy white dress talking to the fence."

"Let me see, Mama," I said, gently pushing her aside. She moved over as much as she could and I peeked out. It was Kambia, all right. She was standing in the dew-drenched grass, underneath the thin, spiky branches of the pomegranate tree. It looked like she was holding a conversation with several of the silver links in the chain-link fence. Her small pink lips were moving quickly, like she was really talking about something.

"Poor thing," Mama said, shaking her head. "Poor, poor thing."

I wasn't real sure what Mama meant by her comments, but I had some idea. She had probably heard the same rumor that I had at school a few weeks ago. It was about Kambia's mom. The rumor was that Kambia's mom was selling her stuff. According to the kids at school, they had got the scoop from J. B. Walker, who owned a pool hall down by the park. J. B. said that some of the dudes who hung out at the hall during the late-night hours had said that Kambia's mom could outdo the five-dollar hookers on Lyons. You could have her for as little as a carton of Salems or a couple pounds of ribs from Bobby's Rib Shack on Grayson Street. "She paying her rent on her back," J. B. said, "and putting all the other nasty women in the neighborhood to shame." I was shocked when I heard the rumor. Kambia's mom's boyfriends weren't boyfriends at all. I didn't know if Kambia had heard the rumor, and when I told Tia about it, she told me not to repeat it. "Don't go around gossiping about stuff that you don't know is true," she said.

"I'm gonna go see what she's up to," I said to Mama.

"Maybe she can go down to the rec center with you to enter that contest," Mama yelled as I opened the back door.

A writing contest was being held down at the rec center in the park. It was open to kids from seven to thirteen. The rules were simple: You had to take a fairy tale and rewrite it for modern-day times. The first prize was a hundred-dollar gift certificate for some fancy bookstore downtown. The story was going to be tacked up on the bulletin board at the center, so it had to be simple enough so that even the younger kids could read it. I had picked as my story "The Three Little Pigs." I wrote it in street rhyme, using plenty of slang, like the stories that some of the older guys on our block told at the neighborhood barbecue each year. I had only found out about the contest last week, but I had worked real hard on a story since then. If I won, it would be the first time that I ever had books that I didn't have to return to the library.

I slammed the back door shut and walked through the wet grass over to my side of the fence. It was chilly out. A cool breeze was ruffling the tiny hairs on my bare legs, and blowing Kambia's unbraided sandy locks wildly. Kambia didn't look up as I approached the fence. She just kept right on talking.

"Who you rapping with?" I asked, walking up and leaning in close. Kambia's olive eyes snapped away from the fence and fixed on me.

"The Lizard People," she said with a spacey look. "I was just talking to them, asking them how their night went, what they did while the rest of us were asleep." I glanced at the fence and back at her.

"There's no Lizard People, Kambia," I said coolly.

"Not anymore," she said. "They just tucked their funny little tails in and started for home. They have to be in before the sun rises too far above the clouds or they'll turn into purple sticks of chewing gum and some greedy kid will come along, spot them on the fence, and eat them."

"Why not orange or blue sticks of chewing gum? Why can't they turn into those?" I snapped.

"They just can't," she said. "They can only turn colors that help them blend into where they live—brown on wood, green in the grass, and dark purple at night. That's when they come out, you know. They come out late at night when the moon is really bright, and waltz to beautiful music on top of the fence until day breaks, then they scurry back into their holes until the sun goes down again."

"Hogwash," I said.

"It's true," she said. "Sometimes the moon oversleeps and forgets to come out of his house, and the Lizard People just spend the whole night sitting on the fence and talking about what it feels like to have a human head and a lizard body and to be able to change your color anytime you feel like it. I wish I could do that," she said. "I wish I could be whatever color I wanted to be just at the snap of my fingers."

"What color would you be?" I asked.

"Multicolored," she said. "Then everybody everywhere would have to like me, because a little piece of me would look just like them."

I changed the subject. "I'm going to the park today," I said. "I got a story that I want to enter in the writing contest there. You wanna come?"

Kambia's eyes nervously darted to her rusted back screen door for a couple of seconds. "When are you going?" she asked.

"As soon as I finish eating my Froot Loops," I answered.

"Does it take you a long time to eat?" she asked, looking over at her back door again.

"Naw, I'm a quick eater," I said.

"Okay, I'll meet you out front," she said.

Kambia was true to her word. When I ran out to the sidewalk in front of my house later, she was right there, staring at the cracks in the concrete. She had slipped a tattered red sweater on over her white dress, and her tiny feet were sporting a pair of worn-out Nikes. Her hair was tugged back with a thick black rubber band, and her bony hands were shiny, as if she had rubbed them with Vaseline.

"I'm sorry I'm late," I said. "Mama made me wash last night's dishes."

"It's okay," she said. "Some guy stopped by and talked to me."

"About what?" I asked. "My mama says it's dangerous to talk to strange men."

"I seen him around some," Kambia said. "He said he was a friend of your sister, Tia. He wanted to know if she was at home. I told him I didn't know. There he goes," she said, pointing down the street.

I followed Kambia's finger with my eyes. At the end of the block, walking fast underneath a row of leafless pecan trees, was a tall, lanky dude wearing a black corduroy jacket, black jeans, and sporting a red baseball cap on top of an extra-long head. The head was a dead giveaway. It was Doo-witty.

Doo-witty reached the curb. He turned around and stared at me. I stared back. At the moment our eyes connected I could tell that we were both trying to figure out what the other was thinking. I was thinking that if Mama or Grandma Augustine had come outta the front door and seen him standing next to our gate talking to Kambia, hell woulda swarmed on him like locusts. I could see Grandma Augustine taking her cane and beating him down to the ground, like he had stole her best dentures. Doo-witty probably was thinking the same thing, too, since he hadn't been brave enough to come up to the house and ask for Tia himself. I looked at his popped eyes and dropped jaw. How in the world could he be turning Tia's brain to squashed cabbage? I turned away.

"Let's go, Kambia," I said, walking off down the sidewalk in the opposite direction. Kambia fell into step beside me.

I didn't say anything more to Kambia as we hurried off down the street. I knew that she wouldn't talk to me. She was always quiet when we walked to school each morning. For almost all of the twelve-block walk she would stroll silently, her eyes focusing in on stuff, taking in information, but spitting none out. She never commented on the shady-looking drug dealers who hung out on the corner of nearly every street that led to our school, their Levi's bulging with freshly packaged dime bags, or the angry dudes with jittery hands who leaned up against the orange brick walls of Parson's Cash-and-Carry, dragging on joints dusted with powdered crack. Kambia would not let these kinds of people into her little world. I was jealous of her for being able to tune out the things that I couldn't help but see, but mostly I was jealous of her for being able to tune me out too. I couldn't do that to her, no matter how annoyed I got with her sometimes.

Although we walked to school together most mornings, Kambia and I were not really friends. I still didn't know hardly anything about her. I didn't know what her favorite TV show was or her favorite record. I didn't know if she liked her ice cream in a cone or liked to scoop it out of a dish. I didn't even know if she had kissed her first boy, and if she had, if she'd done it with her eyes closed or if she had stared at the pimples on his forehead, wondering if her kiss would clear them up. It was as if Kambia were way up high on the top floor of a huge skyscraper and there were no stairs or elevator to take me to the room that she was in. She could keep even me out whenever she wanted. I liked her, even though she gave me very little about herself to like, even though I knew that hanging out with her was probably not the best thing for me to be doing.

Things were just as I expected when Kambia and I entered the small rec room next door to the park. In the center of the room was a long table filled with several large round trays of cookies and a huge glass punch bowl with green punch. The beige walls of the room were decorated with large red-and-white signs telling everybody that this was the big day to turn in their entries, and saying how wonderful they were going to feel for doing it. THERE IS NO GREATER POWER IN THE WORLD THAN THE PEN AND THE MIND THAT DRIVES IT, one poster read.

"How can you drive a pen? It doesn't have any wheels," I whispered to Kambia as we walked over to the table. Kambia broke into giggles.

There was one person seated at the end of the long table, Miss Marshall, who was a volunteer for an afternoon reading program at my school. She was a nice sister who used to live in the Bottom but had worked her way out. She was about Mama's age, slender and shapely, with deep-brown eyes, high cheekbones, and short hair cropped real close to her head. Miss Marshall worked for J&R, the chemical company that was sponsoring the contest. J&R was located just on the edge of our neighborhood. Their huge concrete smokestacks towered over the highest church steeples on our blocks J&R was giving the contest to lend a helping hand to our community—at least that's what one of the signs over the table said. WE WANT TO HAVE A HAND IN THE ENRICHMENT OF YOUNG MINDS, it said in bold letters.

I handed Miss Marshall my paper with a smile on my face. Though I had never actually sat down and talked to her, I had a feeling that I would like her a lot. Some of the other kids at my school had said that she was real cool. She took it from me, returning the smile.

"Shayla Dubois," she said, reading the name on the top line. I nodded.

"Haven't I seen you at the school?" she asked, opening her mouth just wide enough to expose an even row of glossy white teeth. *She must go to the dentist a lot,* I told myself.

"Yes, ma'am," I said. "I'm one of Miss Patrick's English students."

"That's right," she said. "I've seen you in her class." She glanced down at my paper again.

"You did yours on 'The Three Little Pigs,'" she said. "It was always one of my favorites."

"Mine, too," I said.

"Mine, too," Kambia echoed. I had almost forgotten that she was there.

"Well," Miss Marshall said, "so far I have two Little Red Riding Hoods and three Jack and the Beanstalks, but no Three Little Pigs, at least not until now," she said, cutting her eyes to a pleated folder lying a couple of feet away. "I'm sure that I and the rest of the people on the committee will find it good reading."

"Yes, ma'am, I hope so," I said, wondering who the rest of the committee was.

"Well, you girls grab yourselves some cookies and punch before you go," she said, scribbling something on the top of my paper with a black pen.

Kambia and I hurried down to the end of the table.

There were all kinds of cookies on the plastic trays. Dark-chocolate Oreos, sugared ginger snaps, flower-shaped butter cookies, the list went on. We picked up one of each kind and shoved them into our pockets, then Kambia reached for the punch ladle.

"No," Miss Marshall said as Kambia took it in her hand. Kambia dropped the ladle and we both looked back at Miss Marshall. She was staring at my story with a frown on her face.

"No," she said again. "No."

"Is something wrong, ma'am?" I asked. Kambia and I went back down to where she was.

She dropped the paper and looked at me sternly. "This story is not acceptable," she said.

"Excuse me, ma'am?" I whispered.

"You can't enter this story into the contest," she said, blinking her eyes rapidly.

"What's wrong with it, ma'am?" I asked, raising my voice a bit higher.

"This is not the kind of writing my company was meaning to sponsor," she said.

"I don't understand, ma'am. What do you mean?" I asked. "I followed the guidelines. It's simple, and set in modern times. I did it just like the sheet told me to."

"Nowhere in the guidelines did it say that this type of ghetto grammar and language was okay," she barked. "This isn't even a story. It's some type of poem."

"It's not a poem," I said. "It's street talk."

"I know what it is," she said. "I used to live on one of these streets, not too far from here. Don't get me wrong. This type of writing might be just fine for the hood, but you can't expect to excel in the real world with street jargon. What kind of person would I be if I didn't make sure that kids like you knew this?" she said.

I wasn't even sure what the word *jargon* meant. I could feel the tears welling up in the corners of my eyes, but I held them back. I wasn't a crier. Crying was for babies. Tia was a crier.

"I'm sorry, ma'am. I thought that we could do it any way we liked," I said with a shaky voice.

"No," she said. "Certain rules of English must apply. Here," she said, holding it out to me. "You can take it home and redo it if you want. Miss Patrick always tells me that you are one of her brightest students. I know that you can turn this story into something acceptable, something that your community can be proud of. The deadline to turn it in isn't until noon. We don't want people to think that we are incapable of competing, do we?"

"I can't do it over by noon, ma'am. There ain't enough time," I said.

"*Isn't* enough time," she corrected. "And yes, there is, if you want to turn it in."

"I can't do it by noon, ma'am," I repeated. "I'll have to start it all over from scratch."

"It's only a few pages," she said. "It shouldn't take you but an hour or two."

Tears started to slide down my face. I could feel them tingling and dripping off my nose. I wiped them away with my hand as quick as I could. I took the paper from her, but as soon as I had it in my hand, Kambia snatched it from me and placed it back on the table.

"We came to enter the contest," she said to Miss Marshall.

"Excuse me? What did you say, little girl?" Miss Marshall asked.

"We came to enter the contest," Kambia repeated in a very calm voice, too calm.

"I just told your friend that her paper was not acceptable," Miss Marshall said, the frown on her face turning into a scowl.

"We came to enter the contest," Kambia said again. Her voice was still calm, but it was more serious, like Mama's after she had asked me to do something more than two times.

"Now look, little girl," Miss Marshall said, rising from her seat, tugging down the jacket of a nicely tailored linen suit. "I'm not going to repeat myself anymore." She grabbed the paper off the table and pushed it at me. "Take it and go home," she said. Her wide eyes were narrowed with anger, and if a woman as dark as she could have turned completely red, her face probably would have looked like the inside of an overripe watermelon. I reached for the story, but Kambia got to it before me. She snatched it out of Miss Marshall's hand and placed it back on the table.

"We came to enter the contest," she said, glaring at Miss Marshall.

"It's okay, Kambia," I said. "I can enter the next contest. Let's just go home."

"That's a good idea," Miss Marshall said, glaring back at Kambia. She tried to pick the story up, but Kambia clapped her bony hands down on it. She pressed her palms down so hard that her yellow knuckles were tuning white.

"We came to enter the contest," she said again. Her voice was trembling something fierce, and her skinny arms were vibrating.

"Look, little girl!" Miss Marshall yelled, looking down at her.

"I'm not a little girl!" Kambia screamed. "I'm not a little girl! I'm a rainbow-colored crab from the Gulf. I just crawled all the way up here to visit my best friend, Shayla, and we came over here to enter this contest!"

"Get out of here, little girl!" Miss Marshall yelled.

"I'm not a little girl!" Kambia shrieked. "I told you! I'm a rainbow-colored crab from the Gulf! I ain't never, never, never ever been a little girl! Little girls are stupid and bad! They are stupid, stupid, stupid, bad, bad, bad! I'm a crab! I'm a crab!"

"I want you to go, right now!" Miss Marshall shrieked back. She tried to pry Kambia's fingers off the story, but she couldn't get them loose.

"Leave her alone," I heard a voice in me screaming. I yanked one of her hands away, and she withdrew the other and backed away from the table, spilling a shower of lime punch all over the wood-grain tiles on the floor.

"You girls are going to be in big trouble!" she shouted. "I'm going to report this incident to your teachers on Monday, and your fathers and mothers will be notified."

"I don't have a father!" I snapped. "Let's go, Kambia," I said, tugging at Kambia's arm.

"But we came to enter the contest," Kambia mumbled.

"I know," I said. "But it's all right. It's not important. It's really not important. It's really not important."

I pulled at one of Kambia's hands and she let the paper go. I slipped it off the table and stuck it in the pocket of my skirt.

"Come on," I said, leading her by the arm through the rec door.

Kambia and I walked out of the room and sat down at one of the wooden tables in the park. It was still nice and cool out. All around us giggling groups of kinky-haired girls and boys were ripping and running through the brown grass, climbing up and down on the broken-down playscape.

I looked at Kambia. Her eyes were blank. My stomach churned. I felt like I wanted to throw up. What had just happened? How could something so simple have turned into such a big mess? I would never be allowed to participate in any contest that the company sponsored. All I had wanted to do was turn in my story. Now I was in big trouble. Mama would be burning-up mad over this. I stuck my hand in my pocket and fingered my story for a few seconds. There was nothing that I could do with it now but take it home and put it in my blue notebook, where nobody would see it but me. I sighed, then put my head down on the table and stared at Kambia. Her eyes suddenly returned to life.

"All stories come from the Story Bees," she said. "They live far away, on the other side of the world, in a land where the flowers grow words instead of nectar. Once a year, usually around spring, they fly through all the countries until they find a very special person that they can trust. While that person mows their lawn or works in their garden, they sneak up behind them and whisper their favorite stories into their ear. Then they fly back home and let that person share the wonderful stories with the rest of the world."

I got up from the table.

"Kambia, let's go home," I said.

As Kambia and I started for home, her Story Bees story played over and over in my mind. It seemed different from the other silly stories that she always told. It actually made some sense. I decided that in her strange little way Kambia was trying to tell me that my writing was a special gift, and that I shouldn't let Miss Marshall shape my words, tell me how I should express myself. As I watched Kambia walking silently beside me in her tattered sweater I decided that the next time she told one of her tales I would listen. Maybe it would help me figure her out.

Chapter 3

*F*or a while peace flew in and lighted on our back porch. Mama and Tia got along great during the Thanksgiving holiday. They didn't argue once, and Tia even helped Mama cook dinner while me and Grandma Augustine delivered pumpkin pies and butter cookies to some of the sick and shut-in members at Grandma's church. For a couple of weeks it looked like things were going to be just fine, but today Mr. Anger popped his head back into our front door, and now nothing in this house will ever be the same.

What brought Mr. Anger back to our house was the Women of Mahogany Festival, an annual mother and daughter get-together attended by all of the ladies and girls in my neighborhood. The festival is held down at the Fifth Ward Cultural Center.

It starts at first light and goes until the sun glows burnt orange and the clouds turn violet in the sky. There are speeches, workshops, gumbo and baking cook-offs, and, of course, a quilting contest, all designed to bring African-American mothers and daughters together in unity.

This year Mama and Grandma Augustine entered the quilting contest. Their quilt was called "A Black Woman's Harvest." It was a round quilt edged in white lace. The background was made out of navy quilting squares that were embroidered with glossy white stars. In the center of the squares was a huge moon made of bright yellow, diamond-shaped pieces. On top of the moon was an African-American woman wearing a scarlet dress. Her long black hair was tied back with a ribbon made of Kente cloth. In one hand she carried a huge straw basket. In the other she held a blue-and-white

Earth made out of shiny satin. The woman had a big smile on her face as she picked up our world and placed it into her basket.

Grandma Augustine and Mama came in second in the contest, behind a quilt of five slave women picking cotton in an east Texas cotton field. Grandma Augustine said that it didn't matter. She just wanted everybody to see the quilt. It was her best work ever. She had sat up many a night embroidering the stars on the quilt with her arthritic hands.

We were all very happy when we gathered our coats and things to leave the cultural center. That is, until Mama and Grandma looked around and noticed that Tia was missing. We were in the hallway of the crowded center when Mama let loose with a "Where in the hell is that girl?" All the ladies and girls in the hall stopped and stared at us, like we was putting on some kind of play or something.

"What y'all looking at? Go on about y'all business. Folks sho can be ignorant sometimes," Grandma Augustine snapped at a pair of sour-faced ladies with gray fleece coats.

"I haven't seen her, Mama," I said, giggling at Grandma Augustine's remark.

"I saw her 'bout an hour ago," Grandma Augustine said. "She was in some kind of hair-braiding workshop. A whole bunch of gals her age was sitting in a circle weaving colored beads and such into their hair. I hollered at her, but I didn't go in."

"Where was that at?" Mama asked.

"In one of them rooms near the back," Grandma Augustine said.

"Shayla," Mama said in an irritated voice. "Go run back there and get your sister. I'm not trying to be here all day. I have to throw some dinner together before I go to work. Tell her to put some wheels on her behind. She know I can't be late for my shift."

"Yes, ma'am," I yelled as I ran off down the hall.

To tell the truth, I was really happy about being the one to go and look for Tia. I figured it would give me another chance to glance at some of the fancy paintings that were on the white-washed brick walls of the center. Lots of funny-looking pieces had been donated by some artist who had a gallery downtown. They were mostly big squares and long stripes of bright colors, and I have to admit that I couldn't quite figure them out, but I liked them anyway. They reminded me of the images that I sometimes saw when I closed my eyes at night to fall asleep.

I took my time walking down the emptying hallway. Most of the ladies were like Mama, they worked nights. They were filing out of the classroom doors in big clusters, chatting loudly as they inched their way over the black-and-white tiles leading to the huge glass door at the front of the cultural center. A cold front had roared in this morning, freezing the wet sheets on our clotheslines. Through the frosty windows I could see many of the ladies. Their arms loaded with homemade ceramics and baked goods, they were noisily crunching their way through the icy grass toward home.

I didn't bother going inside when I got to the room where Tia was supposed to be. It was empty. There were only a few metal chairs in a semicircle to remind anyone that there had been a class in the room just a little while ago.

I looked back down the hallway. Mama and Grandma Augustine were standing next to the door, glancing at their watches, like they were seriously ready to go. I decided to keep on up the hall and continue looking for Tia. If I went back now, they would jump on me like they was gonna jump on her when she finally showed up. There were about ten or twelve nice-size rooms in the cultural center. I figured it wouldn't hurt me to check them all out.

I walked down the hall, peeping into open doors, until I reached the end of the hallway. As I expected, all of the rooms were empty, with the exception of a piece of forgotten artwork left here and there on the brown worktables. Folks weren't always pleased with their projects after they had made them. I had tossed a couple of badly glittered Christmas cards myself after one of my workshops.

When I reached the end of the first hall, I turned and started up the second one. The rooms were empty there, too, and I soon found myself standing in front of a huge pair of oak double doors. I stopped and thought about what I wanted to do. I knew where the doors led. The doors connected the cultural center with Morgan's Mortuary. Mama said that Morgan Aldrich, the mortuary owner, had put up the land for the center and a heap smart of the money before the city took over and finished building it. Since Morgan had given so much, the city saw no reason why they shouldn't grant his only request, and hook the cultural center up with the funeral home. Morgan had several reasons why this would be a good idea. He said that the cultural center would be a good place for grieving relatives to wait while other family members picked out a casket for the family's deceased loved one. He said that his staff could keep up-to-date by reading the latest medical magazines in the center's small library, and whenever he got a new shipment of caskets in, folks could come over and browse at the new styles, maybe even put a casket on the layaway for when it came time for them to meet their maker.

Since the first day that the cultural center opened only Morgan's staff had used the entryway. It gave most people the creeps. Some folks even called it the Tomb. On Halloween, Friday the Thirteenth, and other days where spooky stuff was supposed to go on, people had been known to say that they had seen a dead person or two with ashy gray skin and lifeless eyes wander out of those double doors, dressed in their Sunday best, hunting for relatives and friends. The last person spotted was Mrs. Alvania C. Davis, head usher at the Tabernacle of the Blessed Redeemer.

Folks say that on a cool Halloween night, a couple of years ago, Mrs. Alvania come stepping out of that entryway with her crisp black usher's uniform and her patent-leather handbag, looking for her husband, Donald T., a fruit stand owner on Dowling Street. They say she wandered in and out of the rooms of the cultural center scaring black folks white with her blank face and ghoulish voice. She walked the center for nearly two hours, until somebody finally told her that she had already burnt up her time on this earth, and that she was gonna take a few more folks with her if she didn't get back in her coffin where she belonged.

I stood at the door, trying to make up my mind. I wasn't afraid of no ghosts. Grandma Augustine attended every funeral in the neighborhood, often dragging me, Mama, and Tia along. The Tomb just didn't seem like any place I needed to look.

I turned away from the doors and started walking back up the hall, tapping my fingers along the wall. I was three doors down when I heard a low moan coming from behind me. I whipped my head around. Then another moan drifted from behind the double doors of the Tomb, low and eerie, like those scary sounds you always hear in horror flicks. I froze. That moan was either Mrs. Alvania, back to look for Donald T., or some other confused dead person. My heart started to thump real fast, like I had just finished doing a lot of jumping jacks. I started to run down the hallway, but something made me stop. There was no such thing as ghosts. Mama said that ghosts were just something that people made up when they didn't have an answer for stuff that they thought they had seen or heard. I walked back to the doors and yanked them open.

My mouth dropped to my belly. It was worse than a ghost. It was Tia and Doo-witty. They were all over each other in one corner of the small room. Tia's polyester sweater was unbuttoned and falling off her loose breasts, and her thick braids were flying in all directions. She spotted me and pushed Doo-witty away from her as if he had suddenly got real bad breath. Doo-witty stumbled and bumped into a shiny radiator on one side of the sand-colored wall.

"Tia, have you . . . you lost your mind?" Doo-witty asked, regaining his balance. Tia just kept staring at me. Doo-witty turned around to see what she was looking at.

"Oh," he said, opening his mouth wide, like a big ole goldfish. I rolled my eyes at him.

"Tia, the festival is over. Mama is ready to go, right now," I said.

"Where is she at?" Tia asked, reaching deep into her sweater and yanking up the straps of her bra.

"She's down the hall, at the front," I said. "She and Grandma Augustine really want to take off. She's gonna be boiling mad when she finds out that you been in here with Doo-witty all this time."

"Oh, please don't tell her, Shayla," Tia said, skirting around Doo-witty. "We weren't doing nothing wrong, just kissing and stuff." I looked at Doo-witty's drooping jaw and shuddered.

"I'm telling Mama," I said sharply.

"No don't, Shayla. I swear we weren't doing anything shameful," Tia pleaded.

"Well, how come you doing it back here?" I asked more sharply. I put my hands on my hips and waited for an answer. But instead of answering me, Doo-witty turned around and looked at Tia. I knew he would. It was an easy question and anybody could have answered it lickety-split, but not Doo-witty. Doo-witty's corn bread wasn't quite done in the middle.

"We just wanted a little space to ourselves," Tia said, pulling up her sweater. "Ain't nothing wrong with that."

"Yeah," Doo-witty repeated. "We . . . we just wanted a . . . a little space to ourselves. Ain't nothing wrong with . . . with that," he said. He reminded me of one of those talking teddy bears that repeats everything you say from a tape recorder sewn into its stomach. I cut my eyes at him again. I wanted to give *him* a hard time, not Tia. He was getting Tia into serious trouble, and he wasn't even smart enough to help her out of it with a lie.

"Come on, Shayla, don't tell Mama," Tia begged. Her warm brown face was knotted with worry. I looked into her eyes. It was almost as if I could see through her eyeballs, see clean down to her heart. Her heart was all soggy and drippy with love stuff.

I leaned against one of the doors and checked out Doo-witty. All I could see was that long head and that jawbone that looked like it was being pulled down by some kind of weight toward the floor. Was Doo-witty in love with Tia? I couldn't tell. He hadn't spoken his mind and I couldn't read his heart. I checked out his clothes. He had on the same outfit that I saw him in that day on the street—black corduroys, black jeans, and a red baseball cap with no writing on the brim. There was nothing at all special about the clothes he had picked out, nothing that would tell me anything about the Doo-witty inside. From head to toe he was a flat zero. I had no idea what Tia saw in him. But there had to be something.

Like Mama, Tia loved hard. When Maurice Jafee, Mama's last boyfriend, left Mama, Tia cried for a whole month. Maurice was good to me and Tia. He took us shopping once a month when he got paid at the gas station, and even bought us each our own boom box one Christmas. But Mama and Maurice didn't get along too well. Mama did care for him. He was a nice-looking Creole brother who spoke a strange kinda French talk. He was real good at cooking and building stuff, but he had this problem of sometimes bringing home things that didn't belong to him. He went to jail twice one year, for jacking radios out of other people's cars. Mama said that she couldn't have that kind of mess in her house. She told Maurice that she was trying to raise us decent and she didn't need him putting the wrong ideas into our heads. She wanted us to know that we could get the things that we wanted through hard work, and not from boosting other folks' things. Maurice said that it was cool. He packed his bags and went back to his hometown in New Orleans, Louisiana.

Tia blamed Mama for Maurice leaving. She said that Mama shoulda gave him a chance to change. She said that he treated me and her like we were his daughters and that Mama was never ever gonna find another dude that would do that. No, if Tia was willing to risk Mama being pissed off over Doo-witty, there had to be more to him. I just wasn't sure what it was.

"I won't tell," I said. "But we better start booking it toward the front, because Mama is already madder than a tomcat in a sack."

"Oh, I'm a lot madder than that," Mama's voice cried over my shoulder, causing Tia, Doo-witty, and me to jump like somebody had jabbed us with a hot fork.

Mama and Grandma Augustine pushed me aside and marched into the the Tomb. Tia and Doo-witty swallowed hard. Mama still had her contest-winning quilt under her right arm. She shoved it at me roughly and walked up to Tia.

"Explain this to me, little girl," she said. "I want to know how in the world you can choose a day like this, and a place like this, to make your Mama's heart bleed blood. You tell me, Tia, why every girl in this place understood what today was supposed to be about but you."

"Mama, I'm sorry," Tia said, blinking her slanted eyes rapidly. "I didn't come here to do this. I just saw Doo-witty outside . . . and it just happened."

"'Just happened,' Tia? The only thing that just happens is death," Mama said, pointing to the second pair of oak double doors leading to the mortuary. "Everything else we got some control over. Do you understand me, little girl? This is not a mistake. It's an intent. You intended to make me look like I done raised you with my head always looking in the wrong direction, like I haven't ever seen nothing you done so I could teach you right from wrong."

"Mama, I wasn't trying to make you look bad," Tia said. "I swear I wasn't. I just . . . when it comes to Doo-witty . . . I don't know, Mama. I can't explain," she said, cutting her eyes away from Mama to Doo-witty, who was just standing there with his hands in his pockets, staring blankly, like he wasn't really sure what the heck was going on.

"Yes, you were, Tia," Mama continued. "You were trying to make me look like a pure fool. I bet everybody in this place know that you was back here with this no-account dumbo, but me. The whole neighborhood will be talking about it for weeks, along with the rest of my business, I'm sure."

"Mama, it wasn't like that," Tia said. "Nobody knows that I—"

"Th-that's right. It just happened," Doo-witty blurted out.

"If I was you, I would shut my mouth, and quick," Grandma Augustine said, shaking her cane at him. " 'Cause right now I'm asking the Lord for all the patience he can give me to keep me from beating all the black off your ass right here in this room. You no-good, foot-grabbing piece of—"

"Mu'dear!" Mama snapped. "Don't make things worse than they have to be. Miss Tia is the problem here, not Doo-witty. He ain't my child, she is. She's the one defying me."

Grandma Augustine got quiet.

"Tia," Mama said. "I admit, you and I have went toe to toe on a lot of things over the years. You just like your daddy, strong willed—stubborn—but I never dreamed you would do this to me."

"Mama, this ain't about you," Tia said with a trembling voice. "Why can't you see that? Why can't you understand that I got feelings just like you? This is about what's happening inside of me."

"Whatever it's about, Tia, I don't want it in my house," Mama said. "There can't be but one woman in my house. I won't have no woman-child. If you feel like your wings done sprouted and you ready to fly, take off—but the only woman in my house is me. Now, it's December, and my insides done cried the last tear of the year I'm gone cry over you. The Lord knows that I love you girls more than anything on this earth. But I don't know how much more of a burden I can bear. You make up your mind, Miss Tia. You can either be a girl or a woman, but I only got room for girls under my roof."

Mama snatched her quilt from me and walked out of the room. Grandma Augustine shook her cane at Doo-witty again, after that she turned and hobbled off behind Mama. I stood for a moment and looked at Tia and Doo-witty. Doo-witty had the same empty face, but Tia looked like someone had reached inside of her and pulled everything out. I walked over to her and threw my arms around her. I gave her a big hug and a kiss on the cheek. "I'm sorry," I said, and hurried out of the room.

As I followed Grandma's blue coat through the hallway, I remembered an ancient African saying that Grandma used to read me from her book of African folktales: "The birth of a daughter is both a joy and a disappointment to a father." I guess the saying was true for a mother as well.

By the time we got home the sun and moon were already starting to exchange shifts, and a line of bright stars was tiptoeing across the sky. Mama marched up our porch steps without saying a word, opened the front door, and went straight to her room. Grandma and I stared after her for a few moments, then we hurried in out of the cold too, dropped our coats on the living-room sofa, and stood trembling in the middle of the floor.

"Vera, I'll light the heaters and get some dinner to going," Grandma yelled at Mama's closed door. "You go on and get ready for work. I'll stay here with the baby."

For a second or two I frowned at the word *baby*. No matter how old I got Grandma Augustine always talked about me as if I were still wetting my diapers. It was like she couldn't see that I didn't suck my thumb anymore. But my frown didn't last for long. What had happened between Mama and Tia had broken something in me also, and right now Grandma Augustine's mothering was just what I needed to hold me together. I watched her pull a clear Bic lighter out of her handbag, then I followed her into our bedroom and stood by her side while she lit the dusty old gas heater in the corner of the room.

After Grandma Augustine had warm blue flames flickering

and dancing in every heater in our tiny house, she headed to the kitchen to start dinner. I dogged her footsteps, following her closely like a hungry kitten.

When she got to the kitchen, Grandma Augustine leaned her cane against a wall. She yanked open the refrigerator and took out a fat green cabbage. She washed the vegetable off in the metal sink, snatched a plastic bowl and a large knife out of the dish drainer, and started to cut it up. I pressed the side of my face into her back and sighed. She paused her cutting.

"Shayla, what's the matter with you, baby?" she asked.

"I don't feel good, Grandma," I answered, breathing in the minty scent of her arthritis medication.

"What's hurting you, baby?" she asked. I shrugged my shoulders, pressed my face closer against her back, and put my arms around her waist. I didn't know what to say. There were a lot of things bothering me. I felt like muddy water, and hurt was swimming through me like catfish.

"I don't know, Grandma," I said. "I just don't feel good."

Grandma Augustine put the knife and cabbage down. I let her go, and she turned around and looked at me. Her normally stern eyes were soft and gentle.

"I know you hurting, honey," she said. "We all are, but sometimes things have to boil to the top before they can cook down nice and smooth. Do you understand what I'm saying?" she asked, taking my chin in her hand.

"No, Grandma," I said. "I just understand that soon it'll be Christmas, and I don't feel good."

"Don't you worry yourself into the sickbed. You just be patient. You'll understand it better by and by," Grandma Augustine said, turning back to her cabbage.

"Okay, Grandma," I said.

"Shayla, do you like boys?" Grandma Augustine asked.

"Boys are okay," I answered.

"Just okay?" she asked.

"Just okay," I said. "I like boys, but not like Tia."

"You're slow natured," Grandma Augustine said. "Your womanhood is dripping out of you drop by drop, like tree sap. I was like that at your age. I was nearly eighteen before I really liked boys, you know, the way your sister, Tia, does."

"Is that bad, Grandma?" I asked.

"Naw, child, ain't nothing wrong with it at all. Some women run fast and hard away from their girlhood, others crawl away like infants. You're a crawler. Ain't no shame in that. The faster you run, the less time you have to notice what's going on around you. You can't see that ole Foot Grabber snatching at your ankles. Like I said before, I came into my womanhood slow. For the longest time I couldn't stand to be 'round boys. They was so loud and rough. You wouldn't know it now, but when I was your age, I was a shy little thing, kept to myself mostly. My mama said that I was like dust. I could settle anywhere but never be a part of nothing. Then one day I was setting outside on the front porch reading a book, and your late Grandpa Theodore come walking by the gate. He had just come from the barber shop, and he was strutting and smiling with his chest all puffed out, like only a man can do. Lord! He was the handsomest thing. I don't know. It seems like right then and there I just floated clean out of my body, floated straight up in the air. When I looked down, I could see that shy little girl with long pigtails sitting on the steps reading her book. I saw that girl put that book down. Then I saw her get up off them steps, open the gate, and go right out into the street. That girl started walking, walking,

walking. She kept right on walking down that street until I couldn't see her no more. Then, I floated back down to Earth and I was a woman."

"Is that what's gonna happen to me, Grandma?" I asked.

"Something like that. It's different with every girl."

"Oh," I said. I looked at the round wall clock over the canned goods shelf. "I wonder where Tia is at?" I whined.

"Don't you worry none, baby," Grandma Augustine said. "Remember what I told you. Sometimes things have to boil to the top before they can cook down nice and smooth."

I nodded my head at Grandma Augustine. Then I left the kitchen, went to my room, and got my blue notebook. *Pain is running from our faucets like tap water,* I wrote. *And my sister, Tia, ain't never coming home.*

After Grandma put the cabbage on the stove to simmer, Mama came out of her room wearing her navy blue work uniform and her red overcoat, and fixed herself a pan of hot-water corn bread. She didn't say a word to me or Grandma while she fixed the bread. She just stood there listening to the grease sizzle, watching the patties turn golden brown in the cast-iron skillet. When she was finished, she wrapped the patties in a piece of used aluminum foil, shoved them into her purse, and headed for the back door.

"Shayla, lock this door behind me, then go up front and latch that one, too," she said, turning the rusty lock on the back door.

"What about Tia?" I asked.

"Miss Tia knows how to knock on this door if she wants to get back in it!" Mama barked. "You do what I told you to do," she said, unhooking the screen door and stepping out.

"Yes, ma'am," I said. I latched the screen door behind her and shut the door. I turned the lock quickly, and I went up to the front of the house and locked that door. When I got back to the kitchen, Grandma Augustine was taking a pink package of hamburger out of the refrigerator. I looked at the bloodred meat and felt sick.

"Grandma, I'm not hungry," I said, and started for my room, holding my stomach. As I passed the wooden plant stand in the tiny hallway that linked my room to the kitchen I heard Grandma Augustine yell something after me. But I didn't catch what it was. I was thinking about Mama. Had she gone crazy? How could she tell me to lock Tia out of the house? She and Tia had always fought, but none of their fights had ever ended like this.

I opened the door to my room and flopped down on me and Tia's bed, hoping that I would feel Tia's warm body lying there in the darkness, but she wasn't there. I was too sad to get my blue notebook out again, so I just added a note to the journal that I keep in my head. *Madness is pushing up through our floors like bean sprouts, and Mama's been abducted by aliens.*

I didn't mean to, but I slept. When I woke up, the moon was high over our house, beaming brightness through my bedroom window. I got up, walked over to the flimsy curtains, and yanked them back. There was a thick frost on the window. I scribbled my name in it and watched as liquid crystals formed on the glass and dripped down it like tears.

I sighed. I wanted to look at the digital alarm clock sitting on the bookcase next to the window, but I couldn't. I didn't want to know what time it was. I knew from the icy silence in the house that Tia wasn't home yet. I wondered if she was still hanging out in the Tomb with dumb ole Doo-witty. Naw, she wouldn't be that stupid. Tia was lovestruck, not foolish. She had already made Mama explode like a frozen water pipe. She wouldn't piss her off anymore tonight. But where was she? I thought about calling down to her friend Maxi's house, but Maxi and her family were out of town for the holidays. Maxi's grandma was really ill. The family had been in Georgia for the past two weeks. I sighed again, pressing my face against the glass, and peered out through the letters of my name at Kambia's house just a few feet away.

I hadn't seen Kambia since Friday afternoon, when our biology teacher, Mrs. Feely, kicked her out of class for the second time. Kambia had refused to take her seat after we got back from lab. For several minutes she had stood in the center of the room with her arms linked into a circle high over her head, claiming to be a newly blossomed sunflower waiting to be pollinated by a bee. Miss Feely didn't think that it was funny at all. She pushed Kambia out of the door and told her to get herself down to the office. Kambia got three days of after-school detention.

I blinked and looked through the chain-link fence that connected my house and Kambia's. There was someone standing on the other side of it. I wiped away the rest of the frost. It was Kambia's mom. Besides the moonlight, a light was glowing in a small window on the side of the house. I could clearly make out Kambia's mom's wide hips and heavy ankles.

She was leaning against the rotten boards of the house, staring underneath it, and she was wearing next to nothing. She had on some sort of lacy shorty gown that barely came down to her butt, and her legs looked really dark, like she was wearing tights or panty hose. As quietly as I could I unhooked the metal latch on the window and opened it just a bit.

"Kambia Elaine. I'm not playing with you, girl. You bring your butt back in this house right now," Kambia's mom cried.

"I can't." Kambia's voice floated in faintly through the window. I bent down and looked through the opening so that I could see underneath her house. Like my house, the foundation sat high up on bricks, to keep the house from flooding when the bayou overflowed. I squinted. There was something moving around down there. I caught a glimpse of white. It had to be Kambia's dingy dress.

"Do you hear me, little girl?" her mother asked while pounding on the side of the house. "It's cold out here. I'm freezing my behind off. You come outta there right now!"

"I can't," Kambia said.

"Damn, girl! I swear you get on my nerves sometimes. You the stupidest thing that any woman ever gave birth to. I knew I shoulda left your ass in Dallas, let 'em put you in a foster home or something. But I thought that you could do something to help me out. Help me keep my head above water. Now, you bring your ignorant behind out from underneath this house right now! I mean it, Kambia. You gone make me go off on you!"

"I can't," Kambia repeated.

"All right, then, fine. I'm not gone stand out here in the cold begging you to have some sense. Stay under there and freeze for all I care, you stupid-ass fool."

Kambia's mom stomped away from the side of the house, crunching the frozen grass loudly in her three-inch heels. I waited a few seconds until she disappeared in the shadow of the front porch and the door slammed, then I opened the window as far as I could and called softly.

"Kambia." She didn't reply. "Kambia," I called again. Nothing. There was no screen on the window, so I just hopped out. The cold hit me before I hit the ground. Kambia's mom was right. It was freezing out. The wind was cutting something fierce through my thin cotton sweater and faded jeans as I walked over to the fence.

"Kambia," I called again, but this time a bit louder. Nothing. I looked around quickly. It was all clear. I climbed over the fence and stepped onto the ground as lightly as I could to keep the grass from crunching. I wasn't sure why, but I didn't want Kambia's mom to see or hear me. I didn't want her to know that I had heard what she said to Kambia.

I bent down again and peered underneath the house.

"Kambia," I called, squinting to see in the darkness.

"Is that you, Shayla?" she called back.

"Yeah," I said, catching sight of her white dress again.

"You can come under if you want," she said. "But just you, nobody else."

"Ain't nobody out here but me," I said, easing under the wood frame. I got down on all fours and crawled through the loose dirt in the direction of where I thought she was sitting. The closer I got, the more I could see of her, until I could almost make out her thin pink lips and the whites of her olive eyes.

"Kambia, what are you doing here?" I asked, stopping in front of her.

"I'm hiding," she said through chattering teeth. It was a little warmer under the house, but not much. Kambia must have felt like an ice cube in her short sleeves.

"What are you hiding from?" I asked, shivering slightly.

"Wallpaper Wolves," she answered. "I'm hiding from Wallpaper Wolves."

"What?" I asked. Her teeth stopped chattering.

"They live in your wallpaper," she said. "They have five-inch fangs, fiery red eyes, purple horns, long sharp claws, and spiky gray fur, but only at night," she whispered. "They look really different during the day."

"What do they look like?" I whispered back.

"During the day they don't have any color at all," she said. "You can see straight through them. They attach their ugly bodies to your wallpaper with five big suction cups that grow underneath their huge stomachs. And when you walk by, they can reach out and grab you with their claws."

"Kambia, that's the stupidest story I ever heard," I blurted out quickly, but then I remembered that I had promised myself I wouldn't hassle Kambia about her stories anymore. I would try and make sense out of them. "Where do the wolves come from, Kambia?" I asked.

"The Lie Catcher makes them," she said.

"The what?"

"The Lie Catcher. He lives high up in the tallest branches of our trees. He has a head shaped like a tube of lipstick and eighty murky green eyes sticking out of his bloated belly. Whenever he hears a person telling a lie, he jumps down from his tree and scoops the lies up with his bony hands before they can spread from person to person, then he takes them back to his home in the tree, mixes them with his evil, poisonous spit, and makes Wallpaper Wolves."

"Why?" I asked.

"I don't know," she said. "He just does. He doesn't like people, I guess. He's really mean and cruel. Anyway, when a family leaves for a picnic or something like that, he climbs down from his tree again, pries open their window, lets in the Wallpaper Wolves, and watches until they attach themselves to a wall."

"Oh," I said.

"Once the wolves are on your wall," she continued, "they can reach out and grab you whenever you walk by."

"What do they do after they grab you?" I asked.

She didn't answer.

"What do they do after they grab you?" I repeated.

"You don't want to know," she said in a trembly voice.

"Yes, I do," I said. She sighed. For several seconds the whites of her eyes disappeared, then they showed up again.

"They whisper horrible, nasty things in your ear," she said. "Then they make you do them."

"What kind of things?" I asked.

"You don't want to know," she repeated.

"Yes, I do," I said again. "I told you I did."

"They are bad, bad, horrible things. Things that hurt," she said, whispering again.

"What kind of things that hurt?" I asked. She paused again for a few seconds.

"I . . . I . . . can't tell you, Shayla," she finally whispered. "If I tell you, they'll hurt me even worse."

I felt myself starting to shiver, and it wasn't from the cold. I knew that Kambia was just telling another one of her tales, but this one was much stranger than the rest. It was really frightening. I didn't want to, but I knew that I had to hear all of it.

"Kambia, how come you can't tell me?" I asked.

Kambia started to hum softly, a nursery rhyme. It was "Three Blind Mice," the same rhyme that she hummed the day she pretended she was going to jump into the roaring waters of the bayou. I started to get really pissed. "Kambia, how do they hurt?" I asked sternly, reaching into the darkness and grasping her skinny arm. It was cold and rigid. "Kambia, stop humming," I said, shaking her lightly. She kept it up. "Kambia, stop singing baby songs!" I said, shaking her a bit harder. She stopped.

"Do you know, Shayla," she said, "that when it's cold outside, it's because God has stuck the earth into his freezer."

"No," I snapped.

"It's true," she said. "God has a really big freezer, big enough to hold the entire universe—stars, moons, and even planets. When he wants it to be cold out, he just picks up a planet or moon and sticks it into that freezer."

"Kambia, what kind of horrible—," I began, but my sentence was cut off by the sound of male voices laughing loudly. Kambia left my side and crawled over to the edge of the house. The men's voices were soon followed by the scrape and tap of footsteps walking down the cement porch steps.

"Y'all come back soon," Kambia's mom called out in a sweet, girlie voice. Then Kambia's front door slammed again.

"I'm going in now, Shayla," Kambia said.

"What about the wolves?" I asked, crawling over to her.

"I gotta go," she said. "I'll see you in school."

Kambia scurried from underneath the house. I saw her bony legs run toward the front porch, and soon afterward heard the front door slam for a third time.

I crawled out on all fours, walked over to the fence, and hopped it back into my yard. I didn't climb back in my window right away. I stood there, still shivering and trying to make sense out of Kambia's story. It had really shaken me up. My heart was thumping hard again in my chest. I looked through my window at the tattered wallpaper over my bed. In the moonlight I thought I saw a pair of fiery red eyes staring back at me. I swallowed hard and blinked, and the eyes went away. I took a deep breath and hoisted myself back up through the window. When Tia got home, I would tell her about Kambia's Wallpaper Wolves story, and how bizarre it was that Kambia was hiding underneath her house. Tia could figure anything out. I looked at the digital alarm clock on the bookcase. It flashed 10:35 in bright red numbers. *Tia will be home soon*, I told myself. *Everything will make sense once she walks in the door.*

Chapter 4

Morning came and went, and before I knew it noon was tapping on the windows. I let her in with a brush of angel's wings and a swish of Satan's tail. That's what Grandma Augustine calls it when it's a nice, beautiful day outside, but you feel all backwater blue inside. It's been two weeks, and Tia hasn't come home or even called. Worry is growing up the side of the house like moss on trees. Grandma Augustine says that she knew that this would happen. She says that the night Tia and Mama fought she had a dream about a demon baby.

In her dream she was back home in her own house, down by Horton's Fruit Stand. It was around nine o'clock or so, and she had just dragged in from her Monday night bridge game. When she opened her front door, there was the demon baby, sitting in the middle of her new crushed-velvet Sears sofa, bawling its head off and yelping loudly like it was some sort of wounded dog. Grandma Augustine says that the child was buck naked, so she could tell that it was a girl child, barely two years old, with glowing eyes that looked as if they had fireflies in them and lightened up her entire living room. Grandma Augustine almost fainted from fright. "I felt real dizzy, but I took my Bible outta my purse and I throwed Psalms at that demon until it disappeared and went back on to hell where it came from," she said.

Grandma Augustine thinks that the baby was sent here by Tia's Foot Grabber. She thinks that it was sent here to tell us that Tia isn't coming home. "Them Foot Grabbers always let you know when they got the upper hand. They can't never leave well enough alone. I was wrong. I thought that things would be fine after everything was brought to the light. I didn't count on that ole Foot Grabber playing a dirty hand."

To even things up Grandma Augustine has been to see Madam Vahilia Racine twice since Tia left, hoping that Madam Racine can mix up another Foot Grabber potion, one that will get the Foot Grabber out of our lives for good. Mama isn't happy about it at all. She says that Grandma is wasting her time, throwing away her money on foolishness, when she can hardly pay her rent each month. "I told you before, Mu'dear, that backwater bayou voodoo foolishness ain't got no place in the real world. You might as well tear your money into pieces and throw it into the fire. You ain't doing nothing but making that crazy Racine woman rich."

According to Mama, Tia is just fine and will be home any day now. She says that Tia is probably holed up somewhere with one of her girlfriends, trying to make Mama change her mind about Doo-witty. "When she gets tired of showing her behind and having to wear them other gals' clothes, she'll come home," Mama says. But Mama doesn't really believe this. The truth is, Mama is more worried about Tia than any of us. In the past two weeks she has missed seven days off of work. She spends most of her time sitting in Tia's space, on the side of the porch, staring at Tia's yellowing bra, which is still clinging to the thorny rose bushes, or looking off down the street, hoping to catch a glimpse of Tia's long braids blowing somewhere in the distance.

And when she isn't doing either one of those things, Mama's cutting out quilting squares. She's filled up every empty box and basket in our house with star-shaped and triangular pieces of old material. Sometimes she stays up all night long sipping tea and cutting, making endless stacks of fabric, like she's trying to make enough quilts to cover the whole world. Grandma Augustine thinks that Mama has cried an ocean of tears on the inside over what she said to Tia, and that she probably wishes she could replace the bad words that she said with good ones. "Once your words fly out of your mouth, you sometimes can't control whether they fly straight or crooked," Grandma Augustine says. "They can get bent in the strangest of ways."

Grandma Augustine says that the only way to straighten out bad words is to keep making good ones until you say what you need to say to who you need to say it to. With this in mind, she decided to take a trip over to Doo-witty's house to have a word with Doo-witty. Mama didn't think that it was a good idea, but she said that at least it wasn't costing Grandma Augustine any money. But, considering Frog's bad attitude and Grandma's temper, she sent me along to make sure that all Grandma did was talk.

It was nearly one when we got over to Doo-witty's house. The lollipop-shaped bus stop signs were surrounded with kinky-haired, warmly dressed brothers and sisters exchanging loud greetings as they waited for the Number Eleven to come moaning and shaking down the narrow blocks. A bright sun was dancing in and out of a cluster of soft marshmallow clouds, and a cool breeze was running up and down the rows of paintless shacks, blowing frost on the screenless windows. Grandma Augustine snatched open Frog's wooden gate and hobbled up the steps in her flowered house duster and brown jacket, as bold as she could, like she was the landlord coming to collect the rent. I skirted around her on the steps and rapped on the door lightly, before she could bang on it with her Doberman-headed cane. Frog appeared almost instantly, her big balloon belly bursting against a tight polyester long-sleeved blue dress. She had combed her wiry gray-black hair into thin cornrows, and though it was the middle of the day, her pop eyes looked heavy with sleep.

"We want to speak with Doo-witty," I said quickly.

"Who want to speak with Doo-witty?" Frog barked.

"I do," Grandma Augustine said, pushing me aside. I walked over to the porch column and leaned against it.

"Miss Earlene, I don't believe I have to introduce myself," Grandma Augustine said.

"I know who you are, Mrs. Dubois," Frog replied. She rolled her eyes a bit, but not enough to set Grandma Augustine off.

"I come to have a word with Doo-witty," Grandma Augustine continued. "I want to talk to him about my grandbaby Tia."

"If that's what you come to talk about, you might as well get off of my porch," Frog spat. "Doo-witty don't know nothing about that gal."

"I find that hard to believe," Grandma Augustine said. "The last time I saw him, he was so tight up on Tia that I couldn't tell where his skin ended and hers began. A man all over a young gal like that don't suddenly know nothing about her."

Frog placed her hands on her hips and glared at Grandma real mean, like an angry German shepherd ready to strike. And she would strike too. Frog was famous in the neighborhood for talking with her hands instead of her mouth. She usually didn't take mess off of anyone. Last year, at the Women of Mahogany Festival, she had slapped a thin, freckle-faced woman dead in the mouth, just for what she called "looking at me funny."

"What is it you after here, Mrs. Dubois? What do you think you gone get from my Doo-witty?" she asked.

"What I'm hoping to get is some information about where my grandbaby could possibly—"

"Well, Doo-witty ain't home, so I guess you cain't get nothing from him," Frog spat again, throwing her usual bits of spit all over the place. Grandma Augustine moved her head back to avoid the shower. "But I can tell you this," Frog continued. "Doo-witty did drag that gal down here a couple of weeks ago. He said that her mama told her that if she didn't stop messing around with him, she could live out on the streets."

"That ain't what was said at all," Grandma Augustine said patiently, but you could see Mr. Anger doing somersaults behind her stern eyes. I took a deep breath and let it out.

I didn't know how long Grandma Augustine could control Mr. Anger. Grandma was pretty good at striking, herself. Once, when I was little, Grandma and me took a trip to the JCPenney on Main. While we were walking down one of the clothing aisles, some small dude came up behind Grandma and stuck his hand in her purse. Grandma snatched that guy's hand out of her purse, turned around, and started beating him like he had actually got a chance to steal something. She beat that guy high and low, until the manager of the store finally pulled her off of him, took him into his office, and locked the door. Grandma banged on the door for nearly fifteen minutes until the law showed up.

"I don't know what was said. I just know what I was told," Frog snapped. "Don't matter anyway. I told Doo-witty that there was no place in this house for that gal. I don't allow none of that modern-day throwing-your-legs-over-your-head-before-you-married mess in my house. I told Doo-witty that that gal could either take her fast-tail behind back to her mama's house or find a friend's place to lay her head at for the night, but she wasn't gone come in here shaming my house like she did hers, at least not with me knowing about it. Doo-witty told her that she was gone have to go somewhere else.

I ain't seen her since then. Now, Doo-witty's been visiting his uncle in Beaumont for the past week. I'll ask him about it when he gets home. If the subject stays in my head that long."

"You do that," Grandma said. She started to hobble back down the steps. I followed her.

"If you see that slut of a gal before Doo-witty get back here," Frog yelled, "you tell her to stay away from my son!"

Grandma Augustine stopped. I bumped into her and fell off the step onto the ground.

"What did you call my grandbaby?" Grandma Augustine yelled back.

"She called her a slut, Grandma. Tia ain't no slut!" I yelled, wiping off my knees.

"You stay outta grown folks' business and don't be repeating what they say," Grandma Augustine said sharply. She walked back up to Frog, holding her cane in her callused hand like a club. I hopped back up on the porch and reclaimed my place next to the post.

"Now, Miss Earlene," Grandma Augustine said. "I didn't come over here to get into a fight with you like my daughter Vera did. I spoke to you plain and simple, like a woman, not some street trash. I would appreciate it if you would speak to me in that same manner, like a woman."

"I'm speaking to you like a woman!" Frog yelled. "I'm speaking to you like a woman that's tired of that gal of your daughter Vera's messing up the plans I got for my son." Frog pointed her finger at Grandma. "Now, Doo-witty ain't smart, and I admit to that," she said. "But he ain't no fool, either, like people around here try to make him out to be. He can do the same things that most people can do. It just takes him a little longer. That's all. I know it ain't no two or three ways about it, Doo-witty ain't much to look at, and I admit that, too, but that's my fault, not his. He didn't ask for his face to come out looking like mine. He didn't get no choice in the matter. Some thangs is just left up to God. But I'll tell you what ain't just left up to God, and that is what he gets outta life. And I tell you now, Mrs. Dubois, that I don't intend to let him throw what little chances he got away on some little short-skirted gal that don't know how to keep her dress down. I'm trying to make things right for Doo-witty. I'm not sure you know this, but there's sorrow in having children sometimes."

Grandma Augustine's cane relaxed a little in her hands. For a few seconds she just stood there staring at Frog with her forehead and eyebrows all scrunched up, like she had something really serious on her mind. Finally her face kinda went all soft.

"Oh, I know about sorrow and children," Grandma said. "I had my daughter Vera late in life. I lost four children before she was born. Two of 'em was born with the shadow of death on their faces, another two was called back to Jesus before I could sew 'em up a christening gown. Now, I understand how you feel about your son, but you also have to understand how I feel about my daughter and my grandbabies. I want what's right for them, too. Tia is only a girl of fifteen, and Doo-witty done already run up on twenty-three. Now, I don't care if he's smart, stupid, ugly, or pretty. He is still a man, and me and my daughter hold him responsible for his actions as we would any another man. But since I'm pretty sure that the devil got his hand in this mess somewhere, and I never did learn to trust the law when it came to black men, I told my daughter that we ought to give Doo-witty the chance to make his feelings known on the subject. Miss Earlene, I'm an old woman. I don't intend to go all over this neighborhood looking for Tia. The last time I saw her she was with Doo-witty. He needs to tell me where she is or where she ain't, and that's all I got to say on the matter," Grandma Augustine said, heading down the steps.

"When Doo-witty gets back, I'll pass the message on," Frog said. She cleared her throat. "I'm sorry about your babies," she called softly.

"Thank you, Miss Earlene," Grandma Augustine said. "But I cried my tears over them babies long before you was even thinking about being born. Come on, Shayla," she added. I started down the steps after her, but then I turned and walked back up to Frog.

"If Doo-witty knows where Tia is at," I said, "tell him to tell her to come home. Tell her that Mama isn't mad at her anymore, and that if she comes home, I'll trade my soft side of the bed for her lumpy one." Frog didn't respond. I hurried after Grandma.

On the way back to the house we passed a plump, curly-haired woman with large brown eyes sitting on the steps of a one-story house, bouncing a giggling baby boy on her knees. I didn't know that Grandma Augustine had had any children before Mama. Grandma was always so strict with Mama, always coming over and taking charge. Who would have thought that death had pulled on the tail of her skirt four times before Mama was born? I tried to form a picture of Grandma's babies. Were they big and strong-built like her and Mama, or small with fine bones like Tia? Did they have Grandma's serious wide eyes and a narrow nose, or soft slanty eyes and a pug nose like Mama's and Tia's? Would any of them have looked like me when they were my age, plump with no chest to speak of? I wanted to ask Grandma about the babies, but I didn't think that she would talk to me about them. I had a feeling that they would fall under "grown folks' business."

I decided to give Grandma's dead babies names so that I could always keep them with me. I named them after my favorite colors—Violet, Fuchsia, Gold, and Blue—so that whenever I saw those colors in a beautiful flower garden, I would see the babies' tiny faces smiling back at me. When I got a chance, I would make a journal entry about it. *Grandma's babies slipped out of her body into nothingness*, I would write. *But I'll remember them every time I see the soft petals of a carnation or pass a field of bluebonnets.*

When we got back home, Grandma Augustine decided to head over to her house so that she could feed her cat, Nat King Cole, and check her mail. She told me that she would be back in a little while, and that I had better get ready for this afternoon.

I sat down on the porch step and pulled my nylon windbreaker closed over my blue-jeans jumper. Nothing at all was right in the world. The crickets were buzzing and the bees were chirping. We still didn't know where Tia was, and I had to get ready for this afternoon.

Mr. Anderson Fox, my sometimes father, had rung Mama last night and told her that he was rolling through town for a visit so he could see how the neighborhood looked and say hi to his little girl. I wondered what little girl he was talking about. From what I heard around the hood, he could have been talking about me or at least three other girls around my age, all with a different mother, all born while he and Mama were still hooked up.

Mama was married to Mr. Anderson Fox for six years. He and Mama had something called a common law marriage, which Grandma Augustine says really isn't a marriage at all, but what the old folks call shacking up.

According to the neighborhood grapevine, Mr. Anderson Fox, like Maurice Jafee, was good at lots of things. He was kinda good at holding down a job at Lulu's Bakery on Grayson, pretty good at going to services every other Sunday at Precious Jesus Baptist

Church, and very good at keeping his old 1975 Ford fixed up and filled with gas. But what he was great at was stepping out on Mama, which was something he did most Friday and Saturday nights. "He had a pretty good heart," some of the older folks in the hood say. "Your mama could always count on him to buy you diapers and stuff like that. But he couldn't be true to just one woman. It wasn't in his nature."

I don't know what was or wasn't in Mr. Anderson Fox's nature. I know only that he left Mama when I was five. He left her for a woman twice Mama's age, a saggy-faced widow with sad eyes and lots of cash in the bank. Mama had to pawn everything that we owned to pay the rent for the next two months. I was young, but I remember clearly that I didn't cry when he left. I felt all empty inside, like I was losing something, but I didn't know what. And I still don't know what. I have no idea how I'm supposed to feel whenever Mr. Anderson Fox decides to make one of his rare visits. Should I feel glad or angry? I'm only sure that I don't like playing daughter every time he feels the need to hear at least one of his kids call him Daddy.

Especially not today. I didn't have time for it, not with Tia still missing. What if Mama and Grandma were wrong? They were both sure that they knew where Tia was and who she was with. I wasn't so sure. If Tia was with one of her girlfriends, we would know about it by now. Tia's friends were all like her—smart, pretty, gossipy girls, who shared perfume and boyfriends. If Tia was with one of those girls, they woulda talked. And why would Frog lie? She hated Tia. She wouldn't protect her. The whole thing was as confusing as Kambia's Linda James mystery novels, except there was no secret passageways or dumbwaiters for Tia to get lost in.

I wanted to go looking for Tia, but Mama had told me not to.

"She went out of here on her own. Let her come back the same way," Mama said. "Ain't nobody gone beg her to have some sense." Should I defy Mama? I hadn't quite made up my mind yet. I would have to think about it later, after Mr. Anderson Fox took off. I got up from the porch steps and went inside.

After Grandma got through feeding Nat King Cole, she came back over to our house. Together she and Mama begged and wrestled me into a bright yellow dress that she made for me last Easter. I fought them all the way, complaining that the dress was way too small and that I looked like a big fat banana, but at two thirty, when Mr. Anderson Fox stepped into the front door, I was primped up like I was going to a church social, sitting in the middle of our burlap sofa next to Grandma with a frown on my face that woulda scared the bogeyman back underneath my bed, if I still believed in him.

Mr. Anderson Fox ignored my look. He walked into the living room, sporting a bright, nicely brushed row of thirty-twos, and nearly knocking us out with his loud musk-scented cologne. He was a nice-looking guy, smooth skinned with a neat goatee, carved cheekbones, and wavy hair. He probably could have been a movie star or at least one of those dudes in the deodorant ads if it wasn't for his eyes. He had what Grandma Augustine called "searchlight eyes." One of them was always looking in the opposite direction from the other. He eased his six-foot frame into a matching recliner across from me and Grandma, pulled a cigarette and a Bic lighter out of his dark gray suit, lit the cigarette, and stared at me through the white twirls of smoke. I scooted back in my seat and rolled my eyes.

"How you doing, baby?" he asked, stroking the rough hairs of his goatee.

"I can't breathe," I said with a nasal voice. Grandma Augustine pinched my thigh sharply with her wrinkled fingers. I jumped, then moved it as far away from her as I could.

"Oh, Lord, you sho is getting big," Mr. Anderson Fox said. "You remind me of your Aunt Leverta. She was about your size when she was your age."

"What age is that?" I snapped, still holding my nose. Grandma Augustine reached over and slapped my hand down. Mama, standing in the doorway, gave me a stern look that I know had to make Grandma proud. I shrugged it off.

I was pretty sure that Mr. Anderson Fox had no idea how old I really was. I was nine when he stopped sending me his usual every-other-year birthday cards—cheap, silly greetings that you could buy in a box of twenty at your local Kmart. There was never anything personal about them, no nice notes scrawled on the bottom, just the preprinted message with his initials underneath. I never got a letter from him or even a picture. He didn't bother to share any part of himself with me. In fact, there were only a couple of things that I actually knew about him. I knew that he was now living alone back in his hometown of Blue Eagle, Texas, where he worked at least four days a week grinding chunks of beef into hamburger patties at a meat packing plant near the town hall. I figured that he knew even less about me.

"Oh, you know what age I'm talking about," he said, with his big grin, but it was starting to fold in a little at the corners, like maybe it was getting tired of spreading across his face.

"No, I don't know what age that is," I said, rolling my eyes again. This time he scooted back in his seat.

"You don't know how old you is?" he asked with a fake laugh. I folded my arms across my chest.

"I know when my last birthday was," I said. "Do you?" He cleared his throat. Grandma Augustine tried to reach my thigh again, but I slid to the other side of the sofa. Mr. Anderson Fox turned his searchlight eyes on Mama with a surprised look on his face, like he had just noticed that she was in the room.

Mama was wearing her new plum layaway sweaterdress. It was clingy, like plastic wrap, and cut real deep in the front. It looked good on her. It made her skin look all velvety chocolate, and her heavy frame seem soft and delicate, not hard like it did when she wore her grocery stocker uniform.

"Vera, you sho do look nice," Mr. Anderson Fox said, adjusting his silk tie. Mama batted her eyes real girlie-like, like Tia sometimes does when she meets a cute guy on the street.

I wished that Tia would come walking through the door, like Mama thought she would. Tia didn't care for Mr. Anderson Fox any more than I did. She remembered the way Mama used to act on the nights that Mr. Fox stepped out on Mama. Tia said that Mama wouldn't cry, get mad, or nothing. She would just pace the floor all night long in the same spot, walking back and forth, as if she were trying to erase her own footsteps.

"Thank you, Anderson," Mama replied softly.

"Yeah, you sho do look nice. You sho do look nice," Mr. Anderson Fox repeated twice, before focusing back on me. I glared at him.

"Oh, you sho can make some ugly faces, little girl," he said with a nervous giggle.

"Shayla, stop that," Mama scolded. I didn't change my expression. Mr. Anderson Fox had no right wasting my time with his daddy-wanna-be questions. He had no right to expect any more from me than I expected from him, which was absolutely nothing.

"She don't mean nothing by it," Mama said. "She just been a little upset lately. The house been going through some adjustments."

"What kinda adjustments?" Mr. Anderson Fox asked.

"None that you need to be worried about," Mama answered. Mr. Anderson Fox turned his searchlight eyes on the room.

"Where's the other one, Vera?" he asked. "She hiding back there in the bedroom?"

Mama hesitated for a minute.

"Where's the other one at?" he asked again. Mama stared at the floor.

"She's visiting with some friends," she said.

"Oh, I'm sorry I'm gone miss her," Mr. Anderson Fox said. "Well, now," he said to me, "ain't you gone ask your daddy what he brought you?" I continued to glare.

"Ask him, Shayla," Mama said.

"Ask him," Grandma Augustine whispered next to me.

"I don't want to know, Grandma," I whispered back.

"You ask him anyway," she said. I shook my head.

"You don't want to know?" Mr. Anderson Fox asked. I shook my head again. His grin disappeared.

"Vera, what's wrong with this gal?" he asked, frowning. "I done come all the way over here just to see this child, and she treating me like I'm some kinda hobo or something, begging for a plate of food. You know that I ain't got time for this mess. You know how busy I am."

Busy. We were all busy. Mama was busy trying to take care of me and Tia. Grandma was busy trying to help her do it, and me and Tia were busy trying to pretend that we didn't mind having to share the same bed and wear the same clothes to school every other day.

Who wasn't busy? I looked in the doorway, past Mama, and saw Mr. Anger running into the room in his red anger suit, just waiting to jump into my eyes, but I waved him away. I didn't want to be angry at Mr. Anderson Fox. I didn't want him to think that I cared enough to let him hurt me. I just wanted him to leave me alone.

"I told you before," Mama said. "It ain't about you. She just got some heavy stuff sitting on her mind."

"Well, that still ain't no reason to treat me like I'm a stepchild. I got feelings too."

"What did you bring me?" I blurted out. His grin reappeared. He reached into his jacket pocket, pulled out an envelope, and handed it to me. I opened it. It was a bunch of fifty-dollar bills. Mama walked over and took the envelope from me. She counted the contents quickly, then stuck the whole thing in her bosom.

"What do you say to your daddy?" she asked.

"Thank you," I muttered.

"You can buy a whole lot of nice stuff with that," Mr. Anderson Fox said. "Anything that you like. What you gone buy?"

I shrugged my shoulders. "I don't know, maybe books," I said.

"Books, girl, you can get books outta the library. You don't need to be wasting no money on that!"

"Shayla likes books," Mama said. "Books and writing. She wants to be a writer."

"A what?" Mr. Anderson Fox shouted. "What she gone write?"

"Anything," Mama answered. "Her teachers say that she can write most anything. They always give her good grades."

"Aw, they just happy that she ain't cutting up and acting a fool in school, like some of them other knuckleheads," Mr. Anderson Fox said. "That's what that's about. But shoot—they know better than that. Writing, that's for them rich kids whose daddies and mamas got time for them to do that kinda mess. This girl gone need a real job when she gets outta school. She ain't gone have no time to be sitting around scribbling on no paper. Writer, umph, that's way whacked-out. She needs to be a nurse or something like that, something that's gone keep some food on the table. Now, you listen to me, baby girl," he said, leaning toward me. "You have your mama buy you some real pretty dresses with some of that money. And when you go to school next week, you tell them teachers that your daddy say that he wants you to take some of them biology classes. Tell them that he gone put you through the best nursing school in Texas when you get out of high school."

"Okay," I said. "Mama, can I go outside?" She nodded. I got up from the sofa and pecked Mr. Anderson Fox on the cheek. He started to say something fatherly, but before he even got the words out, I opened the front door and went out. As I was pulling it shut behind me Mr. Anger tried to squeeze through the opening, but I pushed him back in.

I sat down on the side of the porch and pulled my knees up to my chest. I wanted to cry, scream, or something, but I couldn't. I was just happy that the whole stupid thing was over. The front door creaked, and Grandma limped out on her cane, leaning heavily on her good right knee.

"I brought your wrap out," Grandma said, throwing my yellow cotton sweater around my shoulders. I slipped my arms into it. "You know, Shayla," she said. "When I was round about your age, I used to go visit my Great-Great-Aunt Ophelia up in Deer County, Texas."

"Up in where?" I asked.

"Deer County," she said, tugging the left sleeve of my sweater over my wrist. "Now, there wasn't but two things in Dear County," she continued. "There was mesquite trees as far as the eye could see, and one little ole grocery store made outta rotten plywood that sold all of the town's groceries."

"Grandma, what is this about?" I whined.

"I'm getting there," she answered sharply. "Now, that grocery store was owned and run by Mr. Leotis P. Farmer. He was a pretty good man, let you slide on your bill a month or two, but he was proud. The old folks used to say too proud."

"Why did they say that?" I asked.

"Because Mr. Farmer had had some trouble when he was a child, some kind of accident with lye, that messed up his eyesight. He could only see in shades of black and white—but he didn't want to admit it, didn't want nobody to know that he wasn't like everybody else in town. So, whenever a woman come into his store with a new dress on, he would compliment her on the color of it. 'That's a real nice green,' he would say. Or, 'Goodness, what a lovely pink,' whatever color popped into his mind. And do you know that those ladies never once corrected him."

"Why?" I asked.

"Because if they did, he would close the store for the next few days and sit around brooding about his disadvantage, and nobody in the town would be able to get they sugar, eggs, or milk until he opened back up."

"So the ladies gave him what he wanted so that the town could get what it wanted," I said. "But I didn't want anything from him, Grandma Augustine," I added.

"I know you didn't, baby, but your mama did. I'm not proud to say this, Shayla, but sometimes you have to go down the wrong path to get to the right place. I've had to do it in my life a time or two. It don't make you feel good, but it won't kill you either."

Grandma Augustine patted me on the head, then left the

porch and went back into the house. I stewed on her words for a minute, turning them over and over in my head, like a ham bone in a pot of navy beans. Finally, when I just couldn't stand to think about them a minute longer, I got up from the porch too. Grandma was right. Sometimes you had to go down the wrong path to get to the right place. Mama had got what she wanted, now I was gonna get what I wanted. I was gonna go hunting for Tia.

"Three blind mice, see how they run."

I looked over at Kambia's yard. She sat on the porch in her dingy dress and ragged red sweater. Her shoulder-length hair was parted in the middle and yanked back into two fuzzy balls, and her purple magic bracelet was dangling from her bony wrist. I was really shocked to see her. She usually had to sneak out during the day. I walked over to the fence and hopped it into her yard. Kambia's walkway and front porch were covered with some rather early fat black beetles.

"Yuck," I said, trying to walk around them. I made it up the walkway without stepping on any, but the minute I put my foot on the first step I heard a loud *crunch* and a *squish*.

"Gross," I yelled, and started to scrape the bug gook off the bottom of my shoe.

"No!" Kambia screamed.

"What's wrong?" I asked.

"You killed it," she whined.

"I didn't mean to," I said. "It's just an ugly ole beetle."

"No, it's a Memory Beetle," Kambia said, picking up one of the bugs and staring at it.

"A what?"

"A Memory Beetle," she said. "They keep all of your good memories, the ones that you don't ever want to forget."

"Really," I said. I leaned in close and stared at her fingers. The beetle was kicking its legs something fierce. It was none too happy about being caught up in one of Kambia's tales.

"It looks like any ole beetle to me," I said. "How do you know it's special?"

"Because they always come out extra early, before any of the other beetles, near the end of winter and the beginning of spring. They been doing it for almost eight hundred years. They leave their home on the dark side of the planet Uranus, fly to Earth, and gather up all of the wonderful thoughts that people don't want to forget. They gather and gather until their chubby bodies are almost bursting from people's memories and their dreams, then they fly back to Uranus, put them in golden boxes in their secret caves, and keep them there until someone wants to remember them again."

"Really," I said.

"That's right," she said. "It's a good thing, too, Shayla, because sometimes the bad memories in your head run all of the good ones off."

"What do you mean?" I asked.

She shrugged her shoulders. "The clouds are just pieces of Styrofoam. Did you know that, Shayla?" she asked, looking up at the sky.

"No," I answered, looking up at a mass of fluffy white clouds.

"They are," she said, gently putting the beetle down. "You want to know how?"

I nodded.

"Well," she said, "it was late one night when God unpacked the earth to place it in the sky. He had worked hard all day, teaching his angels how to fly and arguing with his builders over how many rooms he wanted in each wing of heaven. By the time he got around to taking Earth out of the box to place it in the sky, he was dog tired, so tired that when he picked it up and put it between the other planets and the moon, he forgot to clean off all of the funny little pieces of Styrofoam before he went to bed. Well, they stayed on top of the earth all night, which for us was many, many years. So, the next morning, when God finally got around to cleaning them off, we had already started to call them clouds, so he figured what's the use and left them there."

"That's funny," I said, giggling, letting my question about the bad memories drift out of my head. Kambia didn't laugh with me. She just looked at me strange, like a curious puppy, as if she didn't know what I was finding so funny.

"You sure do know a lot about God and stuff," I said. "Did you used to go to church a lot?"

She shook her head. "When we used to live up in Dallas," she said, "my mama would get beat up on a lot. We were always at the hospital for this or that. The nurses and doctors all knew me. Most of the time Mama would get fixed up real quick and we would go right home, but sometimes she had to spend a day or two. When they had to keep her, I would stay across the street at this house for nuns. They called it a convent. Well, anyway, they were always talking about Jesus, God, and stuff, and that's where I got it from."

"How come your mom got beat on so much?" I asked.

"I don't know," she said. "It just happened."

"Oh," I said. "Hey, what are you doing out, anyway?"

"One of my mom's new boyfriends just came over. My mom wanted me to stay, but he told her to make me go outside."

"I gotta go," I said.

"Where ya going?" she asked.

I looked down at the crawling beetles on the walkway. I didn't know what to say. I didn't want to tell Kambia where I was going. I was gonna start at Tia's best friend Maxi's house on the other side of the bayou, and I didn't want to take Kambia through there. I hadn't told anybody yet, but I couldn't help but remember that scary game she had played that day on the bayou after the rains, pretending to be a piece of driftwood and sliding down the hill toward the rushing waters. I remembered how she had stayed down there with the murky waters splashing against her legs until I told her that I believed her because I was scared that she was gonna drown or something in the water. The whole thing still made me dizzy.

But then I couldn't forget how she had stood up for me when Miss Marshall wouldn't let me enter my story into the writing contest because I had written it in street slang. She had fought for my words, while I just stood there crying and saying that there wasn't enough time for me to do the whole thing over. But she had acted strange that time, too, yelling at Miss Marshall that she had never ever been a little girl, and making me drag her from the room. I was starting to like Kambia a lot. Most of the time she was really cool, and I actually liked some of her stories, but sometimes she took things too far.

"I'm going to look for my sister, Tia," I said, not being able to come up with a way to lie to her.

"Can I come too?" she asked.

"Sure," I answered.

On the way to the bayou Kambia was her normally quiet self, the way she always was whenever we walked down the street. As usual she kept her head up high, her olive eyes taking in all the sights in the neighborhood, her mind somewhere that I couldn't reach. I walked along beside her thinking about Tia and stepping over the cracks in the sidewalk, trying not to break my mother's back.

When we got halfway to the bayou, I changed my mind. I didn't want to be anywhere near the water if Kambia decided to play another game. I decided to take the long route down the old Negro Union tracks, one of my favorite places. Grandma Augustine said that back during the time of the Jim Crow Laws, Tom Aldrich—Morgan's father, who owned a funeral parlor *and* an iron mill—made a deal with the railroad company that serviced Houston to run an old engine and a couple of passenger cars from Houston to Dallas, so that black folks could take a trip between the major cities without having to ride in the caboose. Grandma said that her mother told her that most of the folks thought it was a fine idea, but it didn't set too cool with others. "Some folks just saw it as another form of segregation," Grandma's mom said.

Anyway, the Negro Union tracks, as the folks in the Bottom called them, were supposed to be run by Aldrich himself. They were supposed to run on an abandoned rail no longer used by the railroad, located behind some of the better houses in the Bottom, but when it came time for the railroad to turn over the engine and the cars, they wouldn't do it. They had made the deal with Aldrich by letters. They didn't know until he showed up to sign the papers that he was black. They said that they didn't mind if any Negroes rode in their cars, but they drew the line at Negroes being in charge of them. They didn't care how much iron Aldrich was willing to give them for free. They tore up the railroad contract.

I told Kambia that we would have a lot of fun walking near the old railroad. There was a soft-shell pecan tree here and there along the tracks. I told her that if we could gather up enough pecans on the way, I could probably get Grandma Augustine to fix us some of her famous oatmeal pecan cookies. Kambia liked this idea a lot. We cut behind a row of boarded-up, windowless houses and headed for the tracks.

When we got to the start of the rusty railroad tracks, Kambia's face lit up. She ran ahead of me along the short tan grass next to the tracks, singing her "Three Blind Mice" song and cracking fallen pecans underneath the soles of her worn-out Nikes. I followed her with a frown on my face. I had been wrong about the pecans. The season was pretty much over. Most of the pecans on the ground were still in their rotted shells, pitch-black and worm-eaten. There would be no oatmeal cookies for us, but Kambia didn't seem to mind. While I examined nuts by turning them over with the tip of my foot, she just kept walking, singing, and cracking. It didn't take too much to make Kambia happy. There was something really nice about that, and for just a little while I let Kambia's good mood run my worries about Tia out of my mind.

For the past week I had been trying to figure out whether or not I wanted to take a poetry class that was being offered down at the cultural center next month. I liked words, and I was sure that I could probably spin out a poem or two if I thought about it, but I didn't really want to have to do it in front of a whole group of kids, and that was what you had to do in the class. You had to write a poem every meeting and read it at the end of class to the rest of the students. I wasn't much for doing anything that might get me laughed at. Once, when I was seven, I had to give an Easter speech at Grandma Augustine's church. I studied the speech for two weeks. I knew it backward and forward, but when the time came for me to give it, I just stood there in my organdy dress with my hair decorated with poodle-shaped barrettes and my mouth wide open, like a turkey in a rainstorm. All the people laughed, and Grandma Augustine covered her face with her church program. I was a complete idiot. I told myself that I would never get up in front of a group again. But I really wanted to take the class. It was being taught by some African-American sister whose stories were in lots of neat magazines. I wanted to meet her and ask her what it felt like to know that so many people were reading her stuff. I thought that it must be great, but really, really scary.

I looked around and noticed that we had passed the dirt turnoff that led to Maxi's house. Kambia was a piece up the tracks from me, still walking and singing. I yelled at her to come back

"Hey, Kambia, come back. We missed our turnoff." She stopped next to a huge pecan tree, whose thick branches looked like streaks of black lightning against the blue sky.

"Let's go back, Kambia!" I repeated. She didn't move. She stood there all rigid with her arms glued to her sides. She was playing one of her baby games. I trotted up to her.

"Come on, Kambia," I said. "We passed Maxi's house already. We gotta go back. Come on," I said, tugging gently at the back of her sweater. I heard a few of the threads rip as the material stretched.

"I can't move," she said.

"Yes, you can," I said. "Come on. I don't have time for silly games."

"I can't," she said. "I can't walk. I don't have any legs. I have a trunk. I'm a pecan tree."

"No, you're not," I said. "You're a plain ole girl, just like me."

"No," she said. "I'm a pecan tree. I was planted here way back before the Civil War. I saw the end of slavery. I was here before all the houses were built, before there were lights, before the cars, the buses, the radios, the telephones, the TVs, everything."

I walked around to her front. Her face was red from the cold, and her eyes had that same strange, blank look in them that they had had that day on the bayou and the time she went off on Miss Marshall. I didn't like this game at all.

"You are not," I insisted. "You're just a plain ole girl."

"I'm a pecan tree," she repeated.

"You're not a tree," I said. "If you were a pecan tree, you would have branches and leaves. Where are your leaves? Where are your branches?"

She stretched her arms out like an airplane and started to wiggle her fingers. "See," she said. "I got branches and I got leaves. My leaves can even blow in the wind."

"Fine," I said. "But you don't have any pecans. You can't be a pecan tree without pecans. You don't have any pecans."

"My pecans all fell to the ground during the last rainstorm."

"Then how do I know that you're a pecan tree? How do I know you're not an oak or something like that? I'll bet you're not a pecan tree at all."

"Yes, I am. I'll show you," she said. Staying as rigid as she could, she did a knee bend down to the ground and began picking up the rotten nuts and setting them on her head. Most of them rolled back off.

"Kambia, cut it out," I said. "I told you the last time you did this that I didn't like playing this game. You're not a pecan tree or a crab or a sunflower or any of those things. I don't like it when you pretend to be something else."

"I'm a pecan tree," she repeated, picking up a nut. A cool breeze suddenly rushed through the trees. It caught the skirt of her flared dress and lifted it up. I could see straight between her skinny legs. I gasped. There were big, purplish red bruises on her. They started from her crotch and came halfway down her thighs. They were really gross-looking, like maybe she had taken a bad fall or something. But I didn't know how she could have fallen and hurt herself there.

"Kambia, what happened to your thighs?" I asked. She dropped the nut, yanked her dress down, and stood up.

"Let's go, Shayla," she said.

"What happened to your thighs?" I repeated.

"We better go back, Shayla," she said.

"Kambia, what happened to your thighs?" I asked. "Did you fall off a bike or something?"

"I don't know what you're talking about, Shayla," she said. "We better get home."

"You got bruises all over you," I said. "Don't they hurt? How'd you get them?" She didn't answer me. I was getting mad. I knew that she knew what I was talking about. "Kambia, you never tell me anything," I said. "I thought you were supposed to be my friend, but you never tell me nothing."

"I can't tell you, Shayla," she said. "I can't."

"Why not?" I asked. "I'd tell you. That's what friends do, they tell each other."

"I won't tell you, Shayla," she said.

"Fine," I snapped. "I'll ask your mom," I lied, walking past her. She yanked me back by my windbreaker.

"No, Shayla, don't, please!" she cried. "You'll get me into big trouble."

"What kind of trouble?" I asked. She shook her head. "How did you get the bruises?" I asked.

"The Wallpaper Wolves did it," she said in a trembly voice.

"No such a thing," I said, remembering her story from a couple of weeks ago. "It ain't true. Can't you just tell me what happened?"

"The Wallpaper Wolves did it, Shayla. They did. They did. It's true," she said. I looked into her eyes. They weren't blank anymore. They had started to tear up, and I could see the tears lining up to come sliding down her face, but there was something else in them too. Something that bothered me even more than her Wallpaper Wolves story, but I didn't know what it was.

"Why do they hurt you?" I asked. She shook her head and tears started to fall from her eyes.

"They just do," she said.

"Do they hurt your mom, too?" I asked. She didn't answer. "Maybe you should tell somebody."

"No, Shayla, don't tell anybody, okay? The wolves won't like it if I tell on them."

I took a deep breath and let it out. Who would believe me if I told them Kambia's Wallpaper Wolves story? It didn't make sense, not even to me. To tell the truth, I wasn't really sure what was going on. But if I told it, would she be hurt again? A while back I was gonna tell the story to Tia. Tia would have made whatever was hurting Kambia go away. She was always good at looking out for me. But now it was too late. Fear was slithering all over Kambia like water moccasins! I had to tell her something. I had to let her know that she would be safe.

"I promise I won't tell, Kambia," I said.

"Do you swear by Jesus, heaven, the angels, and everything?" she asked, wiping away tears with the backs of her hands.

"Grandma Augustine told me never to swear by anything,

because it was blasphemous," I said. "But I promise by Jesus, heaven, and all the angels that I won't tell anyone."

"Okay," she said, walking off. "We better go back."

I nodded my head and followed her back down the tracks, thinking that I had just done something really wrong.

Chapter 5

Kambia didn't come to school today again, so I had to go home by myself. Usually when she doesn't show up I take the bus, but today I decided to walk. I took a shortcut home, past Harvey Park, near Rawlings Baseball Field, and finally through Peaceful Rest Cemetery.

At Peaceful Rest I stopped time and again to read the dirt-encrusted writing on some of the granite and concrete tombstones, not at all worried about the ghost of Mrs. Alvania, or anyone else that might not be too happy with their final resting place, popping up out of nowhere.

I was looking for the grave of Mama James. She was well over a hundred when she went to sleep one night about three years ago and didn't wake up the next morning. Mama James was like a mother to the whole neighborhood. She was a sweet, kind woman, who had lost both of her legs when she was only seventeen to what Mama said is diabetes, but had still managed to find herself a husband and have eleven kids.

It was Mama James who told Mama that she could do anything. She was the reason that Mama decided to take that special free sewing and design class over on Dowling. She was the reason that Mama tried to get back her dream.

When Mama was Tia's age, she wanted to be a dress designer. Grandma Augustine said that she could do almost anything with a simple piece of fabric, cut it every which way, and make it into something fabulous. She was always getting compliments on the dresses that she made for herself in her homemaking class at school. Her teacher thought that she had real talent, and that when she grew up, she could easily go off to New York or somewhere and get a great job as a designer, but that was before Tia came.

Like Grandma Augustine said, Mama got pregnant with Tia when she was fifteen. She got pregnant by a guy only a year older than her with a pimply face, large feet, and long lashes as delicate as butterfly wings.

They got married just two weeks before Tia was born. They tied the knot at Grandma's church with just a minister, Grandma and Grandpa, and a marble pound cake for the reception.

The marriage didn't last long. Grandma Augustine said that Tia's daddy just plain and simple didn't know anything about being a husband. He got fired from every after-school job that Mama found for him, and spent his evenings lying on the floor in front of the TV watching reruns of *Green Acres* and eating corn chips and bean dip. Tia hadn't even said her first word when Grandpa kicked him out, leaving Mama to raise her baby alone.

It was Mama James who told Mama to forget about all that. She told Mama that just because things went bad for her when she was a girl, it didn't mean that they had to be bad for her forever. She told Mama that after she lost her legs, she thought that the world would come to an end, but eleven children and forty grandkids later, she certainly knew that it wasn't true. She convinced Mama to sign up for the design classes, but unfortunately after four classes the state decided that it would rather spend its money on other things, and told all the ladies in the class that they would have to pay. Mama couldn't afford the tuition, so she dropped out.

But Mama had tried. After years and years of giving up on everything, Mama James had made her see some hope in something. That hope was what I needed. Lately, hurt had been wrapping itself around me like a python, squeezing me something fierce, strangling all of the happiness out of me. I needed to know how to get through the day without feeling so bad. "If you want to know how to make it in the present, look in the past," Grandma Augustine always says. "Hardship and pain are like hand-me-downs. Somebody else done surely wore 'em before you. You find out how they climbed over their wall of trouble, and you'll know how to get over yours."

There was certainly no way that I could ask Mama James how she got over her wall, but I figured that if I stood next to her, or next to what she used to be, I would get some strength.

There had been no new news about Tia. None of her friends were at all helpful with finding her, not even her best friend Maxi. Maxi said that she hadn't heard from Tia since the night of the Women of Mahogany Festival. She said that Tia had come by that night looking for a place to crash, but things didn't work out.

"My mom told Tia that her place was at your house," Maxi said, sitting on her overstuffed sofa in a bright orange T-shirt dress, the bangs of her long hair hanging like thick pieces of black dental floss over her plump baby face. "She told her that she needed to keep her trash on her own back porch and not be trying to sweep it in anybody else's yard. My mom said that Tia needed to go get things straight with her mom before she opened up a package that she couldn't rewrap. 'Mothers and daughters are always getting in each other's faces,' she told her. 'It ain't the end of the world, unless you make it out to be.' That's all I know," Maxi said. "I ain't heard from Tia since then. She could be anywhere." She wiped a corner of her sleepy brown eyes. "I hope y'all find her real soon."

Fear has finally come to sit at Mama's side of the dining-room table. Last night was her night off from work. She didn't even bother with her quilting squares. She spent most of the night sitting on the living-room sofa, staring at the dark blue phone in the middle of our coffee table, as if she had never seen it before.

I watched her from my bedroom. Her eyes were all cloudy, and worry was running all up and down her face. For the first time ever she looked like she might actually drop a few tears. She looked as if she might actually let some of the pain seep out of the hole that Tia has put in her heart.

This morning, before I left for school, she shoved a note into my hands. The note was for Tia's homeroom teacher. It said that Tia had gone to visit Mama's cousin Delores in Washington, D.C. While Tia was there, she had come down with some female problems that were making her too ill to take the bus home. "I don't know when she'll be back," Mama wrote. "Nobody does." I delivered the note to Mrs. Skinner with a sad face, but I don't think that she even looked at it. I think that she already knew about Tia. Everybody knows.

After I found Mama James's stone and stood for a while, I headed for home. On the way back I spotted two shaggy black dogs heading up the winding dirt path that led to the back entrance of the bayou. One of the dogs was stepping briskly, his head held up high, like he was in an expensive dog show or something, but the other dog was limp-hopping, holding his right hind leg up off the ground, as if he was afraid to put it down. When I got home, I told Grandma Augustine about them.

"It's a sign," she said, standing in the kitchen, pouring herself a small glass of foamy buttermilk. "Those dogs represent two liars. One of the liars is sure of himself, positive that what he is doing is the right thing, but the other liar is not so certain. He stumbling over his own conscience," she said. "Trying to keep from stepping in his own mess."

"Mu'dear, what is you telling that girl that craziness for?" Mama asked, coming into the kitchen, her wrinkled navy blue work uniform tossed over her arm. She opened the broom closet next to the stove, took out the old steam iron, and headed for the sink. "Mu'dear, now you know that liars don't come on this earth as no dogs," she said, running a thin stream of cool water into the little hole in the top of the iron. "Liars are just plain ole people like you and me. Though some may act like dogs, I ain't seen one yet with four legs. I swear, Mu'dear, you and them old sayings. Some of them is just plain ole foolishness."

"Foolishness, Vera? Folks been saying the very same thing that I just said since before I was even born," Grandma Augustine said. "Any saying that stays around for that long got to have some truth in it." Mama shook her head. She walked over to the dining-room table, cleared our plastic salt and pepper shakers, plugged the iron into a nearby socket, and started running it over her uniform. Hot, misty steam hissed into the air.

"Mu'dear," she said, pressing down the wrinkles on the hem of her skirt. "Folks used to say that if you swallowed a watermelon seed a watermelon would grow in your belly, but I ain't seen nobody give birth to one yet."

"Good Lord, wouldn't that be a sight," Grandma Augustine said. She and Mama broke into laughter. For a few moments the house stopped shaking and joy pranced into the room. I sighed and grabbed a banana out of the glass fruit bowl over the sink. Then I walked to my room, feeling good inside and wondering how they could have found their silly conversation so funny.

In my room I tossed my book bag onto the floor, flopped down in what was slowly becoming my bed, not Tia's and mine, and pulled my blue notebook from underneath my pillow. I'd been keeping the notebook there since the day that I went searching for Tia. I wanted it close so that I could scribble my thoughts in it when I woke up late at night worried. I opened it and turned to a clean page. *Laughter is tap-dancing on top of our kitchen cabinets*, I wrote. *And happiness is sliding up and down the sides of our sink.* It was a corny entry, I know, but I joyfully read it aloud over and over, until the words were stuck in my memory forever.

I put my notebook away and sat up in the bed. In the kitchen I could hear Mama and Grandma whispering softly. I knew that they had to be talking about Tia. That's the way they talk about her lately, real quiet, as if they are afraid to say her name out loud. In the whispers I often catch hints of phrases from Grandma, like "Call the police" and "You're being too stubborn." And Mama's husky voice answers with a low "Maybe you're right, maybe you're right." But the next morning, when the sun rises high over our tiny little part of the world, and Mama makes her way home from work, they are back to making more whispers, and Tia still isn't at home. I got up from my bed and closed my bedroom door. It's something else that I've been doing a lot of lately. I've been trying to keep the madness out.

The madness that I'm referring to is Mr. Anderson Fox. He is still in town, taking a longer visit than anybody had expected, and chilling out. He is staying with a couple of his homeboys that he knows down at the pool hall, sleeping on their sofa and eating take-out food every night.

It was the take-out food that made Mama invite him over that first time. She said that there wasn't any sense in him spending what little money he had down at John's Three-Dollar Breakfast when we had enough food for an extra plate.

So Mr. Anderson Fox came over—came over with his big toothy grin and his musty aftershave. The first time that he showed up I came down with a sudden stomachache and was too sick to eat my Froot Loops. I sat alone in my room. From my bed I heard Mr. Anderson Fox crack a not-too-funny joke, and then I heard Mama giggle, but it wasn't a happy giggle. It was more like one of those strange giggles that you hear when you squeeze a laughing bag in the toy store. It was fake and hollow. But Mr. Anderson Fox sure didn't think so. He's been coming over ever since then, all because of that giggle.

Mama says that I should be nice to Mr. Anderson Fox. She says that I'm not the only little girl that he has, but that I am the only one that he comes to see. "He really cares about you," she says. But Mama doesn't see his searchlight eyes when he stands in my door. They are not caring eyes. They are curious eyes, curious about things that I'm afraid to figure out.

"Why does he always have to be over here?" I ask.

"Because this is the right place for him to be," Mama answers.

"How so?" I ask.

"You'll see," she says. "In time you'll see."

After I finished my journal entry, I turned to my advanced studies homework—homework made up from tougher high-school-like subjects to help disadvantaged kids excel. It was geometry, the only subject that I can honestly say I truly hate. Geometry is like cartoons without sound to me. There are some interesting shapes and pictures, but nothing pulls together. I took out my geometry book and turned to chapter five, slowly letting my fingers glide over the new, crisp paper, and wrinkling my nose at the fresh ink smell.

There it was, lesson ten, pages and pages of squares, triangles, and circles—the basic structure of all buildings, my math teacher, Mr. Forest, always tells us. "If you know how to work with squares, triangles, and circles, you can build the world." I don't want to build the world. I just want to make sense out of it.

I buried my nose as deep in the book as I could, hoping that a close study of the shapes would make it easier to figure out the stupid radiuses and the intersections. I was halfway through part three when I heard a rap on my door. I turned to find Mr. Anderson Fox entering it. He had a newly shaved head, which made him look like an overgrown chocolate Tootsie Pop. I quickly felt a smile spreading across my face, but then I remembered all of the presents and phone calls that I never received, and I let that smile curve right back into its usual frown.

"How you doing, baby girl?" he asked. I answered with my normal shrug. He hunched his shoulders and started to turn away, but stopped for some unknown reason.

He walked over to my bed and looked down, his musty cologne pushing all of the breathable air from the room.

"Whatcha doing, baby girl?" he asked.

"Geometry," I muttered.

"Oh, man, shoot, they still have that junk," he said. "I thought they had stopped making kids take that mess. You know," he added, rubbing his smooth scalp, "I never could get used to that junk. I mean, I never had nothing for it. I hated it worse than a fat woman hates a girdle. What you think about it, huh?"

I opened my mouth to answer, but the words got stuck in my throat. I didn't want Mr. Anderson Fox to know that I didn't like geometry either. I didn't want him to know that there was any part of me that was like him, any part of me that he could claim.

"It's great!" I said excitedly.

"Oh," he said. "You must be good at it."

"Very good!" I lied.

"So you the one to come to if I want to know all about circles and stuff. You the one to ask."

I nodded.

"Well, I must say," he said, "you sho do know how to make your daddy proud."

I closed my book and stared at him. As usual one of his eyes was going in the complete opposite direction from the other, like a cockroach's antennae, but you could still see the curiosity in them. They were curious, so curious, but about what? What was it that Mr. Anderson Fox wanted from me? What did he want to know about me? He said that I made him proud. Had his father ever been proud of him?

I knew even less about Mr. Anderson Fox's parents than I did about him. I had learned only a few bits and pieces about them from the old ladies in my neighborhood. The ladies said that Mr. Anderson Fox's parents were die-hard church folks, strict Baptists who were always the first people on the steps of their church when the doors opened for Sunday morning services. The ladies said that Mr. Anderson Fox's parents had kicked him to the curb years ago, when he was barely a grown man, showed him the door because of his fool acting and girl chasing.

"Sometimes you have to let your children go," the ladies said. "You got to turn 'em loose and let life whip 'em back on the right path. It's just the way it is. You can't tell some children not to chase wasps in the backyard. They got to get stung first in order to figure it out."

"So you doing real good with that geometry stuff?" Mr. Anderson asked.

I turned my frown up into a half smile.

"That sho is good," he said, pleased. "Well, let me go on in here and holler at your mama," he added. "See what's been going on in her world today." He turned and walked toward the doorway.

"How long are you gonna be in town?" I asked in a fake daughterlike voice.

"Oh, I don't know," he answered. "Right now I'm trying to hook some stuff up. We'll see."

"What kind of stuff?" I asked.

"Some thangs ain't for you to know yet, baby girl." His voice trailed as he strolled through the doorway into the hall. "You'll find out about it when the time comes."

I got up from my bed, shut the door behind him, and latched it. What stuff was he trying to hook up? I didn't like the sound of it. I flopped down on my bed and turned back to my lesson. When I got to the page that I had been working on, I found Mr. Anger sitting there glaring at me from the center of a large circle. I didn't bother brushing him away. I wanted to be pissed off.

For the next half hour my mind skipped back and forth between Mr. Anderson Fox and my homework, like a kid playing hopscotch. Finally, after several page flips without reading a single word, I closed my book up and turned over and stared at the ceiling. I was trying to make out the shape of a huge corn-colored rain stain over my bed when I heard a second rap. This time it came from the window. I yanked back the curtains.

It was Kambia. She was standing there with her head pressed against the glass. Her face was real white, as if all the blood in her skin had suddenly decided to take off for other places, and her eyes were wild-looking, like something had really turned her upside down. I opened the window.

"What's wrong with you?" I asked. "You look like Godzilla is after you."

"Nothing," she said calmly, but her face didn't change.

"Are you sure?" I asked. "You really looked freaked out."

"I'm okay," she said. She glanced back at her house quickly, the way I had seen her do several times before, then looked at me. "Can I come in?" she asked.

Now my face grew all weird. Kambia had never been in my house before, or even asked to come in, though I had asked her if she wanted to on several occasions. Whenever we walked home from school together, I would ask her if she wanted to come in and watch TV or listen to the radio or something, but she always said no.

"I can't, my mom doesn't like me to go in other people's houses," she would say. "My mom says that I'm too clumsy and stupid, and that I'll trip and break something and she'll have to pay for it. She says that she doesn't have any extra money to spend on junk, and for me to just stay outside."

"Oh," I'd say. My mom never worries about stuff like that.

I tugged the window all the way up and moved back. "Sure, you can come in," I said. She climbed into it so fast that she stumbled over her own feet and hit the floor. I bent down and helped her up. I caught my breath. She wasn't wearing her normal dingy white dress. She had on what had to be one of her mom's dresses. It was a really short, shiny red thing, with thin straps and see-through nylon material where the breasts were supposed to be, which would have been really gross if Kambia actually had any breasts, but she didn't. Like me, Mother Nature hadn't yet punched that clock on her time card. She was flat as a Ping-Pong table. The dress was sagging from her shoulders like a miniature hammock. I held back a giggle.

"Are you playing dress-up?" I asked. She didn't answer. She just looked back over at her house really quickly, then she went and sat on my bed.

"Is this your bed?" she asked, running her fingers over the ragged spread.

"Mine and Tia's."

"Oh," she said. "Do you like sleeping with your sister?"

"It's okay, but she kicks a lot sometimes."

"I don't have a bed," she said.

"You don't?" I asked. I couldn't imagine anyone not having a bed. Even the poorest of the poor kids in our neighborhood bunked with somebody. "Well, where do you sleep?"

"On the floor most of the time," she said. "But sometimes I sleep with my mom. She kicks too."

"Really," I said, wondering how big her mother's bed was. According to the neighborhood grapevine, her mother always spent the night with one of her male friends. I couldn't see where there would be room for Kambia to squeeze in. "Your mom must have a whole lot of extra space," I said. She just blinked her eyes.

She got up from the bed and started walking around the room, taking in everything. There wasn't much to see. All me and Tia had was the raggedy bookshelf filled with old *Glamour*, *Seventeen*, and *People* magazines that she and I got from the free magazine table at the library each month; the ancient, box-shaped gas heater sitting in a corner of the room; our broken-down dresser; and a picture of the Last Supper, done all with black people, that Grandma had tacked up on the wall next to our bathroom door.

"You got a lot of neat stuff in your room," she said, her face slowly returning to normal.

"Naw, not really," I answered. "Just a bunch of old leftovers."

She stopped walking and pulled the dress up over her right shoulder. It slipped down further on her left one.

"So, why are you wearing your mom's dress?" I asked. "It doesn't even fit you." She just blinked again, then walked over to the bookshelf and took an old issue of *People* with a picture of Oprah on the cover off the top shelf.

"My mom watches her all the time," I said. "She really likes her a lot. I guess it's because she's black and all."

"My mom likes her too," she said. "But she doesn't get to watch her much. She's too busy most of the time."

She put the magazine back on the shelf, walked back over to the bed, and sat down. I walked over and sat beside her.

"So, how come you're wearing your mom's dress?" I asked again. She shrugged her shoulders, picked up my geometry book, and started to thumb through it.

"Kambia, how come you got on your mama's clothes?" I asked again. She just kept thumbing through the book.

"Kambia," I said.

"I don't have anything else to wear, Shayla," she answered quickly. "My mom and me didn't wash yet. Have you heard from your sister, Tia, yet?" she asked. I hunched my shoulders.

"No," I said. "But my mom thinks that she's still off just showing her behind and stuff with her girlfriends, and Grandma thinks that she might be with Doo-witty. I still don't know what to think, but I'm starting to believe Grandma—a little. I really don't know where she is. I just hope that she comes home soon."

"Maybe they took her," she said.

"Who took her?"

"The men," she said.

"What men?"

"The big, hairy men that live under the pavement in the streets. They take little kids, you know, especially little girls."

"Kambia, I never heard of any men living under the street."

"They do," she said. "They live right underneath the pavement, near the top. All they do, day and night, is sit around waiting for a naughty little girl or boy to run away. They wait and wait until they hear the kid's door slam, and the sound of his sneakers on the street, then they reach up out of the ground and pull him under. Their families never see them again. All because they were naughty and tried to run away from the people that cared about them."

"That's not true, Kambia," I snapped, a little shaken by her Foot-Grabber-like story. "Why do you always have to make up stupid tales like that? There are no men living under our streets. I wish you wouldn't tell such creepy stories."

"It's not a story," she snapped. "It is true. I know, because my mom told me. She knows everything. They take little girls and boys to be their slaves, wash their dishes, cook their food, even comb their hair, and if you don't do it, they grind you up and sell you for wieners at the butcher shop."

"That's just a big ole story," I said, feeling a little ill. "You read it in a fairy tale book or something."

"It's not—," she began, but another rap on the door broke up our argument.

"Who is it?" I asked.

"It's Mama," my mom's voice came through the rotting wood. I got up from the bed, but Kambia grabbed me by my arm real hard.

"Don't tell her that I'm here, Shayla," she begged, her face going all white again.

"It's okay," I said. "It's just my mom. She won't mind. She's real cool."

"No, Shayla," she said again. Her voice was real trembly, and her eyes seemed even wilder than when I first saw her at the window.

"Don't, don't, Shayla," she begged. "Please don't tell." She hopped off the bed and scooted under it, like a puppy afraid of thunder and lightning. I bent down and looked underneath.

"Kambia, come back out. It's fine," I said. She shook her head.

"Don't tell on me, Shayla," she pleaded again. Then there was that look again. That scared look that I had seen the night underneath her house and on our way to search for Tia. I felt a lump forming in my throat.

"Okay—I won't," I said. I pulled the ends of my bedspread down, hurried to the door, and unlatched it. My mom walked in, yanking down the skirt of her freshly ironed uniform.

"What took you so long to open this door, girl?" she asked.

"I was doing my homework," I lied. "What's up?"

She glanced around the room. "That little gal from next door, Kambia, her mama is at the back door asking for her. Have you seen her?"

"No, ma'am," I said.

"You certain?" she asked. "You haven't seen her at all today?"

"No, ma'am, I haven't seen her. She didn't come to school."

"Well, you better come tell her mama that, so that she can be satisfied and go looking for her somewhere else. I don't want her hanging in my kitchen for too long. Your grandma is about to have a fit. You know how she can be about things."

The scene that greeted us when we entered the room would never have been a picture on one of Mr. Anderson Fox's cheap, sappy greeting cards. Kambia's mom was standing in the middle of the kitchen doorway in one of her teeny, tiny working outfits, a silky black robe that barely came down to the start of her heavy thighs, and a shiny pair of extra-high silver shoes with the backs cut out. She had twirled and curled her red hair up into a fancy do that reminded me of those squirming snakes that you always see on top of Medusa's head, and she was wearing cactus green eye shadow that had seeped into tiny creases around her chestnut eyes. Her thin lips were smeared with a thick layer of plum lipstick that made them looked bruised and swollen, and her long press-on nails were sporting several coats of raspberry paint.

Across from her, at our small dining-room table, sat Grandma Augustine with her usual steaming cup of afternoon tea. Normally she was cheerful while she was having her daily dose of Lipton, but today her flabby arms were folded across her chest like she was trying to hold herself in, and you could clearly see the sour look of disgust on her wrinkled face.

Mr. Anderson Fox, however, didn't seem to be as put off by Kambia's mom as Grandma Augustine. He was just standing at the sink with a package of moon-shaped cheddar cheese in his hand, with his big toothy grin on his face. His searchlight eyes were moving up and down Kambia's mom's figure. Mama walked over and snatched the cheese out of his hand. He looked away from Kambia's mom. I took a deep breath and walked over to her.

"Yes, ma'am?" I said, lowering my eyes to keep her from noticing the guilty look on my face.

"I'm Jasmine Joiner," she said in the same high voice that she always used with Kambia. "I'm Kambia Elaine's mom. You her friend, Shayla, right?"

"Yes, ma'am," I answered softly. "She hangs out with me sometimes."

"That's right, that's what I figured," she said, yanking her robe closed over her huge chest. She had big ones like Tia. I wondered if Kambia's would ever get that big.

"Anyway, I'm looking for her," she said. "She got some stuff she was supposed to do at the house, and the minute I turned my back she had sneaked her little ass out of the door, or the window. I'm not sure which. I didn't see her go. I just know that she ain't where she supposed to be. Have you seen her?"

I shook my head.

"Open your mouth and answer her," Mama said.

"No, ma'am," I lied again. "She ain't been by here in a while."

"You sure?" she asked.

"I'm sure," I said.

"Damn," she said, stomping her feet. "Now where in the hell could she have run off to. Man, she gets on my damn nerves sometimes. I knew it! I knew it! I shoulda left her right where she was and come on down here by myself. Lord knows I woulda had less of a headache."

"Leave the Lord out of it," Grandma Augustine suddenly said.

"Mu'dear," Mama called.

"Excuse me?" Kambia's mom said.

"You heard me, Miss Thing," Grandma snapped coolly. "I said leave the Lord out it. He ain't got nothing to do with that child not wanting to be in your house, and you know it. The kind of mess you doing off in there."

"And what kind of mess is that?" Kambia's mom asked with a smile on her face, only it wasn't really a smile. It was more like a teasy grin, like she was trying to make fun of Grandma.

"I ain't got to tell you what goes on in your house," Grandma Augustine said. "The whole neighborhood know about it."

"Know about what?" Kambia's mom asked. "Ain't nothing

going on in my house that ain't going on in everybody else's. All I'm doing is paying my rent."

"Yeah, but how you doing it?"

"Hard work," Kambia's mom said. "The same as any-damn-body else. In fact, I work harder than any-damn-body in this neighborhood. Why, half of the women right here, on this here block, is on food stamps, WIC, or some other type of government handout. But me, I'm taking care of myself."

"So I heard," Grandma Augustine said. "So we all done heard."

"What did you hear?" Kambia's mom asked. "What about me do you think you know? Do you think you can prove? Who you gone find that'll put *all* my business in the street?"

"Every man in this neighborhood," Grandma Augustine said.

"And who would they tell it to?" Kambia's mom asked. "They wives, they girlfriends? I don't think so. I wouldn't advise anybody 'round here to start telling my business. I know enough to turn this whole damn neighborhood upside down."

"It won't be long before you do that," Grandma Augustine said.

"Look, old lady, I ain't never claimed to be no saint. I like men—and I like money. I ain't never put on no pretense at all. My mama taught me a long time ago that you couldn't cover up bad meat with good gravy. All it takes is one taste to figure it out. I am what I am, but I'm not the devil. I'm just a businesswoman, taking care of what needs to be taken care of—any way that I can. Anybody that wants to live my life for me—can pay my rent. Until then, how I pay my bills is my concern."

"There may be a small bit of truth in that," Grandma snapped, "but most of it is just plain hog slop. What you doing is as devilish as it is ugly. You setting a bad example for that child of yours, teaching her the wrong way to do things, when the right way is just as easy."

"Easy for who?" Kambia's mom asked. "Look," she said, "I don't know nothing about easy. I just know about getting stuff done. It don't matter how and what it takes." She pointed at me. "If you see Kambia Elaine, tell her that I said that she better get her behind home. She wasting my time—and my money, and I'm getting real tired of fooling with her." She turned in the doorway.

"I'll pray for your soul," Grandma Augustine said, picking up her teacup. Kambia's mom whipped around and flashed her chestnut eyes.

"I don't need no prayer," she said. "I ain't got nothing for church at all. What I need is for folks to stay outta my business before I start getting in theirs."

"I ain't got no business for you to get into," Grandma snapped back.

"Everybody's got business," Kambia's mom said. "You can find a little dirt on everybody's sheets." She stepped out of the door and banged it behind her.

"Somebody ought to call the law on her," Grandma Augustine said, looking really annoyed.

"Call 'em," Mama said. "I hear at least two or three of 'em in there every Tuesday and Thursday night. Besides, like she said, who can prove what goes on in her house? What man do you think gone stand up in a court and say anything about her? He'd be telling on his self at the same time. Naw, she right about that. She's well in control of the situation. All anybody knows about her is rumors. Nobody wants to get involved with that kinda mess if nothing gone come of it. Besides, if we start calling the law on every woman in this neighborhood that's doing what she's doing to make ends meet—half of the women that we know will end up in jail."

"There's a difference between getting yourself a friend to help out and putting it out on the market," Grandma Augustine said.

"True," Mama answered. "But ain't nobody can prove that that's what she doing for sure."

"I can prove it," Grandma Augustine said. "I know what I done seen with my own eyes. I know clabber when I see it. I ought to call the state in on her. I'll call in them social services people if I can't call in nobody else. They'll come out here," she said. "They'll turn her sorry tail every which way but loose—a trifling cow." She glanced over at Mr. Anderson Fox. "What do you think about a sorry wench like that?" she asked. Mr. Anderson Fox cleared his throat loudly.

"I don't know," he said. "I ain't been around her long enough to form an opinion." He cleared his throat again. "Anyway, don't the Good Book say something about not judging folks?"

"It do," Grandma Augustine said. "But the truth is the truth. God ain't never told nobody to say that they saw fresh water in the stream when all they really saw was mud."

"That's true also," Mama piped in. "And Lord knows I do feel for that child Kambia, having to live with a two-dollar hussy like that, but right now I got my own worries, and Kambia's situation don't seem like anything too desperate. There ain't nothing I could put my finger on for sure—if anybody was to ask me." She shook her head. "And good grief," she cried. "You know what happened the last time somebody called them state folks and complained. I know you ain't forgot what went down because of that."

Grandma sighed. "Naw, I ain't forgot," she said. "I ain't forgot at all. You right, them state people can stir up all kinds of trouble. They really good at finding mess not only in the backyard that you told them to look in, but in your backyard as well."

"Yep," Mama said. "Lord knows they can."

What Mama said was nothing but the truth. About three years ago there had been a problem at Aunt Jimmy Lynn's day care. One of the kids had fallen and cut a pretty nasty hole in his head. Even though it was an accident, his mama, Carol Ann, a bartender down at J. B. Walker's pool hall, had raised all kinds of mess about it. She took her little boy out of the day care and told everyone that Aunt Jimmy Lynn, a good-hearted elderly woman, who had run the small day care from her home without a license for twenty years, was way too old to be keeping other folks' kids.

Most of the people in the neighborhood thought that Carol Ann was just popping and jawing about nothing, since she knew all about Aunt Jimmy Lynn and the day care before she put her kid in it. But a few folks, especially the mothers, were really sympathetic to her complaints. In fact, they were so sympathetic that one of them even called the state and told them that Aunt Jimmy Lynn was running the center without a license.

Before you know it, the whole neighborhood was swarming with state *and* city folks. They were peeking in everybody's kitchens, trying to see if there were any rotten canned goods on the shelves. Pretty soon not just Aunt Jimmy Lynn's, but all of the home businesses in the hood were closed down—beauty parlors, restaurants, appliance repair shops, every little make-a-buck place that people had been using to bring in extra cash each month. Many of the hardworking folks that hadn't been on welfare before had to go begging to the state, hiding their heads in shame as they cashed their checks at the local store.

After that folks just turned their heads if they saw or heard something that they didn't like. When it came to other people's business, they saw very little, heard very little, and knew very little.

Lots of things got overlooked. Right or wrong, people thought that it was safer that way. Nobody wanted to be punished for trying to help out someone else.

"Yep," Mama said. "Calling the state on her is bound to cause a full-blown mess of trouble. For now I'll just keep my feelings about Miss Jasmine Joiner to myself. I suggest you do the same," she said, cutting her eyes at Grandma. "Ain't no sense in bringing no more misery in this house if we can help it."

"I guess you're right," Grandma said slowly. "It don't make sense to open up a can of bait if you ain't sure you got hooks to stick it on." She looked over at me. "Shayla, you go finish your studies," she said sternly. "You ain't got no business listening to grown folks' talk."

I left the kitchen gladly, a little unsure of all that they were talking about. A lot of the conversation had gone right over my head. They were pissed off at Kambia's mom for stuff she was doing with her boyfriends, I knew that, but I wasn't sure about *everything* that was making their faces go all scrunchy.

I went back to my room and closed the door behind me. After making sure that the lock was in place, I bent down and looked under the bed. Kambia was still there, all right. She was lying on her back with her eyes closed real tight like a newborn kitten.

"Hey," I whispered. "Your mom was here looking for you, but she just left." Her eyes popped open. Then she crawled out from underneath the bed and sat back down on it. I sat down beside her.

"Are you hiding from your mom?" I asked. "I do that sometimes. Sometimes when I want to write something really personal in my journal. I go off all by myself, where nobody can find me. I write and write until my hand gets really tired, then I come out of my hiding place."

"What do you write, Shayla?" she asked.

"I don't know, feelings, junk like that. Sometimes the start of a story or a poem."

"I used to like to write stuff," she said. "In my old English class, the one that I had before me and Mama moved to Dallas. It was only for kids that got good grades on they tests and junk. I really liked it, but then I started missing a lot of time outta school, and I got kicked out."

"How come you missed so much time out of school?" I asked. She put her hands in her lap and started wringing them. Her face got all white again, and she got all trembly.

"They catch me sometimes," she said in a really low voice. "I can't always hide from them. Sometimes they find me no matter where I am."

"Who finds you, Kambia?" I asked, stroking her arm. "Your mom?"

"No," she said. "They do."

"They who?" I asked, knowing full well what the answer would be.

"The Wallpaper Wolves," she said. "They get me sometimes, Shayla. It don't matter where I run or how far I go, sometimes they get me."

"Kambia," I asked, "is there any way that you can get rid of the wolves? Maybe you and I can run them off. There's got to be a way to chase them away forever. I'll come over one day and we'll get rid of them together."

"No, Shayla," she said. "You can't ever, ever come in my house. If you do, they'll get you, too. When we were in Dallas, my mom used to keep some of her little nieces. They got them, too. There's no way to get rid of them, Shayla. You just have to hide and hope that they'll never find you."

"Okay," I said.

I pulled Kambia to me and gave her a big hug, the way Tia used to do me when I was really upset about something. She felt cold. I closed my eyes and tried to make sense, once again, out of her Wallpaper Wolves story and her mom. What really went on in her house? I thought about going into the kitchen and telling Mama the wolves story, but I had promised Kambia that I wouldn't. "Your word is your bond," Grandma Augustine always says to me. "If people can't trust the words that come outta your mouth, they can't trust you." I pulled Kambia closer to me. I could feel her bony ribs through the thin material of her dress. It felt like she hadn't eaten in a while, but then if I had Wallpaper Wolves hanging on my walls, I guess I probably couldn't eat either. I took a deep breath and let it out, and pulled her dress straps up over her shoulders for the second time. As I did the sound of pounding came from the window.

"Kambia Elaine!" Kambia's mom's shrill voice yelled out, between her blows to the side of her house. Kambia flinched, but she didn't move. "Kambia Elaine," her mom repeated. "If you're under that house, you better bring your behind out! If you don't come out, I'm gonna make you real sorry!" Kambia already seemed pretty sorry to me. I wondered what her mother could do to make her feel worse.

Chapter 6

This morning, as I was cleaning the living-room window, I looked out and saw a yellow bicycle come rolling up the street with no rider. It ran right past our front porch and kept on going toward the end of the block until I lost sight of it. When Grandma Augustine arrived, I told her about it, thinking that she would tell me that it was one of her famous signs, but she told me that somebody had probably pushed the bicycle from the part of the street that I couldn't see from the window. She said that it had probably rolled for just a little while before it fell into some bushes somewhere at the end the block.

At first I was a little shocked at Grandma Augustine's response, but then I remembered that today was the day that she was supposed to keep her opinions to herself.

Today was Mama's birthday, the only day of the year that she got to have her say in everything. It was supposed to be a very special day for Mama, and for us. We were all going to have a great time together doing fun things and trying to forget about Tia, for just a little while. It was going to be Family Day, Mama said. She even took me out of school for it. She phoned my homeroom teacher and told her that I had some important family business that I needed to take care of. "It's a bit of an emergency," she said. "She can make up her work tomorrow."

The plan for the day was a good one. We were going to have a really light breakfast of fruit or something, do a little necessary housecleaning, then take off to town for a nice lunch and a movie, but nothing at all turned out right.

During the housecleaning Grandma Augustine tripped over a mop bucket and fell pretty hard. She didn't break anything, but her bad leg was giving her a fit, so Mama made her go lie down in her room. Our day out was ruined. There was no way that Grandma could make a trip downtown on the bus. Disappointment circled the room and landed on all of our shoulders, especially Mama's, but she didn't let it get to her. She brushed it off, put on her brightest smile, and said that we would just have to do the best we could to keep it a happy day. "As long as we are together, everything is fine," she said. "What matters is that we spend time with one another." I nodded, but I didn't agree. The day was already a complete mess. Grandma couldn't walk and Tia wasn't home. There was no way to see a crystal vase in broken glass, but I held my tongue and put a smile on my face as well.

Mama decided that the best thing to do was to go on to Plan B, our lunch. Since Grandma was down for the count and Mama had no intention of cooking on her birthday, she said that we would just have to settle on a nice lunch from Bobby's Rib Shack. He was having a special on smoked pork sausage, Grandma's favorite. Mama figured that it would cheer Grandma up if we brought her some.

So after making sure that Grandma was resting comfortably, we took off for the restaurant. It was a normal midmorning weekday as Mama and I strolled down the street, feather-duster quiet. Most of the people in our hood were maids and janitors. They either left for work at the crack of dawn or returned home at it. Either way, by eleven o'clock the neighborhood was usually silent. It was the one time of the day that even the jukebox at Perry's 24-and-7 took a rest. If you concentrated real hard, you could hear the bumblebee-like hum of the cars on the freeway right behind our tiny houses as they sped off down the concrete loops to places that many of us had never seen.

But I didn't mind the quiet very much. I was with Mama and we were actually walking hand in hand, like we used to do when I was real little, before the other kids in the neighborhood said that it was a babyish thing to do. It felt good. It was the first time in a long time that I actually felt close to Mama. Me and Mama were like collard greens and mustard greens; you could throw us in the pot together and we would come out pretty good, but to be honest, we were much better by ourselves. It wasn't that we didn't really love each other or that we didn't get along, like she and Tia. It was just that when it came to connecting, we never quite seemed to be in the same room together. I was always in the bedroom, while she was in the kitchen.

For some reason it was Grandma Augustine that I was in step with most of the time. She and I always seemed to be picking okra in the same patch, even if her picking ways were a little backward sometimes. But with Mama it just wasn't the same. Last year I had come home from school one day, real early, in tears because some girls had called me a bad name. Normally I ignore that kind of stuff, but it had happened to me right in the lunchroom, in front of everybody, in front of what I thought had to be the whole school.

"Hey, fatty fat, you look like a messy rat," a group of thin, pretty girls with fresh hairstyles and cool clothes sang over and over. The taunt was really silly, but it hurt me as bad as a toothache. I ran right home and I told Mama about it, thinking that she would understand and offer some comfort, but she didn't. "Just watch what you eat from here on out, Shayla," she said. "Put yourself on a little diet, and tell Tia to roll your hair up at night. You'll see next year. You'll look just like they do. They won't be able to laugh at you anymore."

No matter what I did, I couldn't make her see that I didn't

want to be just like the other girls. I wanted to be myself. I wanted the girls to like me for who I was. I left her room feeling empty and sad. Later on, in the evening, when I told Grandma Augustine about the ugly name that the girls had called me, she had a much different way of dealing with it. "Mean names can be hateful things," she said, "but just remember that they are like sticker bushes. They can cling to your body and prick you hard, but no matter how much they hurt, it's all on the outside. They can poke holes in your body, but not in your soul." I left Grandma feeling a heck of a lot better.

But today I wasn't with Grandma, I was with Mama. And even though we weren't talking, I could tell that we were thinking about and feeling the same things. I started to remember some of the fun times we used to have together, me, her, and Tia, going to the park, having a picnic on the bayou, and sitting on the front porch shelling pecans. But that was a long time ago, before she got messed over by a ton of Mr. Anderson Foxes, before her hands got hard and calloused from working so many bad jobs, before she learned to sell her giggles to Mr. Anderson Fox in the hopes of getting child support, and before Tia's womanhood swept down like a tornado and sucked out a little piece of all of our hearts.

With nobody to stop and chat with along the way it didn't take very long to reach Bobby's Rib Shack Number Three, called that because the first two had been burned down by grease fires. Bobby's Rib Shack wasn't much to look at. It was just that, a shack, a few termite-eaten boards thrown up in the shape of a box, whitewashed with cheap paint, and topped with an oversized roof made out of leftover aluminum siding from Bobby's Auto Body Shop. There was no window to speak of, so the tiny plywood door was always left open, allowing clouds of fluffy white barbecue smoke to pour out of the building and rise high into the air. Bobby, a skinny, light brown man with rust-colored freckles, was outside when we got there. He had just finished his first pit of meat and was catching a quick drag on a Salem before he had to get back to work.

"How you doing, Ms. Dubois?" he asked, flicking a cluster of burning ashes onto the black dirt next to his feet.

"Fine," Mama answered. "I can't complain about much. I got a place to lay my head, and food in the refrigerator. I can't holler about the way life is treating me."

"I know what you mean," Bobby said, bringing his cigarette back up to his lips. "Every day that the Lord lets me open my eyes is a good day to me. It's plenty of them that didn't this morning."

"Ain't it the truth," Mama said. "Ain't it the truth."

"Well, what can I do for you today?" Bobby asked. "We got plenty of everything but sausage. I just put it on the pit a little while ago. It'll be 'bout twenty minutes or so before it's ready."

"Shoot," Mama said. "That's just what me and Shayla come over here to get." Bobby dropped his smoked-up cigarette onto the ground and stomped on the butt. He looked at me and smiled.

"Shayla," he said. "Lord Jesus, every time I see you, you look like you done sprung up a couple mo' inches."

"Yeah, she growing just like a cornstalk," Mama said. "Up and out at the same time."

"It happens," Bobby laughed. "You ought to see my son, Bobby Junior. He growing every which way he can. Me and his mama can barely keep him in clothes." He smiled at me again.

"Shayla, I hear you into all that writing stuff, trying to take poetry classes, and whatnot," he said to me. I nodded.

"Well, good for you," he continued. "It's nice to have a little hobby. Enjoy it as much as you can. Before you know it, you'll be a full-grown woman like your mama. It'll be time to settle down and get your mind on serious things, work and stuff."

I bristled at the comment but held my tongue, like I did when most adults said things that I didn't like. My writing was serious. Besides my family, it was the only thing that I really cared about, but I couldn't make anybody believe it. I certainly couldn't make Mrs. Wells down at the cultural center believe it, last month. She was the one who decided to cancel the poetry workshop, even after me and the other kids made it there well ahead of time, even after we begged her not to.

There were three of us that showed up on that cool Saturday morning for the workshop—a sweet, dimpled girl named Tamika with soft eyes, and a tall, cocoa brown boy, about Tia's age, that everybody called the Rap King because he always wrote raps during his classes, and me.

We had all been really curious about one another, but not curious enough to ask each other why we had shown up there. Instead we just sat quietly with our backs against the wall, thumbing through the pages of our new poetry notebooks and reading our poems quietly to ourselves.

It was nearly an hour, our butts were sore and our eyeballs tired, when Mrs. Wells, a middle-aged woman with a tender face, caring eyes, and auburn hair, finally came strolling down the hall, wiping her plastic sunglasses on the tail of her khaki dress.

"I'm sorry, children," she said, giving us a pitying look. "I'm sorry, but the poetry class is canceled." Mouthing a silent "what," all three of us kids looked at one another, then back at her with shocked faces. It was as if she had told us that all of the water in the world had just dried up and we were going to die of thirst.

"Excuse me, ma'am," Tamika said in a soft, whispery voice. "Excuse me, but did you say that the class was canceled?"

"Yes, dear, I did," Mrs. Wells said. "I made the decision to cancel it a couple of days ago. There just wasn't enough interest in it. Not enough children signed up."

"But we're interested in it," I said, looking at my two almost classmates. "We really wanted to take it. We showed up extra early, way ahead of time. We even brought our poems and everything."

"I appreciate that, dear," she said. "And believe me, I'm really glad that you three came. But I just couldn't have asked Miss Bookman to come all the way down here, on a Saturday, for three kids. I phoned her and told her that the center was really happy that she had volunteered to teach the class, but we just didn't have enough kids that wanted to take it. I told her that perhaps we could do it at some later date. When we were really sure that somebody wanted to take it."

"We somebody," the Rap King spoke up, in a booming voice that seemed way too deep for his fifteen years. "You say ain't nobody showed up or seemed interested, but what are we? Ain't we students? We here. How come she couldn't teach us?"

"Like I said before, young man," Mrs. Wells said, shaking her head, "I'm very happy that you three wanted to be here, but don't you see? A class with three children in it just wouldn't be fair. You wouldn't even have enough students to share your work with. Now, I'm sorry, kids," she said, backing off down the hall toward her office. "But we'll just have to try it again another time. Maybe things will turn out better then."

"And maybe not, ma'am," I said. "We probably won't ever get a whole bunch of kids in here that want to read poetry and stuff. Most kids are only into watching TV and playing video games. We're never gonna get a full class. How come we can't just have a class with what we got? It's not fair to blame us for what the other kids don't want to do."

"Nobody is blaming anyone," she said, backing away farther. "It's just the way things have to be, right now. We'll make some other arrangements later on, if it looks like things are going to change." I ran after her and grabbed her arm, not hard like Kambia sometimes did to me, but firm and desperate-like. I wanted her to give me an answer that I could place some hope in.

"When, ma'am?" I asked. "When can we try to make some other arrangements? Can we try again soon?"

"We'll see," she said, pulling loose and striding off down the hall. "We'll see."

"Man, what a crock," the Rap King said after she had disappeared. "I shoulda known they wasn't gone have nobody come teach us no poetry. Shoot, I done wasted my whole Saturday morning for nothing. I coulda been hanging out with my crew," he added, heading off down the hall in the opposite direction, toward the double glass doors. "This is just plain ole messed up."

"It sure is," Tamika said, following him. "My sister told me that this was just a big ole joke. I shoulda listened to her. I coulda stayed in the bed and got a couple of more hours of sleep this morning. We don't never get to have nothing good down here. All we ever get is the same tired junk."

I sat back down on the floor, still clutching my new poetry notebook, and watched Tamika and the Rap King walk off through the doors. Were they right? Had it all been a joke? It occurred to me that what Mrs. Wells had done to us was much worse than telling us that all the water in the world had dried up and that we were going to die of thirst. She had told us that there was plenty of water, but that no matter how thirsty we were, we weren't going to get a drink. Sadness poured over me like hot lava. I felt like running down the hall and screaming, but as usual I tucked the unhappiness deep inside of me, then I got up from the floor and left the building.

On the way home I stopped at the bayou and tried real hard to make up a poem about how I felt about the day's events, but I couldn't. There was a blankness in me. My words had disappeared into nothingness, just like Tia, just like Grandma's babies, just like any feelings I had once had for Mr. Anderson Fox, just like the pages of my poetry notebook as I tore them off one by one and tossed them into the murky waters. I'll bet Bobby would have been proud when he saw the pages sinking into the water. He would have thought my throwing away the notebook was a pretty mature thing to do.

"Yeah, that's right," Bobby said now. "It won't be long before you'll be a grown-up, before you'll have to start paying bills and buying your own clothes. You better enjoy the good times now. Pretty soon life ain't gone be nothing but worries."

"That's a fact," Mama chimed in. "That is most certainly a fact. Bobby, I really do want that sausage. I believe that me and Shayla will hang around a bit until it gets done."

"Fine with me," Bobby said. "By the way, did I tell you about Mrs. Barker's oldest daughter, Zaire?"

Mama shook her head. I sighed and started walking away. I knew what Bobby was going to talk about. Mrs. Barker's daughter Zaire was only twenty-eight and had already been married four times. There were always several rumors going on about her latest husband. I had already heard most of them. I decided to pass up any new ones. I walked around to the back.

In the back of Bobby's Rib Shack was what he called the dining area—several large round tables that were made out of huge telephone wire spools turned over on their sides, touched up with a hint of walnut varnish and surrounded by three or four beat-up metal folding chairs that Bobby got on a discount from one of the hotels downtown. In the center of each table was a pair of gray plastic salt and pepper shakers stamped with "The West Side Eatery," where Bobby's wife, Wynona, had picked them up cheap. They were each complemented by a matching gray vase filled with dusty-pink Styrofoam lilies, which Bobby's youngest daughter, Kenya, had made last year in her fifth-grade art class.

I flopped down at a table close to the shack so that I would be the first thing that Mama saw when she rounded the corner. I was rocking back and forth, on an extremely wobbly chair, when my eyes nearly jumped out of my face. It was Frog; Frog—and Doo-witty! They were sitting there at one of the tables just as big as you please, sitting there with what looked like a two- or three-pound platter of Bobby's Juicy Pork Ribs. Doo-witty was eating real slow, taking a nibble at a time, but Frog was putting 'em away like she hadn't eaten since man discovered fire. I couldn't believe it. Doo-witty was back in town and nobody had told us. I got up and ran over to their table so fast that I don't even think that they saw me coming. I reached them just as Frog was picking a large piece of meat out of her front teeth with her fat fingers. When she saw that it was me, she plucked it out of her mouth quickly and flicked it on the table next to her plate.

"What are you doing running over here like somebody was choking to death or something, little girl?" she barked at me. I turned to Doo-witty. He stopped nibbling on his rib and stared at me. As usual his pop eyes were blank. There was nothing in them at all, at least nothing that I could see.

"Where's Tia at?" I blurted out. He just kept staring at me. "Doo-witty, you're back in town," I said. "Did you bring Tia, too?

Where is she at? Did she come home with you?"

"T-T-Tia wasn't with me," he stuttered. "I-I went outta town by myself. I went to see my uncle, do a little work for him."

"What?" I asked, puzzled.

"I was working for m-m-my Uncle Mosley," he said. "He had me helping him clean out . . . out his attic and paint his house and junk. That's where I-I was at."

"Did you bring Tia back with you?" I repeated, wondering if he understood my question. "Where is she at?"

"I-I t-t-told you," he said. "I didn't . . . didn't take no Tia with me. I-I went off to my uncle's alone."

"Well, where is she at, then?" I asked. "She gotta be with you. There ain't nowhere else for her to be. Me and Grandma looked all over. She had to be in Beaumont with you. You and she went off together."

"T-T-Tia didn't go nowhere with me," he said. "I left her with her girlfriend Maxi, that plump girl that likes to talk a lot. I ain't seen her since I took off."

"What are you talking about!" I yelled. "I been down to Maxi's. I been to all of her friends' houses. Ain't nobody seen Tia since she took off with you!"

"I-I left her here," Doo-witty said.

"You didn't!" I screamed. "You didn't! She ain't here. Nobody's seen her!"

"I-I d-d-did," Doo-witty stuttered back. "I left her here, r-r-right here," he said.

"You left her where?" Mama's voice came booming over my shoulder. I turned around to see her standing beside me holding a large, greasy sack of barbecue.

"You left my child where, Doo-witty?" she asked again. "Where did you leave my baby?"

"I-I left her here, in Houston. She didn't . . . didn't go with me," Doo-witty answered.

"What?" Mama said, confusion and anger slowly starting to creep into her face. Her eyes were real wide, like she was surprised, but her forehead was scrunched into pissed-off wrinkles.

"You heard him!" Frog suddenly spoke up, wiping a big glob of barbecue sauce off one of her bulging jowls. "He said that he don't know nothing about that gal. That's exactly what I told your mama a while back. I told her that my Doo-witty didn't know where that gal had got off to. Y'all wouldn't listen to me. Now I guess y'all will listen to him."

"You talk sense to me, Doo-witty," Mama said. "If my child was anywhere 'round here, we woulda seen her by now. Don't you think we know that? Don't you think that we got sense enough to figure that out?" Doo-witty didn't answer. Then Mama did something that I had never seen her do before. She reached down and grabbed Doo-witty by the collar of his black jean jacket. "If Tia was 'round here, we woulda seen her by now," Mama said, stretching the material. "Now, your mama say that you smarter than we all think that you is, and that you can pick up on most anything that other folks can, so now you pick up on this. You quit playing the fool with me and tell me where my baby is at!" she screamed. Doo-witty just sat there, his face unchanging, his pop eyes still blank, and that jaw of his drooping toward the floor. "Where is my baby at?" Mama yelled again. She tugged Doo-witty so hard that he raised up out of his seat. Frog raised up out of her seat as well.

"Now, wait just a second, Vera Dubois," she said. "You just wait one damn minute. Don't nobody yank on my child like he some kinda damn animal. You get your hands off of him!"

Mama glared at Frog. "Shut up, Frog!" she yelled. "Doo-witty is a man, not a child. Let him fight his own battles. You take his balls outta your purse and let him wear 'em himself." Frog bucked her eyes real hard, like she was seriously put out. I thought that she would come back at Mama with some fighting words, but she didn't. That flabby face of hers just seemed to fall right onto the table. Anybody seeing her woulda thought that Mama had smacked her a good one.

"I don't have nothing of his in my purse," she said quietly, and sat down.

"Now, Doo-witty," Mama continued. "Tia tells me that she believes in you. She tells me that she trusts you, so I'm gonna trust you too. Please, in the name of all goodness, tell me where my baby is at?"

"I d-d-don't know, Ms. Dubois," Doo-witty repeated weakly. "Like I said, she didn't go w-w-with me. I-I went by myself. You can call my uncle and ask him. T-T-Tia stayed here. Sh-sh-she stayed here with Maxi. She was gone hang out with her for a while. I-I swear she ain't been with me. I just g-g-got back this morning. Me and Mama stopped for a-a early lunch. I ain't heard from her. I would tell you if I had. I-I don't want no harm to be done to Tia. I c-c-care about Tia. She real special to me. She said that . . . that she was gone hang out here," he repeated. "That's wh-wh-what she told me. I swear. If Maxi don't know where she at . . . at, she just done up and run off. That's all there is to . . . to it. She just done up and run off."

Mama let Doo-witty go. She fell into a chair next to Frog, her arms drooping at her sides like a rag doll. The barbecue fell to the ground. I bent down and picked it up. For a minute everything seemed to stop, the way Tia said that it sometimes did for her. A stillness settled over the table, and nothing at all made a sound or moved. It was as if Grandma Augustine's and Kambia's God had turned off the world, crushed all Mama's hopes. Mama never really believed that Tia was hanging out with one of her girlfriends. She thought what we all had come to think—that Tia was with Doo-witty, that she had run off with him to teach Mama a lesson, and that she would turn up in town at the same time that he did. It was that one bright spot in the pit of darkness that Tia had thrown us all into. Frog looked at Mama and sighed. She shook her head. Her faced turned very un-Frog-like. It was gentle and caring, a face that only Doo-witty normally got to see.

"You better take your mama home, girl," she said. "Ain't no more for her to do here. She done got all the answers that she gone get." I grabbed Mama gently by the arm, but she shook me off and got up by herself.

"I'm all right, Shayla," she said. "I'm fine. We better go see about your grandmother. I'm sorry to interrupt your lunch, Miss Earlene," she mumbled. "Lord knows that I am."

Frog nodded.

Mama looked at me again. "I'm all right," she repeated. "Don't look so upset, Shalya. I'm just fine."

But Mama wasn't just fine. On the way back to the house everything seemed to give way in her. That little hole in her heart stretched wide open and a flood of pain came bursting through. For the first time ever Mama dropped tears, huge, heavy tears that slid out of her heart and onto her face. As I walked along beside her I wished that I could gather them up with my hands, catch them as they rolled from her eyes, and save them. They were another part of her that I had never seen before, a part of her that I hoped never to see again. When we reached home, I wouldn't bother trying to write a note in my blue notebook. There were no words that would express how I felt today. Grandma Augustine's Foot Grabber had won at last. He had snatched the bricks out from underneath our house and the whole thing had fallen completely down. Once we got in the door, Mama would finally call the law. She would tell them about Tia and Doo-witty, about all the fights, and about why she had waited so long to call. After that, she'd spend the afternoon sitting on the porch, in Tia's space, sitting and staring into the garden at the thorny rosebush where Tia's bra is still hanging, praying that Tia comes back home to pull it off.

Chapter 7

"*P*uberty is the most wonderful and the most difficult time in a girl's life. It's the caterpillar time, a time when she wraps herself in a cocoon of awkwardness and stays there for several months until her woman wings sprout. Once they sprout, she is no longer an ugly, belly-crawling insect-girl, but a beautiful young lady who can flutter all over the world, filling it with her grace, knowledge, and charm."

That's what Kambia and I learned today at the "Now I'm a Woman" workshop in our school cafeteria after our classes let out. The workshop was held to teach girls me and Kambia's age about the joy of turning into women. It was supposed to explain why our faces were covered with small white pimples, why many of us were starting to need a little extra room in the front of our T-shirts, and why some of us had tiny hairs peeping out of places that we no longer liked for our mothers to see. "It's as common as popcorn at a movie," the heavyset school nurse said. "All over the world girls your age go through it. It's nothing to be ashamed of. It usually starts either before or after you get a visit from the lady in red."

I thought that the workshop was messed up. I didn't like the way that the woman talked to us, as if we had never seen that little fluff of hair between our mothers' legs, or had never been sent to the store to fetch a box of Kotex. "What does she think that we are, dorks or something?" I whispered to Kambia while the talk was going on, but she didn't laugh or anything. She just sat there on the floor next to me, with her legs crossed, tugging the hem outta her dingy white dress as if she suddenly thought that it ought to be longer. I reached over and grabbed her hands a couple of times to try and get her to stop, but she didn't pay me any mind. She just kept yanking at the nylon thread until she had a zigzagged line of it trailing on the floor.

After the talk there was a short question-and-answer session, in which nobody was brave enough to ask anything, then the woman gave us all a Confidential Girl Pack and let us go home. On the way home Kambia and I opened ours up. There was nothing interesting in them, just a package of tampons, a pamphlet on cramps and stuff like that, and a Snickers. I ripped my Snickers open and ate all of it, but Kambia just pinched off the top and tossed the rest of it away. She said that she wasn't very hungry.

Kambia has been saying that a lot. Lately, she never seems to want much to eat. At lunch she picks at her food, eating a couple of spoonfuls of peas or whatever vegetable we are having, and only a few bites out of her meat. She's always been skinny, but now she's pencil-lead thin and kind of sick-looking. Her scrawny arms are no wider than the batteries that my mom puts in her flashlight, and if you stood two baseball bats up against her bony legs, you could probably block them out entirely. There are dark, blue black circles underneath her eyes where there used to be warm, butter yellow skin, and her glossy, red blond hair looks like a dust mop that hasn't been shaken out in years.

"Kambia, why don't you eat something?" I ask her. "You look like one of those zombies out of *Dawn of the Dead*."

"I can't eat too much, Shayla," she says. "I'm trying to get so thin that the wolves won't want to grab me. They don't like extra-skinny girls. There isn't enough meat on them. I want to get so little that when I walk in the room they can barely see me. I'll be safe then. They'll have to leave me alone."

"What if they don't?" I ask.

"They will," she says. "I'll be as thin—and as fragile—as a dragonfly wing. If they touch me, I'll crumble into tiny pieces and all they'll be able to do is sweep me up off the floor."

"I hope you're right," I say. "I hope that you can make them go away forever and ever."

When Kambia and I got back to my house, we sat down on the front porch, and I decided to get rid of the rest of my Confidential Girl Pack. I already knew most of the stuff on the pamphlet, and I didn't have any use for the tampons. I hadn't started my period yet and Mama didn't wear them. But I thought of something fun to do with them, like they do on TV. I walked to the kitchen, got a pitcher of grape Kool-Aid, and poured a glass. Then, while Kambia looked on, I placed a tampon in the glass and watched it explode and absorb up all of the liquid. After the tampon was full, I pulled another one out of the box and did the same with it.

I had gone completely through my box when Grandma Augustine came limping out of the front door, dressed in her favorite pair of maroon polyester stretch pants and matching blouse, and asked me what I was doing. I burst into giggles, but Kambia just got real nervous-looking. Grandma Augustine sighed.

"What are y'all doing that mess for, out here on the front porch?" she asked. I shrugged my shoulders. Kambia copied me.

"Lord, young gals these days, they don't know what to get into," she said. "Y'all pour that mess out, put them things up, and go find something else to do."

"Yes, ma'am," I said. I gathered everything up, took it back in the kitchen, and threw it away. When I returned, Kambia was gone and Grandma Augustine was sitting in her favorite metal rocking chair, rocking back and forth.

"Where's Kambia?" I asked.

"She run home as soon as you walked in the house, like I was a wicked witch. I guess she figured that I was gone push her in the oven," Grandma said.

"Naw, she probably just wanted to get in the house before her mom called her," I remarked. "Her mom is always needing her to do something."

"What her mama needs to be having her do is eat," Grandma said. "That child is getting thin as a paper doll. I bet she don't weigh twenty pounds. I know her mama got food in that house. Lord knows her mama ain't got no Lena Horne figure. It's gotta be plenty food in that house somewhere."

"Kambia is real picky about what she eats," I said.

"Umph," Grandma Augustine said. "Umph—umph, I'll believe that only if I see it with my own eyes. Ain't a child in the world will pass up a full belly for an empty one. Naw, something just ain't right about that child being so skinny. Her mama ain't watching out for her like she suppose to. She ain't putting what that child needs first." She shook her head. "I seen mothers like her before, give they kids lunch meat, while they eat roast. It's just plain sorry. I got a good mind to go on ahead and call them state folks on her. They'll get her straightened out, and Lord knows that she needs to be told a thing or two. Yeah, I gotta good mind to let them find out why that child is looking so peaked. I'll let her know that other folks *can* have a say in her business, whether she like it or not. It might be true that can't nobody say for sure what all she up to, but any fool can see that whatever she doing, she spending more time on it than she is on her on child."

"Maybe," I mumbled in my head. I really didn't know. When I thought about Kambia's mama, all I could imagine was a redheaded woman with heavy ankles and too much makeup. That's all she was to me. Even though I had heard her yell at Kambia that night when Kambia crawled under the porch, and saw how Kambia acted that day she came looking for her at our house, I still didn't know what sort of woman she was. Kambia had never really said one bad word about her mother. If she was as awful as Grandma Augustine thought that she was, wouldn't Kambia say something? Wouldn't any kid say something? Kambia told me that it was her decision to stop eating. I would have to believe her. I had promised that I would. It was the only thing that I could do. It was the only thing that I knew how to do.

"Oh, well," Grandma said after a while. "This ain't nothing that I needed to be talking to you about anyway. Besides, maybe it's best to give the fleas a chance to jump off the dog before you spray them with flea killer. I'll just wait and see what she gone do. It makes more sense to just wait it out and see what happens. It don't make no sense to stick your hand in a pot when you don't really know what's in it. Lord knows you can get burnt that way."

Grandma shook her head once more, then crossed her hands in her lap and looked out into the street. Across from our house, on another small concrete porch, a group of teenage boys were gathered around a large boom box, their dark, kinky heads nodding up and down at a blaring rap tune. Next to the boys, in the center of a porch that was attached to a leaning shack with no screen door, sat two little girls with slick brown hair and matching plaid dresses. They were happily building a dollhouse and some miniature furniture out of an old cardboard potato chip box, cutting out pieces of the board with a carving knife and coloring them with bright crayons. Grandma Augustine sighed again.

"It seems like everything in this neighborhood goes on right here on the front porch," she said. "Everything but birth and marriage, 'cause Lord knows I done seen enough people pass away rocking back and forth in they porch rocking chairs, just like me." She ran her fingers through her short curly hair. I noticed that a fresh crop of gray had sprung up around her temples.

"You got new gray hairs," I said.

"I know," she answered. "Pretty soon I'm gone have a head of snow. With all of the mess that's been going on for the past few months, I don't know why my hair ain't the color of cotton." She shook her head again. "Where in the world could that gal be?" she asked. That's when I noticed that her hair wasn't the only thing that was changing. There were several new clusters of deep wrinkles etched into her forehead, gathered around her stern eyes, and over her mouth. I patted her arm, then sat down beside her rocker, trying to think up an answer to her question.

Tia is still a no-show, even though Mama finally called the police. She called them the day that she and I saw Doo-witty and Frog at the barbecue shack.

The policemen came quickly, which is rare for our neighborhood. It normally takes cops a day or so to respond to non-emergency calls. So we were all very shocked and surprised when two of them rolled on over to our house that very afternoon. One was the color of devil's food cake, the other a bowl of vanilla pudding. They both wore crisp black uniforms, and shiny black shoes that squeaked when they walked up our concrete porch steps.

After a brief "Good afternoon," the policemen asked Mama all sorts of questions, questions that Mama obviously didn't like answering. While they grilled her, she fluttered nervously around our tiny house, from room to room, in her burgundy housedress, like a lost moth. She lighted in each room just long enough to go over it with the buff of a dust rag and the swish of a broom, as if she had endless amounts of housework that she simply had to keep up with.

The policemen wanted to know everything they could about Tia. How long had she been gone? Who had she left with? Had she run off before? What made her take off in the first place? And most importantly, why had Mama waited so long to report her as missing? Mama answered all the questions as best she could in flight, telling the policemen exactly what had happened between her and Tia, and how she originally thought that Tia was just trying to piss her off and would come home on her own after she was sure that Mama was sorry for the things that she had said to her.

The police seemed satisfied with Mama's answers, and they left right away to talk with Doo-witty, Frog, Maxi, and all of Tia's girl-friends, but they didn't find out any more than we did. Nobody changed their story. They still said that they had no earthly idea where Tia could be. At first, just like us, the policemen didn't believe any of them, but after they checked out their houses, they said that there was nothing to prove that any of them was lying. They even took Doo-witty down to the station and gave him a lie detector test; but they said that they didn't know if he even understood everything that they were asking him, so it didn't help much. In the end, all they could do was put Tia's name and a picture of her into their computer in their missing persons section, and hope that something turned up on her in the future.

Nobody at our house has given up hope, but it hurts too much to think about her, so most of the time we try not to. Whenever one of us starts talking about her, the other two try and change the subject. Mama says that it's the only way. She says that it's the best way to keep from being all broke up over her. "If we don't talk about her so much, we won't miss her," she says. "We have to dwell on other things, fill our minds with something else."

The something else that Mama has been filling her mind up with is Mr. Anderson Fox. Since the day that we found out about Tia, he's been sticking to Mama like masking tape, coming over every day and following her around the house like a bald-headed shadow. He says that he wants to help Mama get over her troubles, help her get through all the pain that she's feeling. He's been doing this by hanging out in our kitchen every chance he gets, scarfing down all the food in our refrigerator, and spending long hours talking on the living-room phone to his homeboys and homegirls back home. Grandma Augustine says that she doubts that Mama will be able to pay her telephone bill this month; but Mama doesn't seem to care. When Mr. Anderson Fox comes over, she always greets his big toothy grin with a big smile, the kind of smile that lets him know that it's okay for him to keep coming back. When he comes over, I still mostly stay out of his way. It's the only way that I know of to keep him from trying to play daddy to me.

After a while of rocking in her chair and looking like she had just lost her best Sunday hat, Grandma Augustine decided to go back to her own house. She wanted to spend a little time playing with Nat King Cole, and then take a nap. She told me to go in the house and do my homework until Mama got home from the store, where she had gone to get some butter beans for dinner. I said that I would, then helped her up out of her chair and watched as she opened the gate and went off around the corner. When she was good and gone, I climbed back up on the porch and started for the front door, but as soon as I made it to the door, Kambia called me.

"Shayla," she whispered as I yanked on the door handle. I let it go and looked toward her side of the fence. She was squatting down beside it, next to her mom's window, with a large brown paper bag in her hand. I hopped off the porch and walked over to her.

"What you got in the bag?" I asked.

"I need you to go with me somewhere," she whispered quickly.

"Where?" I asked.

"Down to the bayou," she said. "I need to go down there right now."

"To the bayou!" I couldn't believe it, not the bayou again. Why did it keep popping up no matter how hard I tried to avoid it? It was like getting a whole bunch of mosquito bites after you sprayed yourself all over with bug spray.

"Why do you need to go down to the bayou?" I asked. "If you want to play a game, we can do it right here."

"I don't want to play a game, Shayla," she said. "I just need to go. It's something that I gotta do, and I want you to come with me."

"I can't," I whined. "My mom's not home, and my grandma told me to stay here and do my homework. My mom will be seriously pissed if I'm not here when she gets back."

"Please, please, Shayla," she begged, real desperate-like, as if going was the most important thing in the world, as if the planets would drop from the sky if she didn't do it. I gave in.

"Okay, Kambia," I said. "But I can't be gone long. I gotta come back soon."

"It won't take long, Shayla, I promise," she said. She hopped up, ran over to the gate, opened it, and went out. I ran to my gate and did the same.

If Kambia were the weather, I would describe her as bright and sunny, without a cloud in the sky. She didn't walk quietly beside me with her eyes taking in everything, and not saying anything, like she normally did. Clutching her brown bag tightly, she skipped down the sidewalk, pointing and chatting about everything—the men in cutoffs shooting hoops at the park, the tiny wiener dog in Old Lady Tompson's yard, the beer cans lying in the gutter in front of the 24-and-7, and anything else that caught her attention. It was as though another Kambia had been beamed down from some distant star to take her place. I hurried along beside her, trying to keep up with her.

When we got to the bayou, it was plain to see that Mother Nature had already taken her change-of-season stroll through the area. The blackberry bushes that lined the entrance were bursting with rich, plum red berries, just waiting to be plucked to make blackberry cobbler. As we pushed through the bushes we popped off a couple and tossed them into our mouths, before we started up the winding trail, with Kambia still skipping and me lagging behind.

Once on the trail Kambia continued to point and make a remark about everything. And there was a lot to say something about. The bayou had sprung back to life. The tall, skyscraper-like pine trees were covered with brand-new dark, spindly leaves, and the pecan trees were heavy with hard, bright green pecans. The murky waters of the bayou had gone from muddy winter brown to greenish gray spring, and the high cliffs that overlooked it were sprinkled with cottony dandelions and towering sunflowers blowing gently from a cool breeze.

"Man, it's pretty out here. I could stay all evening," I said to Kambia. She kept skipping, still grasping her bag. Everything seemed to delight her, especially the small fluffy-tailed squirrels that we saw scurrying from tree to tree.

"They look so funny when they do that," she said. "It must be really great to be able to live in a tree."

My fears about coming back to the bayou with Kambia started to ease up. We had got so close since the day that she pulled that silly baby game on me. I couldn't imagine that she would do it again. In fact, Kambia hadn't played any of her games in a while. She hadn't pretended to be a tree, a flower, or anything like that. For the past month she had been just plain ole Kambia. She still told lots of stories, but in them she was always herself. Maybe she had grown out of all of her baby foolishness. Maybe she was starting to grow up.

I turned my mind to something else. I wondered what was in her bag. Even though she had said that she didn't want to come to the bayou to play a game, I figured that it must be something that you could have fun with. Not a Nintendo or anything like that—neither one of us had money for that kind of junk. I thought maybe it was a jump rope or even a bunch of Barbie dolls, if she still played with them. I did sometimes, even though Tia told me that it was a little-girl thing to do.

"Hey, whatcha got in that bag?" I asked her again. She just kept skipping and making comments, more to herself than to me. I got the feeling that if I left, she wouldn't even notice.

After a while Kambia stopped moving, which was fine with me because I was out of breath trying to keep up with her. I didn't know that anybody could skip for so long. She stood in the middle of the path and looked up it. There was a large group of girls, around our age, in short flowered dresses and light sweaters, hanging out on one of the cliffs a little ways up the path. They were kicking back underneath some of the trees, deep in conversation.

"Hey, you wanna go see what they're up to?" I asked. She shook her head and kept looking around.

"What are you looking for?" I continued. She spotted a thick cluster of leafy bushes just a little ways before one of the curves in the path, and pointed to them.

"What's behind them, Shayla?" she asked.

"I don't know, more trees. It's kind of like a little woods or something. I went back there once, but I didn't like it too much. It looked like a place where winos and stuff used to hang out," I said.

"Come on, Shayla," she said, heading for the bushes.

"What for?" I asked. "There's nothing good back there to see."

"Come on, hurry," she said. She ran up to the bushes, squeezed through them, and disappeared. I ran after her.

"Girl, wait up!" I called.

Kambia raced blindly through the bushes until she found a small clearing surrounded by a group of baby pecan trees. I ran up to her, once again out of breath.

"Hey," I said, breathing hard. "What are you gonna do back here? I told you that there wasn't much to see." She just looked down at the ground. Confused, I yanked a tiny limb off of one of the trees, broke it in half, and threw part of it onto the ground next to a pile of dried-out twigs. She looked up at me.

"Do you think that anybody can see us?" she asked.

"Naw," I said, glancing back at the bushes. "I can't even see the trail anymore."

"Good," she said. "I don't want anybody to see us. I don't want anybody to know that we're back here."

"How come?" I asked. She just glanced back at the ground.

"What are you looking at the ground for?" I asked. She looked up at me again, then she slowly started to open her bag. I moved in closer to try and get a peep.

"Hey, what's in your bag, girl?" I asked for a third time. She still didn't answer.

She stuck her hand deep down into the bag and pulled out a spade, the same kind that Grandma Augustine uses to dig in her gardens.

"What are you gonna do with that?" I asked. She just squatted down, brushed the twigs out of the way, and started digging a hole in the dirt.

"Are we gonna plant flowers back here?" I asked, dying of curiosity. "They're not gonna get much sun. We should plant them out in the open."

"No, Shayla," she said quietly. "We're not gonna plant flowers."

"What then?" I asked. She just kept digging. The earth was really soft. With every push and scoop of her spade she brought up a large heap of black dirt.

"Kambia, what are we planting?" I asked. "I don't have time to make a garden. I told you that I have to get home soon." She continued to dig. I sighed and tried to imagine what it was that she could be burying. With no help from her my mind pulled up all sorts of silly, ridiculous things. I thought of watermelon seeds, old plastic containers, even the body of a pet hamster or bird that she might not have told me about. But the one thing that kept swimming through the creeks in my brain—was treasure. I told myself that she might be a kind of a Pippi Longstocking, a young girl whose pirate father had been washed away at sea, leaving her with tons of gold that she had to bury to keep it away from thieves. Since the gold was really heavy, she had to bury it in small piles. There would be just enough in each pile for her to buy herself a fancy dress, a horse, or something like that. It was a fantasy that I would have liked to live myself.

Kambia dug and dug until she had a large, round hole, deep enough to hold two basketballs stacked on top of each other.

When she was finished, she straightened up for a minute to stretch her back, then bent down and opened up her bag again. I bent down beside her. She stuck her hand in, and I waited with excitement to see what she would bring out. When her hand emerged, I nearly fell over from shock. It was underwear! That's what she had in her bag, a small bundle of flimsy, ripped panties with torn elastic around the legs. I recognized the pair that she was wearing that first time I met her on the street, the really awful pair that made me stick my hand in the gutter for her. I couldn't believe it! The underwear was really stained up. They were covered all over with tiny reddish brown splotches. For a minute I felt really sick from the sight of them, but I was too curious to let it get to me.

"Kambia, what are you doing with ratty old underwear?" I asked. She just shoved them in the hole real quickly and started to cover them over with the dirt.

"Kambia, why are you burying that stuff?" I asked. "I don't understand. What are you doing bringing your underwear out here? Your mom's gonna be really mad at you. You better take those back home and wash them. Why are they so messed up?"

"I can't take them home, Shayla," she said, losing all of the happiness that she had had in her voice. "I have to get them away from me. They're evil."

"Evil?"

"Yes," she answered, continuing to scoop the dirt into the hole. "The wolves make them that way."

"How? What do they do to them? Is that where they got all of those funny stains on them?"

"Yes," she said. "The wolves rip them up with their big sharp teeth, then they chew on them until they are all gross-looking from the poisonous spit in their mouths."

"I thought you said that the Lie Catcher was the one with the poisonous spit."

"They have it too," she said. "They all have it. I can't wear these anymore after they touch them. They make me feel real bad on the inside. They make me feel like a dead dog or something. I don't want to feel that way, Shayla. That's why I have to bury them way back here, real deep, where nobody can find them, then I can start to feel better," she said, with shaky hands and an even shakier voice. "If I bury them way back here, they'll never find them. They won't be able to use them to hurt me again."

I squatted down and placed one of my hands on top of hers. It felt like her body did the other day, very cold, like somebody had dipped her in ice water.

"I'll help you," I said. "We'll make sure that nobody ever, ever finds them."

I started helping Kambia scoop the pile of dirt back over the hole. As usual I didn't know what else to do. Had she started her period and just didn't want to admit it? Grandma Augustine said that when she started hers she really freaked out. She said that she stayed in her room for three days crying, until her mom finally tricked her out of it with some homemade peach ice cream. Grandma Augustine didn't want to see an end to her mud-pie-making days; maybe Kambia didn't either. Maybe she wasn't ready to wear her woman wings. I didn't know what to think. This afternoon at the workshop when I told her that I hadn't started my period yet, I hadn't bothered to ask her if she had started hers. I simply figured that she hadn't, since she had never told me that she had the cramps or anything. And then there was the thing we did with the tampons and Kool-Aid. She seemed to think that it was a pretty fun thing to do.

Man, I had more questions about Kambia than a history test. I patted my part of the dirt mound down gently, like I was flouring a piece of snapper, and looked at her. There was no emotion in her face, no fear, no sadness—nothing. There was just that same spacey look that she got when she was starting one of her baby games, but somehow I knew that this wasn't a game. Whatever was wrong with Kambia was hurting her deep. It was tearing into her bony body and ripping her into bits. It wouldn't be long before she did crumble like an old dead dragonfly wing. It wouldn't be long before she couldn't fight her monsters off.

"Kambia, you gotta tell somebody about your wolves and how they make you do things," I said. "You gotta let somebody know that you're being hurt."

"No," she said. "No, no, no, I can't tell, Shayla. I told you that. Everything will turn all bad." She stood up. "You promised me that you wouldn't tell either," she said. "If you break it, I won't be your friend anymore. I'll never, ever hang out with you again."

"I never tell anybody your secrets. I'll keep this one, too," I whispered, feeling a little hurt myself. I couldn't believe that she thought it was necessary to threaten me after all these months, after all of the time that we had spent together, after all the times we'd played together, and shared tears. We were friends—and friends didn't tell on friends. With Tia gone she was the closest thing that I had to a sister, the row of orchids in the field of weeds that had been strangling me since the day that I walked away and left Tia with Doo-witty. How could she still not know that I would never do anything that would cause her pain? I had bitten my tongue when Grandma mentioned sending someone into her house to get on her mother about not feeding her, and I would keep biting it until *she* told me to stop. I would bury my feelings and concerns along with her gross underwear.

"Okay," she said, walking back toward the way that we had come in. I followed her quietly. She turned and faced me, her eyes going from spacey to happy again. "I think that this is really gonna work, Shayla," she said. "I really think that it will keep the wolves away."

"I don't understand how it will, Kambia," I said softly. "But I hope you're right. I hope you're right about everything."

When we got back, Kambia sneaked into her yard the same way that she had come out, and I went back to my house. When I walked up the front steps, Mama was standing in the screen door waiting for me, looking like she was expecting special company. She was dressed in purple from head to toe. She was wearing a full violet skirt and a violet cotton blouse that was topped with a lavender head scarf, which was pulled back over her curled hair. I started to yell something nice to her about her outfit, but I noticed that Mr. Anger was standing right beside her. His anger suit was glowing like hot coals. I figured that I had just better keep my nice words to myself. I dragged myself up the steps like a kid going to the principal's office. She opened the door for me with a scowl on her face.

"Shayla, where have you been?" she yelled. "I been all around to Mama's house looking for you. I was worried to death!"

"Nowhere," I said. "Me and Kambia just went to do some stuff. We went for a walk down on the bayou."

"Down on the bayou!" Mama yelled. "By yourself! Girl, I done told you that I don't want you wandering around this neighborhood no more like that. Lord knows what coulda happened to you!"

I rolled my eyes. "That's silly, Mama," I said. "I always go down to the bayou. I been going down there by myself for two years. Nobody wants me."

"How you know that?" she asked. "How do you know what can happen to you all alone?"

"I was with Kambia," I said.

"Kambia, that little gal ain't nothing but a toothpick. How is she gone stop anybody from grabbing you?"

I shrugged my shoulders.

She pointed her finger in my face. "Besides," she said, "none of that matters. Your grandmother told you to stay here, and that's what you should have done. You getting too big for your drawers, little girl. It's time you learn that you don't run nothing here but your mouth." I flopped down on the sofa and folded my arms across my chest. Mama glared at me and stomped off into the kitchen.

I pulled my lip in and sucked on it a good while. Mama had really pissed me off. Ever since we found out about Tia, she'd been watching me like a cat watching her kittens. I knew that she was just upset over Tia, but I still didn't like it. I stretched out on the sofa, near the side that had the fewest number of springs popping through, and closed my eyes. In the darkness I heard noises coming from the kitchen—Mama's voice, and his, Mr. Anderson Fox's. He was here again, to try and make things better for Mama. I tried to block him out of my mind with something nice, but there wasn't anything. All I could think of was Kambia and her ratty stained underwear and how we had buried it in the ground like it was a vampire or something that could come back to get us. It was certainly the strangest thing that I ever did. In fact, I'll bet that it was the strangest thing that anybody ever did.

If I told Mama, she would probably tell me that I was crazy. She would tell me to tell Kambia to stop being so silly and throwing away her clothes, when she has so few anyway—and that would be true. Kambia has next to nothing. In school the mean kids call her

Raggedy Ann because she always wears the same dress, but the nice kids try and help her. They are always bringing her old clothes from home, things that are well worn but still kinda good-looking. But Kambia never takes the clothes. She doesn't tell them that she doesn't want them or that she thinks that they are ugly. She just tells them what she tells me whenever I try to give her some of my old things. She tells them that her white dress is a special gift from a friend, one of the nuns at the convent she used to have to stay at. She tells them that it has special powers like the blood of Jesus or Mary's tears, and that if she takes it off, her soul will burn in hell forever. The kids don't believe her, any more than I do, but they never tell her. They simply nod their heads and go away. "Poor Kambia," they say. "When did she start to mix her stories up with her real world? How did she get so messed up?"

I thought about Kambia until my brain couldn't take it anymore. Finally I decided that I just plain and simple didn't know what to do, so I got up off the couch and decided to find something to get my mind off of the subject. Homework wasn't on the list. I didn't have any. I figured that a homemade batch of peanut butter cookies would give my brain a break. They were a favorite at our house, better than a Sunday evening revival, Grandma Augustine sometimes said. I smoothed down the wrinkles in my tie-dyed dress and headed for the kitchen, hoping that Mr. Anderson Fox had eaten all that he could out of the refrigerator and was ready to go home. It was the one thing that could make my day.

When I got to the kitchen, I realized that I couldn't have been more wrong. Mr. Anderson Fox was nowhere near ready to go. He was sitting next to Mama, at the dining-room table, with a large plate overflowing with leftover cabbage, hot corn bread, and juicy meat loaf. He had a big blue paper towel tucked into the collar of his wine-colored shirt, and several bottles of hot sauce lined up in front of a large glass of the grape Kool-Aid. He was seriously ready to chow down. I mumbled something ugly about him underneath my breath and walked over to the sink.

"Shayla, come over here and sit down," Mama said to me. I walked over to an empty chair and sat down in it. Mr. Anderson Fox smiled at me.

"How ya doing, baby girl? That sho is a pretty dress you got on," he said. I mumbled something at him again. Mama took a deep breath and let it out, then she picked up one of the hot sauce bottles and started to shake it gently with her heavy hands.

"Shayla," she said, staring at the sauce and not at me, "you know that your daddy here has been staying with Duke and Morris from the hall since he come into town."

"I know, Grandma Augustine told me," I said with as little care as I could get out.

"That's right," she continued, starting to shake the bottle real fast, her voice getting real itty-bitty, like I was a four-year-old. "He's been paying them every other day to sleep on they sofa and wash his clothes in they machine."

"So," I snapped. She cut her eyes away from the bottle for a minute and looked at me sternly, then they were back on the bottle again. She stopped shaking it and started to yank off pieces of the orange label, dropping the shreds next to Mr. Anderson Fox's plate. He brushed them onto the floor.

"Anyway," she continued, "he hasn't been able to keep much money in his pocket that way, having to give them money to do every little thing."

I shrugged my shoulders.

"Well," she said. "Me and him talked about it, and we both

figured that as long as he was over here most of the time anyway, he might as well just stay with us. It'll give him a good chance to get to know you again. He can spend a lot more time with you," she said. I swallowed real hard.

"I thought that he was only gonna be here a little while," I said. "I thought that he had a job that he had to go back to and all."

"Oh," Mama said. "Yeah—he does, he does, but he just taking a little time off for a while, trying to work out some old problems, get back in touch with the people that he cares about. Like I said, he really wants to spend time with you. I think it's a good idea for him to lay his hat here for a while, but I want to know what you think," she said, putting the bottle down and picking up another one.

What I thought? When did it matter what I thought? Did anybody ask me if I wanted Mr. Anderson Fox to come down here in the first place? Did they ask me if I wanted him staring at me with his searchlight eyes? Was I asked about how I felt about the clothes that he never bought me, the toy baking oven that I never got, or the school book club that I couldn't join because Mama didn't have enough to pay the club dues? Why was I being asked now? Why wasn't I asked how I felt about having to eat free lunch and wear hand-me-down shoes, or about the other Shaylas with his face and his big toothy grin that were running around the neighborhood, the ones that I would never get to call sister, the ones that always went the other way whenever they saw me. Did anybody ever ask me how I felt about them? The question was dumb, dumb and senseless. It was like putting a fresh layer of paint on peeling walls, knowing that the old paint was just gonna push out from underneath it.

I looked down at the bottle of hot sauce that Mama was holding and imagined myself grabbing it and pouring it over Mr.

Anderson Fox's head. I would splash it all over him, watch it run down into his searchlight eyes, and let *him* feel some pain for a change. Maybe he would scream and run, and say that I was the worst daughter in the world, and wouldn't ever want to come back. It would make me real happy. I bet it would make all of the Shaylas happy. But I wasn't big on hurting other people, especially not Mama, and as much as I hated it, Mr. Anderson Fox did seem to be the one thing that was holding her together. He was the putty that had plugged up the hole in her heart. I couldn't unplug it.

"I don't think anything about it, Mama," I said, cutting my eyes at Mr. Anderson Fox. He stabbed a piece of meat loaf, brought it up to his mouth, and chewed it slowly, all the while focusing his good eye on me.

"You don't think anything about it, Shayla?" Mama asked with a faint voice that sounded wounded and desperate. "You don't have any feelings on it at all?"

"Whatever you do is okay with me, Mama," I lied.

"Okay," she said. "I just want you to be happy." She looked up at me. "I'm sorry about yelling at you earlier," she said. "I just been a little wound up. Things will be better now, though. Things will be a lot better."

"I know, Mama," I said. I got up from the table and walked back over to the sink. Behind me I heard Mr. Anderson Fox gasp and break into a fit of coughs. His meat loaf had gone down the wrong way.

"I hope you don't choke," I called behind me in my fake daughterlike voice. I turned around to see him pick up his glass of Kool-Aid and take a drink, and set it down. As he set it down his searchlight eyes rested on mine once more. And then it all became clear to me. I figured out what that curiosity was in his eyes, what it was that he wanted to know about me. He wanted to know if he could jump over my hurdles as easily as he had jumped over Mama's. He was trying to read me, trying to open up that journal that I kept in my mind, the one that I never let anyone see. He was looking for a part of me that he could grab on to, like Tia's Foot Grabber and Kambia's wolves. It was the way that Mr. Anderson Fox survived, the way that he got over; but he wouldn't find that part on me. There were no doors on me that he could yank open and crawl through. He wouldn't play me like he thought that I would let him play Mama, like I knew that he had played every female that had ever passed his way. I thought up a journal entry to write down later. *Mr. Anderson Fox is swarming all over our house like yellow jackets,* I scribbled in my mind. *But I'm gonna make sure that he's the only one that gets stung.* I smiled at him brightly. I wondered if he knew that he was a big fat bug. I wondered if he knew that I was gonna squash him into the pavement.

Chapter 8

Sara leaned against the house and watched the gnats dance around the glowing porch light. Up and down, back and forth they flew, sometimes breaking off just a second before hitting the glass lamp, other times flying into it with scary force. Sara had seen the flutter-dance hundreds of times, seen the gnats with their tiny heads and wings of lace spend hours trying to dance their way under the dome covering, only to be burned to death by the hot bulb underneath. She thought the gnats were stupid. She couldn't understand how they could do the same thing every night, exactly the same way, and expect something different to happen. Didn't they see the dried-out bodies of their friends lying broken at the bottom of the glass dome? How could they think that their flutter-dance could lead to anything but their own death?

I read the opening paragraph to my new story aloud to Grandma Augustine and Mama over and over again as we walked down the busy street. I was trying to get their two cents on the beginning of it. I knew that they would tell me if it sounded like hogwash or if it just didn't quite make sense. I could always trust them to throw out the truth when it came to one of my tales. "The best criticism in the world comes from the ones that you love the most. If you really want to know what's what, ask someone that you share blood with," Grandma Augustine always says.

It is good advice, and I've been taking it a lot lately, firing parts of stories at them every chance that I get, letting them help me work my plots and stuff out. Their help means a lot to me since story writing is how I've been filling up most of my time for the past few weeks. I've been writing tale after tale, challenging myself with more mature plots and vocabulary, trying to forget about the pain that's still clinging to the walls of our house, draping itself over everything like huge cobwebs of hurt.

"Walking into this house is like sticking your hand into a fire ant mound," Grandma Augustine said the other day.

When I'm not thinking up stories, I'm thinking up things to do to Mr. Anderson Fox, putting too much salt into his food, spilling bleach on his favorite red shirt, knocking his toothbrush into the toilet, you name it. When he's not at the house, which isn't often, I sneak around like Kambia's Lie Catcher and do whatever I can to make his life miserable.

Both Mama and Grandma have been really worried about the change in my behavior, but they each have different answers for it. Mama seems to believe that the things I keep doing to Mr. Anderson Fox are mostly accidents, brought on by my being upset about Tia. "Be a little bit more careful when you're doing the laundry, Shayla," she said when she saw the red shirt. "Try not to act so carelessly with the bleach. Don't let your worry rattle you so much that you can't get things done."

"Yes, Mama," I said, sweet faced, but if you looked real close, you could see Mr. Anger peeping out from my eyes, where he's made himself at home since Mr. Anderson Fox painted his name on our mailbox. I'm not sure why Mama can't see him, but Grandma does, and she doesn't like what she sees.

"I know what you doing, missy, and I understand it," she told me after she saw the shirt. "But I don't like it one bit. You letting that man turn you into a child that even you wouldn't want to know. You letting him pull off the best parts of you and throw 'em into the darkness. You can't fight wrong with wrong. All you can do is pray for the best and try to make sure that the evil don't get the best of you."

In order to make sure that I did just that, Grandma Augustine thought it was time that I attended some kind of church service, to chase my little demon away before he got hold of me like Tia's had got hold of her. Since I wasn't at all open to a traditional Sunday morning service, where you had to dress all fancy and be in church all day, she suggested that we go to a Saturday cleansing revival at the Tabernacle of the Blessed Redeemer. When she told Mama about it, Mama thought that it was a good idea too, not because she thought I was in danger of losing my soul to the devil, but because she hoped it would help calm my nerves. In fact, she was so high on the idea that she decided to tag along as well. We would try and make it the family affair that we didn't have the day we found out about Tia not being with Doo-witty. We were going to chase all of our troubles away on the family plan. So this afternoon, after all our housework was done and Mr. Anderson Fox had took off for the pool hall, we put on simple shift dresses, covered our hair with scarves, and started for the church, with me pestering them with my latest tale.

"It sounds like it's going to be a really good story," Grandma Augustine said when I finished reading the paragraph for the fifth time. "Though I don't know why you started off talking about death."

"Everything dies, Grandma," I said, slowing down to keep up with her pace. Mama, standing on the other side of her, slowed down too.

"I know that, baby," she said. "Lord knows, I done told you that a million times."

"Yes, you have," I said. "Lots of times. And you're always dragging me, Mama, and Tia off to some funeral or wake."

"That's true," she said. "But, baby, that's reality, not make-believe. In make-believe there is so much more to talk about than things and people passing. Why don't you talk about how beautiful it is when you wake up on a cool morning and see that the grass has been all covered over with dew? Or you can write about how great it is when you find an extra couple of dollars in the bottom of your purse. Sweetie, there's so many wonderful things in this world. Can't you find a way to bring those to life? The Bible say to 'leave the dead to bury the dead.' You do that—and write about something happy. Write about something that'll make you feel better, not worse."

"I'll think about it, Grandma," I said. "But there's no need to. I feel just fine."

"No, you don't," she said, shaking her head. "But you will after the revival."

I slowed down and lagged behind her and Mama. I just couldn't believe that they both thought that the cleansing revival was a good idea. In my twelve years I had never seen them agree on anything, not the color of a dress, how much pepper to put in a recipe, nothing. How could they see eye to eye on the silly old cleansing revival? What was it anyway? It was just a bunch of ladies, all dressed the same, shouting and shaking, trying to get close to God. The last time that me, Mama, and Tia went I didn't understand any of it. It just made me wonder why the ladies would be willing to embarrass themselves to worship. I couldn't see how they could make a fool out of themselves for spirituality.

"People have been known to do some of almost anything to show they beliefs," Grandma Augustine says. "Ain't nothing wrong with a little jumping and hollering if it makes you closer to the man upstairs." *Closer to* was the part that gave me the most trouble. Mama had attended the revival when she was down on her luck, because Grandma had told her that God favored a clean soul. She had sung, danced, and even shouted like the rest of the ladies, but when it was over, and she had found herself a new job—and a new man, too—she was back to her normal non-church-going self. I don't think that it brought her any closer to God, at least not as far as I could see. She was still known to stretch the Ten Commandments just a bit to make them fit what she wanted to do. But here she was again on her way to another revival, on the way to worship a God that she didn't even act like she believed in. Out of all the millions of things that could have bound her and Grandma together, this was the one—and the most unlikely thing. I just didn't get it at all, not the ceremony, not her agreeing to participate in it, not them both thinking that I would be able to stomach Mr. Anderson Fox if they dragged me to it.

I watched them as they walked down the dirty sidewalk ahead of me. They were so much alike, same broad shoulders, wide back, heavy limbs, and slender waistline, strong woman bodies, crafted from hard work—and pain. I remembered one of Grandma Augustine's African proverbs: "You do not teach the trails of the jungle to an old lion. You let him go quietly, hoping that one day your paw prints will be good enough to follow his."

When we got to the Tabernacle of the Blessed Redeemer, you would have thought that something major had happened, like Noah sailing in on his ark. There were ladies everywhere. They stood in front of the red-brick church in small groups, pairs, and singles, waiting for the ceremony to begin. They were all dressed in some shade of white, the members of the church decked out in their ivory floor-length robes, the visitors, like us, adorned in plain off-white. It looked like everybody on the entire block had been suddenly turned into angels.

"Don't everybody look like they in a mind to praise Jesus," Grandma Augustine said. Mama nodded. After a few Christian hellos the three of us went and stood next to a telephone pole and waited for the rejoicing to begin.

The ceremony started some ten minutes later when the revival leader, Sister Ashada Waters, came walking up. She was a tall, coal black woman, with sharp eyes, a catching smile, and fine cheek-bones. Though she was well over sixty, she still wore her gray-black hair in curls down her back, and hardly ever covered her long, sturdy legs with hose, even in the dead of winter. Grandma Augustine said that Sister Ashada could out–Bible verse and out–Scripture most of the ladies in the church. She was well liked by everybody and was always the first one asked whenever any of the church members needed a godmother for one of their babies. When she passed us, both Mama and Grandma Augustine made sure that they greeted her with a very respectful greeting, adding a hug and a kiss to their normal handshake.

With Sister Ashada in place the ceremony kicked off quickly. "Mother to daughter, daughter to mother, both to God," the ladies chanted as we filed into the small, dome-shaped sanctuary. I thought that it was a rather silly chant, but my partner, an older lady with ashy brown skin, and wearing gardenia-scented cologne, really got into it. She chanted at the top of her lungs, her shrill, cracking voice lifting high above the other ladies'. I thought about putting my fingers in my ears, but I knew that either Grandma or Mama, standing right behind me, would probably give me a you-know-better smack on the head.

The ladies chanted their mother-daughter chant until the last two women, a middle-aged set of twins with matching head scarves and watery eyes, came marching up the red-carpeted aisle of the sanctuary. We all bowed, walked orderly over to one of the long mahogany benches, said a short prayer, and took a seat. I settled next to Grandma so that I could lean over and ask her about the parts of the ceremony. She smiled at me, then reached over and patted my knee. Just then the church broke into "Precious Lord." I glanced over at Mama and saw the sides of her lips curve up into a smile. "Precious Lord" was one of the few hymns that she knew.

"Precious Lord, take my hand. Lead me on, let me stand," she started to sing loudly. Grandma joined her, and soon I was the only person on our row not singing.

I looked around the sanctuary. Every inch of the whitewashed walls was taken up by some type of extraordinary adornment. On the wall next to me were two stained-glass windows. One of them was a picture of Jesus. He was clothed in a robe of scarlet and stood in front of a polished table with a silver pitcher in one hand and a silver cup in the other. A huge shower of clear water was pouring from the mouth of the pitcher, downward into the cup. But halfway to the cup the water turned from clear to maroon. It splashed deep inside the cup, overflowing the brim of it with a liquid that looked like red wine.

The second window showed something entirely different. It had a picture of three male slaves with obedient faces. They were dressed in tattered rags and were kneeling in front of a plain wooden cross that was set way up high on a hill that was surrounded with lush green trees.

Grandma Augustine said that the window was the first thing the congregation put into the church. It was supposed to represent the black man's own commitment to God, a commitment that he himself had made, and not one made for him by his slave master. Though I wasn't really sure about the commitment to God thing, I thought the picture was really cool. The slaves in it reminded me of the black people Mama and Grandma liked to put in their quilts, the ones that always saw the world through black eyes. The quilts were really great, but they would have been even greater if Mama and Grandma didn't always spend days, sometimes even weeks, fighting about types of fabric, patterns, and stitches.

After substituting cotton, nylon, and rayon for the panes of glass in the window, my eyes scanned the rest of the room, taking in the other decorations. Here and there were nicely crafted wall hangings made out of colorful squares of felt that were cut into Christian symbols—crosses, fish, and doves. Next to the wall hangings were delicate wreaths of silk violets. But the crowning glory of the room had to be the huge mural over the altar. I had never seen it before or even heard Grandma Augustine mention it, so I figured it must be new. It was about twenty feet long, and I wouldn't even try to guess how wide. It was a painting of a road, a golden road, made out of square blocks of concrete that sparkled underneath a bright, warm sun.

On one side of the road was a grove of dark-leafed fruit trees bursting with juicy red apples, plump oranges, and honey-colored pears, just waiting to be plucked, like the blackberries that me and Kambia ate down on the bayou.

On the other side of the road was a beautiful crystal-clear stream that was flowing toward a pair of golden arches. The arches weren't like the ones at McDonald's. They were hazy-looking. There was a misty fog surrounding them, as if they were from the twilight zone or something.

A large wooden plaque underneath the mural said that it was

called *The Road to Heaven*. I looked at the bottom right corner of the painting and spotted a set of initials, but I couldn't make them out. I decided they must be the initials of some big-time artist that the church had paid to paint the mural. I wondered if they would get him to paint anything else, and what it would be if he did.

After the ladies got through singing "Precious Lord," they broke into a series of foot-stomping hymns, rhythmic spirituals that sounded more like club music than church music to me. During the spirituals the ladies were as moved as the first time we came. Some stood in front of their benches, waving their hands and swaying back and forth, the heels of their two-inch pumps tapping on the bare floors, but others got overcome in another way. They jumped up from their seats, scrambled to the aisle, and started to dance up and down it, shaking tambourines or simply clapping their hands to the beat of the song. Mama was one of the hand clappers. When the music struck her, she popped up, made her way into the crowded aisle, and joined some of the regular church ladies. She smacked her huge hands together as hard as she could, strutting past the benches like a drum majorette.

"Go on, girl, praise Jesus!" Grandma yelled to egg her on. I scooted down real low in my seat.

When the music finally stopped, and the ladies were all sung out, the second part of the revival started. While the ladies took their seats again and began fumbling in their handbags for a mint to relieve their tired throats, Sister Ashada strolled up to the podium with her leather-bound Bible in hand.

"Mother to daughter, daughter to mother, both to God," she began. The ladies echoed her. She opened her Bible to start.

For nearly an hour Sister Ashada spoke on womanhood. She talked about how wonderful it was that women could give birth to children or adopt other people's children and raise them as their own. "The ability to mother a child is the greatest gift from God," she said. She talked about household chores, how women could be both bread bakers and breadwinners, but how men seemed to have a problem being put into more than one role. "Women are the chameleons of the earth," she said. "They can change to suit any environment. Men don't do it as well." The ladies nodded their heads and shouted "amen's." I did too, but only because Grandma shot me a you-better-respond look. I blurted out my "amen," thinking that it would be much better than a thigh pinch.

After Sister Ashada finished talking on woman things, she reminded the women that they must be both good mothers and good wives, not obedient, but a helper to their husband, "a strong link in the bond of marriage," as she put it. Then it was time for the sprinkling ceremony. We all filed in twos up to the podium, where we were sprinkled with the sand of Jesus' footprints (wheat flour) and then told that we could go home. Chatting and hugging, the ladies started to leave the church.

Me, Mama, and Grandma Augustine waited until the sanctuary was nearly empty before we strolled into the foyer. That's when I realized that I really had to go to the restroom, but Mama was ready to go.

"Can't you hold it?" Mama asked. "It's only a few blocks back to the house. You can use it when you get there."

"I can't," I said, crossing my legs like a toddler. "I gotta go now." Mama shook her head.

"Okay," she said. "But me and Mu'dear gone head on home, 'cause I told your daddy that I would be there thirty minutes ago. You can catch up with us. And don't you be playing around, little girl," she added. "You come straight home."

"Yes, ma'am," I said, starting to look around for a sign that said Restroom, as she and Grandma headed out of the church.

Looking for the sign was exactly what I had to do. I didn't have a clue as to where the restroom could be. The last time we came to a revival, Tia and I were able to slip out early before the rest of the ladies. We went to the park and used the bathroom next to the jungle gym. But still, I didn't mind the hunt. It gave me a little time away from Grandma and Mama, and especially Mr. Anderson Fox.

I glanced around the foyer. There were two cedar doors next to a large potted rubber plant. One of the doors was plain, with nothing at all on it, but the other door had a huge black cross painted in the center of it, with the words LET HE WHO IS WITHOUT SIN CAST THE FIRST STONE written underneath. I chose this door. It was the more creative.

The doorknob didn't turn easily when I went to open the door. So I turned it back and forth a few times until I heard a loud *snap*. Then I tugged it open.

When I got inside, quick as an owl could catch a moth, I realized that I wasn't in the bathroom. I was in a hallway, a dim hallway that smelled real strongly of fresh paint. However, I could see, even in the darkness, that the walls were not wet. Where the paint smell was coming from was a real mystery. Ignoring the pressure in my bladder, I headed down the hall, determined to find out about the paint smell. At least that's what I told myself. The truth of the matter was I was just being plain ole peep-through-the-window nosy. I wanted to find out more about the church. Along with Kambia's mom, it was the other big rumor maker in the neighborhood. There were three huge ones that were currently going around.

The first rumor was that the members of the church were like Jehovah's Witnesses or something. They believed that when the world came to an end only the people of their faith would be saved. When they did their sprinkling ceremonies, they made sure that they sprinkled their guests with a different type of sprinkling powder, a darker shade of wheat flour, so that any nonmember that tried to save herself by slipping into an ivory robe and pretending to be part of their flock could be herded out easily, and tossed from the sanctuary, long before Jesus came swooping down from the sky.

The second rumor was a little bit more down-to-earth. It said that the church was really a cult, that it pulled innocent people in with its cleansing revivals and cleaned out their wallets along with their souls. I didn't believe this one at all. We had never been asked to give even a dime at the revivals. During the ceremonies they never even passed a collection plate, but some ladies donated money anyway, laying a dollar or two at the foot of the altar before they left the church.

The third rumor was the craziest of them all. According to the rumor, everybody in the church was related. They were all from the same blood. You could tell this because most of the members of the church rolled their *r*s when they spoke and always shook hands with their left hand. They had inherited these behaviors from an ancestor with a speech problem and no right arm. I didn't believe this rumor, either. To me all the rumors were just hood gossip made up by folks who needed something better to do. But still, I was hoping to find out something bad about the church, something horrible that I could take home to Mama and Grandma, something that would keep them from bringing me to the revival again.

I continued on down the hall, the smell of paint getting stronger with each step, until I reached another door exactly like the first one, cross and all. There wasn't a lock on it, because it popped right open when I turned the knob. I walked on through it like I was a renter coming to look at a new apartment.

I was in a small room with nothing but a winding flight of brown-carpeted stairs right smack dab in the middle of it. At the top of the stairs was another door like the ones that I had already come through, and I might have thought twice about going through it, as well, but my bladder suddenly started to act up again. I don't know if it was from the pressure or the excitement, but I knew that I had to find the bathroom—quick. I could dig up something bad about the church the next time that I came.

I bounded up the stairs like my clothes were on fire and I needed to get to some water to put them out. I reached for the doorknob, but before I could turn it, the door sprang open and Sister Ashada stepped out. She still had on her lace scarf, but she had removed her robe to reveal a plain, straight-cut, pumpkin-colored suit that gave a warm glow to her brown skin.

"What are you doing up here, little daughter?" she asked me. "This part of the church is for church members only."

"I had to use the restroom, ma'am," I blurted out, wondering where she could have possibly come from and how you could cut out parts of a church for only certain people.

"Way back here?" she asked. "Little daughter, you are a long way from the bathroom. Didn't you see the door in the foyer at the front of the church?"

"I saw two doors, ma'am," I answered. "I took the one that had the cross on it. It musta been the wrong one."

"Indeed it was," she said. "Where is your mother, little daughter?" she asked, with a Grandma Augustine no-nonsense look on her face.

"My mom and grandma went home. I'm supposed to catch up

with them after I go," I said. I squeezed my legs together real tight and started to wiggle around. "Oh, I gotta go real bad," I said. She rolled her eyes.

"Come with me, little daughter," she said. "We can't have you defiling the Lord's house. We'll get you to a restroom."

I followed Sister Ashada through the door into another hallway, this one barely large enough for both of us to get through. The smell of the paint was much stronger here. It smelled like someone was using enough paint to have the entire church done. I thought about asking Sister Ashada about it, but I had already been caught stealing a slice of pie out of the window. I didn't want to be caught ripping off the whole thing.

Sister Ashada led me to a small bathroom. There was only one stall in it, sitting next to a shower with a glass door. Beside the shower was a small porcelain sink with a plastic bottle of hand soap and a stack of oversized paper towels on it.

"Go quickly, little daughter," she said. "Then you take yourself right back out of here the same way that you came in. I'm sure that your mother is looking for you." I nodded—and she left.

I did my business quickly, just as I was told, washed my hands, and left the bathroom. But the minute I stepped away from the bathroom, my little demon started to tug on my arm. My curiosity kicked up something fierce again. I couldn't help but give in to it, because now I had three really good things to search for. I could search for something bad about the church, find out how Sister Ashada could have been standing behind the door when I went to open it, and try to find out where the paint was coming from. I was in one of Kambia's Linda James mystery novels for sure this time, on the trail of God only knew what, but willing to risk getting into serious trouble for it.

I stood in the middle of the hall for a moment and checked it out. There were six other doors in the narrow hallway, six places that I could poke my nose into. For a second I tensed up. I knew that Sister Ashada had to have gone through one of the doors. If I ran into her first, she would be madder than a baby with a wet diaper, and probably forget her religion altogether and give me what Grandma Augustine called a good, old-fashioned blessing out. But I guess I didn't care too much. I started down the hall, gently tugging on the handles of the other doors.

The first four that I tried to peep into were locked, and when I bent down and looked through the crack underneath, all I saw was darkness, so I moved on to the last two.

Not hesitating at all, I tugged open the fifth door, thinking that I was going to find some secret passageway or something. I was D for disappointed. The only thing in the room was a small altar, made out of a gold-plated cross that was stuck in the middle of a table that had a red blanket thrown over it. Leading up to the altar was another red blanket. This one was worn, like somebody had kneeled on it to pray a lot. I had heard that Sister Ashada and Brother Maurice, the other leader of the church, had to pray in private six times a day. I figured that this must be the place where they were doing it. I closed the door quietly and continued on to the last one.

The smell of paint slapped me in the face the minute I made it to the last door. The fresh fumes seeping from underneath it were sickening, and for a moment I got dizzy, but then my head cleared up. In fact, it was so clear that for a second it occurred to me that what I was doing was really wrong. I was creeping around the church like the ghost of Mrs. Alvania, hanging out in a place that I didn't belong, because I couldn't deal with the place where I should actually be—home. I had no business being in the congregation's personal space without asking their permission. I certainly didn't like it when Mr. Anderson Fox did it to me. But I had come too far just to run back down the stairs and go home. Linda James wouldn't give up on a mystery just because somebody might get mad at her. I walked over to the door and gently pulled it open.

The first thing that my eyes fell on was paint tarpaulins. They were spread out all over the floor, but you could still see a hint of the blue linoleum showing through. There were all kinds of paint splotches on the tarpaulins, big ones and small ones, all in shades of green, yellow, red, blue, and orange. The floor looked like one big abstract painting, like the ones down at the Fifth Ward Cultural Center.

I tiptoed into the room like a robber. Besides the tarpaulins, there wasn't much else to see but another door with the same cross on it sitting next to a heating vent. The room was pretty much like the sanctuary. It was shaped in a circle, but with no stained-glass windows or pictures on the wall. But the paint on the tarpaulins had to be coming from somewhere. And if it wasn't on the walls, there was only one other place that it could be. I placed my hands on my hips and looked up. That's where it was, all right.

There was a mural on the ceiling just like the one in the sanctuary, the *Road to Heaven* one. It was about as long and just about as wide. It had the same golden arches, the same golden road, and even the same fruit trees. It was an exact duplicate of the one in the sanctuary, with one exception. There was a traveler coming up this winding golden road, a young woman, with catlike eyes, full lips and bosom, and a thin waist. She strolled, eyes forward, her head covered by a simple white head covering.

I caught my breath. It was Tia! She was the girl in the mural.

Tia was the Christian girl with the calm face on her way to heaven.

I stared at the painting. My eyes had to be playing tricks on me. How could a painting of my sister get on the ceiling of the tabernacle? Who could have done it? And when? To make certain that I wasn't just spacing out, I walked directly underneath the painting and stared up at the girl until I thought my eyes would fall out of my head. It was Tia, all right. There was no doubt about it. I knew my own sister. I had slept next to her for twelve years.

I left the painting and walked over to the other door in the room. Behind it I heard voices, low mumbles that barely made it through the wood frame. I was sure that at least one of them belonged to Sister Ashada. A lump formed in my throat. I didn't want to do it, but I had to go talk to her. She had my sister on the ceiling and I wanted to know how—and why? I raised my hand to rap timidly on the door, but changed my mind. What if they just ignored it? So I did what Grandma Augustine did the day that we went over to see Frog. I yanked the door open like it belonged to me and went inside.

As soon as I stepped into the room, my eyes fell on three figures—a man and two women, one pretty tall, the other only a few inches higher than me. They all had their backs to me. They were facing another mural that was obviously just getting started. There was only a line drawing of some trees on the wall. I knew right away from the pumpkin-colored suit that the taller woman had to be Sister Ashada, and I started over to her. But that's when I picked up on the other two people in the room. What I saw made me stop and stand as still as a cobra about to strike.

Without seeing his face I knew that the man standing next to Sister Ashada, with an extra-long head and wearing a black pair of jeans with a matching black jacket, could only be Doo-witty; and if it was Doo-witty, then I couldn't be mistaken that the person standing next to him, wearing a short-short yellow miniskirt, with thin braids trailing down to middle of her back, *was* my sister, Tia.

My heart started pounding. I called out her name really softly at first, but when she turned around and faced me, I screamed it out loud.

"Tia!" I yelled, and ran over to her. And then that's all there was, just me and her hugging and kissing each other, and remembering what we both felt like. I hugged her so hard I thought that I would squeeze all of the life out of her, and I'll bet that she probably felt the same way about me. I just couldn't believe it. It was actually her, not a picture of her, or a memory. I felt as if everything had just jumped back into place in my world, like the pieces of my quilt were finally sewn together.

Tia and me held each other longer than we had ever done in the past. For several moments we stood there breathing in each other. We pulled apart and just stood there, shaking and crying.

"Tia," I said, wiping away my tears. "What are you doing here? Me, Mama, and Grandma been looking for you forever. We been walking the streets searching for you at everybody's houses. Mama even called the police. You been gone for months. Why didn't you come back home?"

Tia wiped some tears out of her eyes with the back of her hand. She looked over at Doo-witty, who was standing there with his normal blank look in his eyes.

"I wanted to, Shayla," she said, still shaking. "I really did, because of you and Grandma and all, but it just wouldn't have been the right thing to do."

"What are you talking about?" I asked, confused. "We all missed you so much. You shoulda been home with us. Mama has been suffering a whole world of hurt. Nothing at all has been right."

"I know," she said, glancing at Doo-witty again. "I know. I been hearing from Doo-witty about Mama, and y'all. I know that it ain't been good at the house since I left. Believe me, Shayla, I know it all. But like I said, I just couldn't come back. It wouldn't have been right. Nothing would have been right."

"Why not? I don't understand what you're talking about Tia," I said. "I don't get it at all." Tia reached out and caught my hands in her hands, covering them with her tear-soaked flesh.

"Shayla," she said. "Do you remember when we had the conversation in the bathroom about me and Doo-witty?"

I nodded.

"Do you remember that I said that he keeps everything from turning off in me, that he keeps me from shutting down?"

"I remember," I said, recalling the deep talk.

"Do you recall that I said that I didn't know why that was or why anything was, for that matter? I told you that I couldn't figure it all out."

"Yes, I remember," I said. "But I still don't understand why you couldn't figure it all out at home. I don't know why you had to be somewhere else, other than with us, to try and get things right."

"Shayla," she said. "You know how Grandma Augustine always says that you have to first make sure that the tail of your own slip isn't showing before you can tell another woman that she needs to pull her slip down? Well, that's what I been doing," she said. "I been trying to make sure that my slip was in the right place."

"I don't get it, Tia," I said. "You ain't making no sense. What are you talking about?"

"Things crowd me, Shayla," she said. "They crowd my head.

Everything seems to push so deep inside of it, so deep there's no room for me, for Tia. Shayla, there's no room for me."

"I . . . I still don't . . ."

"If there's no room for Tia, then there ain't no room for you or Grandma or Mama, especially Mama. Shayla, Mama gave me a choice. She said that I could either be a woman, or a girl in her house, but that I couldn't be both. She crowded my head with so much woman stuff that I had to sort it out. I couldn't be an in-between. I needed to know which side to stand on. If I had come back home, all me and Mama woulda done was fight some more. It wouldn't have be right for her—or me."

"Is that the only reason why you didn't come home?" I asked. "Tia, Mama's been long sorry about what she said. She even been crying and everything. She probably woulda just got over it if you had come back home. Why didn't you call or something? Why didn't you send a note? Your not coming home was what wasn't right!" I yelled. "You tore everything apart! Everything turned into a big mess because of you! You're just plain ole selfish! You messed everything up all because of stupid ole Doo-witty!" I said, glaring at Doo-witty.

"Doo-witty's not stupid," she said, real calm-like. In her slanted eyes you could see just a hint of red, but they weren't nearly as red as mine. I could feel Mr. Anger pacing back and forth in them in his red anger suit.

"He is stupid!" I yelled. "And so are you! You picked him over us! That makes you just as dumb as he is!"

Tia tried to let go of my hands, but I held them tight, gripping them with all my strength. For the first time since everything went down, I was really, really angry—at her, at Mama, at Doo-witty, at everything and everybody. It wasn't fair what Tia had done. It wasn't fair what any of them had done. I tore out all of the pain pages that I kept in the journal in my head and threw them at her feet.

"I really hate you, Tia," I screamed. "You're selfish and mean! You and Mama are just alike, all you ever do is find a way to mess up other people's lives!"

"That's not true, Shayla!" she yelled back. "I wasn't trying to mess up things for anybody! I was just trying to get things together!"

"You and stupid ole Doo-witty," I said.

"He's not stupid!" she screamed.

"That's right, I'm . . . I'm not," Doo-witty chimed in.

"You are, you are. You are stupid, stupid, stupid!" I yelled, sounding a lot like Kambia.

"He's not! He's not," Tia yelled back. She wrenched her hands out of my mine and flew over toward the wall, where Sister Ashada was standing, staring at us patiently, like a nursery school teacher listening to her students squabbling over a toy. I shot her a mean glance.

Tia reached the wall and started to slap the line drawing on it with her hands. "He did this!" she yelled. "He did all of it, Shayla. This one, the one outside, the one in the sanctuary. Doo-witty painted all of it!" She pushed past me and ran out of the door into the next room. I followed her out. "Look!" she said, pointing up at the painting on the ceiling. "It's me. It's me. Doo-witty did it. He put me on the ceiling. He's not stupid, Shayla!" she yelled. "He's not!"

"That's right," Doo-witty said, coming up behind me. "It's my work. I did it all. I do know how to do something good."

"What?" I said, quickly going from anger to confusion. Tia walked over to me.

"Shayla," she said, beaming, still pointing up at the ceiling. "I don't know how to explain it, but Doo-witty can do this. Nobody taught him how. He just can. He can take images in his head, mix them together, and come out with works of art, just like you do with your words. He can paint anything, Shayla. You just have to tell him what you want, and the next thing that you know he's doing it. It's kind of a miracle, Shayla, like God found a way to make up for the parts of him that he didn't work on long enough."

I turned around and looked at Doo-witty. I still saw nothing in his eyes. I still didn't know who or what he was. My world had been righted, but turned upside down again. I didn't know how to make sense out of it. Sister Ashada walked over to us.

"This is my baby sister, Shayla," Tia said to her.

"I know," she said. "I knew it when I saw her in the hall. God does work in strange but glorious ways. You remember that, Daughter Tia," she said. She patted Tia on the cheek lovingly. "You have much to tell your sister," she said. "You two have many vines to unravel."

Tia nodded.

"Dwight," Sister Ashada said to Doo-witty. "Come pray with me. Prayer is better when it's shared."

"Yes . . . yes, ma'am," Doo-witty said. He started to follow her out, but instead stopped and looked at me. "When I was little, they put me in a dumb class," he said in a clear, nonstuttering voice that made me wonder if the words were actually his or if there was some tiny, normal-talking guy hiding in his jacket pocket, yelling out the things that he wanted to say. "I couldn't read and write so good, so they put me in a special class for really slow kids. They said that it was a class for kids that couldn't do the basics no matter how hard their teacher worked with them. They just couldn't keep up. Do you know what I mean?" he asked.

I nodded. I used to tutor some of the kids in my English class who couldn't stay on top of their lessons. Some of them were simply hard at catching on to stuff, they just had to try a little more, but others didn't seem to understand anything, no matter how many times you explained it to them. They were always either way behind or completely lost, like Doo-witty.

"I didn't like it too much," he continued, his face actually starting to turn sad, his facial muscles sliding and moving as if he had just realized that he had some control over his own expressions. "I didn't care for it at all. It made me feel like I was a big rock or something, just a big ole rock that folks could simply throw away or bury, so they didn't have to see it no more."

"You're not a rock, Doo-witty," Tia whispered softly. "And I'll never throw you away." She smiled at him, then stuck her arm through his. Doo-witty's face pulled itself into a smile also, but the smile looked very odd on him, not fake like Mr. Anderson Fox's grin, just strange, like it didn't really belong on his face at all, though I don't know anywhere else on his body you could have put it.

"Anyway, like I said," he continued, patting Tia's arm, "I didn't like it too much, and my mama, she didn't like it either. Sh-sh-she'd come up every . . . every day and fuss at my teacher," he said, beginning to tumble over his words randomly, as he usually did. "Every day she would come up and tell my teacher off. 'Doo-witty ain't no idiot,' sh-sh-she would say. 'He ain't no genius, but he ain't n-n-no fool, either. Just like most kids, he laughs and he cries, but most importantly he tries.' She would say that last part over and over to my teacher. 'He laughs and h-h-he cries, but most importantly he tries.' It made me feel good inside when she said it. I felt like I-I was n-n-no different from the kids in the regular classes. Do you know what I mean?"

"She knows," Tia answered for me.

"Anyhow," he went on, "to go back to wh-wh-why I didn't like the . . . the class too much. It was because there wasn't nothing to do all day but stuff with your hands, just painting, drawing, and that type of thing. I guess they thought 'cause we couldn't r-r-read and write too well that we didn't need to even do it at . . . at all. So all they had was simple things t-t-to do with your hands."

I looked confused again. He started to shake his head.

"Naw, naw, d-d-don't get me wrong," he said quickly. "I learned to like all that, but at the time I wanted to . . . to know things like the other kids. Do you know what I mean?" he asked a third time. This time I answered aloud, for myself.

"Yes, I do," I said. "I know exactly what you mean." I pretty much had to. Like Doo-witty, I always felt just a little crappy when I ran up against another kid that was way smarter than me, one of those kids who always knew all the answers and let you know that they knew them.

"Anyhow, I got good at it," Doo-witty said. "The painting, I got real . . . real good at it. I'd paint anything, stuff in my head, stuff outside the window, whatever I saw, but . . . but mostly I painted Mama. I-I just had to paint her."

"Why?" I asked. I didn't know why anybody, even Doo-witty, would want to paint mean ole Frog.

"Mama got sick," he said in a pained voice. Serious sadness started to tug his jaw back down. "Mama g-g-got real sick with some female problems. They came up on her all of a sudden. One day she was just fine, plain ole Mama. But the n-n-next day she was full of fever and hurting so bad that she barely even knowed who I was. She d-d-didn't know her own Doo-witty."

"I'm sorry, Doo-witty," Tia said, grasping his hand.

"So am I," I mumbled, wondering if Frog had actually had the problem that Mama had lied and said that Tia had.

"So that's it," he went on. "I had to p-p-paint Mama, because she got too sick to come to school. She had t-t-to have an operation. I painted her just the way she looked standing at my teacher's desk, the . . . the way she looked with one finger pointing at . . . at the teacher and another one on her hips. I-I made her mouth just like it was too, when she said those words about me trying. She looked real n-n-nice saying those words," he said.

"Oh," I said, "I'll bet she did."

"She r-r-really did," he whispered. "I was g-g-glad that I had some paintings of her after sh-sh-she couldn't come up to school no more." He pulled away from Tia and pointed up at the ceiling. We all looked up. "Th-th-that's what I did with Tia," he said. "I put her on the ceiling so that I would have her when she stopped coming around. I made it so sh-she'd still be with me after she left. Only she didn't leave. So . . . so now I got her *and* a painting. Tia loves me and I love her," he said. "I wouldn't never want no harm to come to her. I-I-I'm sorry that I lied, but that was what Tia wanted. I-I-I'll do anything that Tia wants me to. I'm n-n-not a bad person. I just don't talk or look so good, and I-I don't know t-t-too much book stuff. But my mama say that none of that makes me stupid. It just mean that I ain't like most folks."

He started to tear up, and for the first time I saw something other than blankness in his eyes. "I wish . . . wish to . . . to God," he stuttered, his words getting a little more tumbled by emotion, "I-I wish . . . wish to . . . to God that I woulda been born like Tia, but I wasn't. I-I just don't . . . don't know why p-p-people think that they have to . . . to hurt . . . hurt me because of it. I don't do nothing to nobody. Wh-wh-why do . . . do everybody always have to do stuff to me." I opened my mouth to say something, but before I could, he pulled Tia to him and hugged her. "I-I-I'll see you later," he said, then he left the room.

I looked at Tia. I didn't know what to say.

"I didn't have nowhere else to go," Tia said. "I ended up here 'cause there was nowhere else."

"Frog wouldn't let you stay with her, would she?" I asked.

"No," she said. "She wouldn't. After I left the Tomb, me and Doo-witty went 'round to his house, but his mom said that she didn't want me there. She said that I was just causing problems in Doo-witty's life. She said that I was just playing him for a fool, having fun with him. So we left," she said, shrugging her shoulders. "Then I went over to Maxi's, but her mom wouldn't let me hang out there, either. She said that I needed to get things straight with Mama. She told me not to be tracking no trash into her house. Maxi's mom is real strict about stuff," she said.

"I know. Maxi told me," I said. "Her mom doesn't play, does she?"

"Nah," she said. "It's okay though. I understand. Anyway, that's how I ended up here," she said. "Doo-witty brought me here. He had been painting for the church for a while. He knew that they had some rooms that you could crash in when you were having problems. He said that Sister Ashada was real good at helping you get things right in your head. It's true," she said, beaming brighter. "She's been like a second mom to me. She was really there when I needed her."

"Oh, that's really nice," I snapped, feeling a bit hurt. "So I guess me, Mama, and Grandma wouldn't have known how to help. We were never there for you."

"That's not what I meant," Tia said quickly, a hurt look spreading across her face to match my own. "That's not what I meant at all. I just meant that she and the church were real good at helping me out."

"You mean hiding you out?" I said. "They had no right. Tia, you had no right to let them."

"You don't understand, Shayla," she pleaded. "You don't understand. With them I never shut down. You just don't get it."

"Well, help me to get it!" I cried, a lot more loudly than I had intended. I could feel Mr. Anger starting to pace back and forth in my eyes again. "I don't understand this. I don't understand any of it. What are you really doing here? And what's all this about Doo-witty painting?"

"I can explain things," she said. "I can explain all of it."

"Well, do it then!" I shouted. "Do it right now!"

"I will!" she yelled back.

"Good!" I yelled even louder, and rolled my eyes at her.

"Look," she began. "The church took me in to help me get my stuff together. They said that my coming into the church would help me clear all of the junk out of my head, and also help Doo-witty get the stuff in his head down on canvas. Shayla, Doo-witty's an artist," she said, starting to beam again. "He's a real live artist. He can barely read and write, but he can take paintbrushes and paint and make a whole world of his own."

"Tia, get to the point," I said angrily.

"Shayla, this is the point," she said. "Look, Doo-witty found out a couple of years ago that he had some real talent. He was working for some dude downtown painting furniture when he just up and got the idea one day to start adding touches of his own. He would paint flowers, animals, landscapes, even people that he knew, just like he did with his mother. He would paint all kinds of things, anything that he had a mind to create."

"He musta been good," I said, feeling myself start to calm down a bit.

"He was, Shayla. In fact, he was so good that pretty soon he didn't even need the furniture anymore. He just painted on whatever he saw—fabric, paper, the wall, it didn't matter, because everything that Doo-witty painted, people bought. Folks would come from all over downtown. They would snatch his work up as soon as he finished it, and come back for more. They just couldn't get enough."

"Wow," I said, genuinely amazed.

"Yeah, wow," she echoed. "Anyway, one day Sister Ashada and some of her congregation passed by where he worked and saw his art. They had been looking for someone to paint murals in the church for a while, so they hired him on the spot. Just like that Doo-witty became a real commissioned artist. Can you believe it?" she squealed.

"I . . . I guess," I said.

"Shayla, the abstract paintings in the Fifth Ward Cultural Center, they're Doo-witty's," she said. "The church just told everybody that they were from some big-time artist because he asked them to."

"Why would he do that?" I asked.

"I don't know. He just wanted to keep it a secret," she said. "He hasn't even told his mom yet. He wants to surprise her when he finishes the murals. He wants to wait until he has something big to show her. Man, is she gonna strut around like a church deacon with a new suit when she finds out, especially when she hears about the contest and all."

"What contest?"

"I found an art contest for new artists in the back of one of those art magazines that they have down at the center. We sent in some of his work—and guess what? He won," she said.

"What did he get?" I asked, excited.

"Paints, brushes, chalks, pastels, everything that he needed to keep him working. But you know what?" she asked.

I shook my head.

"He didn't keep any of it. He donated all of it to an afternoon art program at a junior high school that couldn't afford supplies for their kids, hoping that maybe one of the boys and girls would have a better chance at becoming an artist too."

"Oh, really . . . man," I said, a bit thrown. How wonderful and *strange* it was, Doo-witty giving away the very thing that could prove he was something special in the world. I glanced up at the ceiling again. How was Tia able to see what me, Mama, and Grandma couldn't see?

"I'm sorry, I didn't know," I said. "I didn't know that Doo-witty could do all of this."

"Neither did I. I didn't know until I saw the painting in the sanctuary," she said. "That's when Doo-witty told me everything. It's good, isn't it?"

"Yes, it's real good," I said. "Very good."

I sighed and tried to make sense of the whole thing. Who would believe it? Doo-witty, an artist. I felt real bad about the way that I had been treating Doo-witty. I was wrong about him. He wasn't nearly as slow as I'd thought. I thought I knew what smart was. I thought it had to do with books and reading and talking good, and all the things that the schools tell us make somebody a so-called normal or bright person. Without meaning to, I had placed Doo-witty in a bottle and turned the cap on it, the way people sometimes did with me. I thought that Tia couldn't love him just because he didn't seem like the rest of us, but she saw a smooth, polished stone where we saw a rock. We treated him like he didn't even deserve to breathe the same air that we breathe. I was glad that Tia didn't.

I once read a story called "Cinder's Fellow." It was a Cinderella story, only not like the usual one. In "Cinder's Fellow" Cinderella's prince wasn't at all princely. When she met him at the ball, he was all stuck on his good looks and how much money he had. The whole time that they were together, he kept asking her if he was the most handsome guy that she had ever seen, and telling her how many grand rooms he had in his palace. Cinderella finally got so fed up that she just up and went home, way before midnight, without her golden carriage or anything. She was sick of rich, fancy junk, so she just left her carriage right where it was, before it even got a chance to change back into a pumpkin, and started for home. But on the way home it started to rain real hard, and a cool wind was blowing something fierce. Not knowing what else to do, she ducked into a stable. In the stable she met a guy. He wasn't a hunk or even smart, and he had a slight limp, like Grandma Augustine's. To tell the truth, there wasn't all that much to him, but he *was* young, about her age, with kind eyes and a sweet smile. Anyway, he saw how cold and wet she was, and he gave her his old, moth-eaten coat to put on. Then he made a nice bed of hay for her to sit on while she got warmed up. Cinderella fell in love with that guy, right then and there, in the middle of a smelly stable, on a cold, rainy night. He was everything that she wanted in a prince—somebody that made her feel like a princess. Maybe that's what Doowitty was to Tia. He was her stable guy, the one person in the world that made her feel like royalty. That's why she could love him. That's why in her eyes he could never have been a dummy.

"I'm sorry, Tia," I said again. "I'm sorry that I treated Doo-witty like he was stupid."

"It's okay," she said, pulling me to her for a hug. "It's okay. You couldn't have known." She kissed me on the forehead, like Grandma sometimes did when she was about to tell me something that I didn't want to hear. I tensed up.

"You're not coming home yet, are you?" I asked. She shook her head.

"I can't," she said. "I still need to sort some things out. The point is I still need to pull it all together. I need to figure things out for me, Mama, and *Doo-witty*." She kissed me again. "Shayla, I can't be with you until I can figure out how to be with myself. Just do me a favor," she said. "Don't tell Mama and Grandma that you saw me."

"Tia, they're really worried about you," I said, pulling away from her. "I don't think it's fair."

"It's not, but I still need you to do it," she said, caressing my cheek. "I need you to let me be the one to put what happened between me and Mama back right. It's my responsibility, not yours. I promise I'll come back as soon as I can. But right now, I just need a little more time," she said. "I know that Mama is going through a world of hurt, but trust me, if I come home right now, it ain't gonna make things better. We just gonna start back fighting, and there won't be no peace in the house for anybody."

"Okay," I said, finally seeing a little of her point. "I'll give you some time, if you promise to come home soon."

"I'll try, I'll really try, Shayla," she said.

"I know you will. I trust you to do the right thing," I said, heading for the door.

"Don't worry," she said, waving good-bye. "I'll come home as soon as it feels right."

"Tell Doo-witty I'm really sorry," I said, and left the church.

My footprints left a trail of happiness as I walked back to the house. I didn't like lying to Mama, but Tia was alive and well, and that's all that mattered. So I just piled the promise that I had made to her up with the ones that I had made to Kambia, the ones that I didn't really like keeping but had no choice but to keep. As I skipped down the cracked sidewalk I realized that Grandma Augustine had been right about two things. I had been revived by the revival. It had cleansed a part of me that I didn't even know was dirty, the part of me that kept me from seeing beyond the surface, the part that kept me from seeing people and things for what they really were. And Grandma was also right about the world itself. There were so many good things in it to write about. When I got home I would flood the pages of my journal with new, happier entries. I would create my own kind of painting from the joy in my heart.

Chapter 9

Once, when I was about seven, Mama took me and Tia to a Christmas party down at Parsons Park. The party was held in the rec room where me and Kambia got into it with Miss Marshall over my story. It was a party just for kids like me and Tia, kids whose parents didn't have enough money to buy them nice Christmas presents or fix them a big holiday meal.

During the party all of us kids received a gift, a really nice toy donated by a Christian church group on one of the better sides of town. My toy was a gray wind-up dolphin that paddled its plastic fins and swam when you placed it in water. I loved the dolphin, not because it cost more than any of the cheap dime-store toys that Mama usually gave me and Tia for Christmas and birthdays, but because I thought that someone very kind must have gone to the store and picked it out just for me. I placed the dolphin in the bathtub with me each night.

But my fun with the dolphin didn't last very long. A couple of weeks after I got it, the tiny fins on it stopped moving, and whenever I placed it in the tub, it fell over on its side like a dead goldfish.

I cried over the dolphin for two days, bawling my head off whenever I spotted it lying broken and useless in a corner of my room. At first Mama was really nice to me about the crying, but after a while it started to get on her nerves. While I was at school one day, she tossed it in the trash along with some other junk. When I came home from school, I began to cry some more, but she quickly found a way to put a stop to it. She told me to close my eyes and try to remember the good times that I had with the dolphin before it turned into just another piece of garbage. "Don't worry about the bad things," she said. "Just dwell on the good." That's what I did today when what was supposed to be a good day suddenly turned into something really awful. I closed my eyes and I tried to remember the daylight before the darkness.

The daylight in my life is, of course, the time that I spent with Tia. Almost everything has been great since the day that I found her. I go to see her each afternoon after school lets out. We have a long talk and eat cookies from my school's cafeteria. We are closer now than we ever were before, and I'm even learning to like Doowitty. He is good to Tia. He brings her a flower each afternoon from the florist shop on Cage. He brings her a mum, sometimes pink, sometimes red, but always with a yellow ribbon tied around the stem. When Tia sees the mum, she squeals like a contestant in a game show, then they both burst into giggles and follow the giggles with sloppy kisses. The whole thing makes me kinda queasy when I see it, but as long as it makes Tia feel good, it makes me feel good too. It also does something else for me. It helps me forget about what's going on at home.

Since the day of the revival Mama has been in a get-outta-my-face mood. She's been snapping at us over even the littlest of things. Yesterday she went off on Grandma over a pair of sewing scissors. She said that Grandma took her best pair without asking her and didn't even bother to return them. But Grandma Augustine said that she didn't have them, and when she showed Mama the scissors lying underneath an old bundle of quilting squares in the bottom of Mama's sewing chest, Mama got even madder. She yelled at Grandma for old and new for nearly an hour, until Grandma finally got tired of it and went home.

Grandma says that Mama has "I-shoulda-known-better-itis."

She says that Mama caught it the day of the revival, when she realized that she had made another mistake with Mr. Anderson Fox.

Mr. Anderson Fox is stepping out again. He's been going out all night and coming back in just before the street lamp goes out in front of our house. Mama has stayed up all this week, pacing the floor like she did when I was kid, wearing a hole in our already-worn linoleum. Grandma says that Mama knows she should have let Mr. Anderson Fox get right back on the Greyhound that he came in on, but she just can't do it. She says that Mama is too blinded by maybes. Maybe Mr. Anderson Fox will want to stay in Houston, maybe Mr. Anderson Fox will want to make her his wife, maybe Mr. Anderson Fox will want to find himself a job and help pay the phone bill.

Right now the phone is the biggest issue where Mr. Anderson Fox is concerned. Using the phone is all that he does when he's at home. But now his phone calls are no longer to homeboys. They are just to homegirls, women that he recently met down at the pool hall, instead of the sisters that he used to rap with from back home.

Grandma Augustine says that what Mr. Anderson Fox is doing is a shame before the Lord. "He hanging his hat at one house and trying to leave his shoes at another," she says to Mama. "If I was you, I would take the phone clean out of my house. Let him call his friends from the gas station. Let him have to buy a roll of quarters to reach out and touch his women." But Mama doesn't seem to agree with Grandma Augustine. She says that Grandma is overreacting. She still just says that it's not unusual for a man as good-looking and fascinating as Mr. Anderson Fox is to have a lot of male *and* female friends. "A charming man is like a hot pizza," she says. "The minute he comes in the door, everybody wants a piece of him." She's not surprised that so many people want to add Mr. Anderson Fox's number to their address books.

But the stuff with Mama and Mr. Anderson Fox isn't what caused me to see weeds where I usually see tulips. It was the thing that happened after I went to pick up Kambia. That's when I had to try real hard to recall the fun times that I had had with Tia just a day earlier.

I left to go pick up Kambia at the regular time, 8:15, an hour before we were due at school. We liked to make sure that we had plenty of time to get there, since we had such a long walk.

I was really looking forward to seeing Kambia. When she called me last night to tell me that she was coming to school today, I nearly flipped. She had been sick since the day we buried her underwear. She hadn't been to school at all and hadn't been outside even once to play. I really missed her. There was so much that I wanted to tell her about the things that were going on in my house. She was a good listener. She could listen to you for hours on end and never say a word, but after you were finished, she would spit it all back out at you like a human tape recorder. She could make comments about parts you didn't even remember saying.

When I got to Kambia's house, I opened her gate and waited in front of it like I always did. I knew better than to tap on her screen door. The last time I did, one of Kambia's mom's so-called boyfriends—a shirtless, mean-looking guy with a big gap in his front teeth—came to the door and yelled something ugly at me. Since then I've been keeping my distance from it.

I waited for Kambia until my feet went to sleep from standing in one place for so long, and I had to pick them up one at a time and wiggle them awake. It wasn't like Kambia to be late. She was always on time. I had never known her to be even a minute late when she told me to meet her somewhere. Confused, I started up the steps, determined that I would at least try to peep in the keyhole of the door and find out what the heck was taking her so long. As I started up the walkway she came stepping out of the house, and I totally freaked out.

Kambia looked horrible, like she hadn't got over whatever made her take to bed in the first place. I don't know how it was possible, but she was even skinnier. She was knitting-needle thin. She looked like she hadn't eaten since Martin Luther King marched on Washington. Her hair had gone from dull to plain ole gross. It was tied back in two matted ponytails that looked like they hadn't been washed in weeks. I had seen her pale before, but this time she was vampire white. With her ghostly skin and lifeless green eyes she coulda won first prize in anybody's Halloween costume contest. I took her arm. It was ice cold, like it was the day that she hid out from her mother in my room.

"Kambia, what happened to you?" I asked. "You look terrible. Are you still sick?"

She shook her head weakly, like it was too heavy for her narrow shoulders. "I'm fine, Shayla," she said in a really faint voice. "I'm sorry that I'm late. My mom had something that she wanted me to do."

"What?" I asked. She just hunched her shoulders.

She walked real slowly over to the steps, holding herself underneath her stomach with a real pained look on her face, like she was seriously hurting.

"Kambia, what's wrong?" I asked, scrunching my forehead into worry wrinkles. "Does your stomach hurt? Maybe you should stay home. I don't think that you're well enough to go to school."

"I'm fine, Shayla," she said softly. "We better go to school.

We're gonna be late. I can't miss any more time outta school. Our homeroom teacher says that if I do, they gonna leave me back." Her face changed from pained to sad. "I don't want to be left back, Shayla," she said. "I wanna be with you. I don't want them to leave me back by myself. Let's just go. I'm really fine."

"No, you're not," I said, shaking my head. "Kambia, you look like somebody beat up on you." I skirted around her on the porch steps and tugged the waist of her dress. "I'll talk to our homeroom teacher," I said. "I'll tell her that you're still really sick. She won't think that you're goofing around. I'll ask her if I can pick up your homework from the rest of your teachers. Come on, let's go back in the house."

"No!" she yelled, snatching my hand away from her dress so hard that I nearly fell backward. "No, Shayla, I'm not gonna go back in the house. Don't make me, please," she begged. "I just wanna go to school. Walk with me to school, Shayla," she began to whine. "Just walk with me."

I sighed and looked into her eyes, the way I always did. It was the only part of her that I could really understand. It was the only part of most people that I could understand. Grandma Augustine always says that if you can read a person's eyes, you can read their very existence, what they were before, what they want to be, what they'll end up being. In Kambia's eyes I saw the same spacey, desperate fear that I always saw when something was really upsetting her. It was the same fear that I had given in to that first day, when I stuck my hand down the gutter for her, and the same fear I had given in to every day after that. It was stronger than anything that I had seen before.

"Okay, Kambia," I said. "But if you get sicker on the way, we're coming back."

She clamped her cold hands down on mine. "You're my best friend, Shayla," she said. "Did I ever tell you that?"

I shook my head. "You didn't have to," I said. "I already knew." I skirted back around her and helped her down the steps.

We started down the street, with Kambia barely walking, still holding herself beneath her stomach, and me wishing that I had been brave enough to go and speak to her mother in the hopes that her mother would have convinced her to come back in the house. I couldn't believe that her mother would let Kambia leave the house looking so bad. I couldn't believe that she didn't know how sick Kambia was.

Who was her mother? I knew what she did, but I didn't know anything else about her. Did she know about Kambia's wolves and the way that Kambia spaced out sometimes? My own mother and I weren't always mixing the same batter, but I could always count on her. Like most moms, she would take off work when me or Tia got sick and sit at our bedside until we were better, making us homemade soup and stuff like that. No matter how many times Grandma would tell her that she could go back to work, she wouldn't do it. She would just tell Grandma that me and Tia belonged to her, and that it was her responsibility to take care of us when we were sick, not anybody else's. I couldn't imagine anybody's mother not feeling the same way, not even Kambia's.

After we had walked down the street awhile with Kambia's pace getting a little slower and her steps getting really shaky, I realized that I had made a mistake, but as usual I didn't know how to correct it. I looked around for an adult that could help me out, maybe do Kambia's mom's job and convince Kambia to go back home, but as I scanned the streets I found that I was out of luck. Most of the people had already come home from work and gone to bed. The only adults still out weren't really adults at all. They were what Grandma called the "will-never-be-nothing's"—the bald-headed teenage dope pushers that had recently started hanging out on the few corners that the big-time dealers no longer wanted to work. With Mr.-Anderson-Fox-like grins and a slick rap, they conned the younger kids outta their lunch money, selling them a joint instead of a hot meal. The only service that they could offer me I didn't want.

So I just kept following Kambia and praying that some miracle would happen that would make her turn back. If we made it to school, the only thing the nurse could do for her was send her home. She couldn't even give her an aspirin for the pain. Handing out any type of drugs was strictly forbidden at my school. When we went by Perry's 24-and-7 lounge, I longed for the sound of a rap tune blaring from its jukebox, but the club was as silent as a head nod, having been shut down by the cops nearly two weeks before for selling drinks to a couple of girls just a year or so older than me.

After we passed Perry's, we somehow managed to make it past the neatly cut green lawns of the Fifth Ward Cultural Center, and the concrete tombstones of Peaceful Rest Cemetery. I didn't know how Kambia was doing it, but she was managing to do exactly what she said she wanted to do, make it to school. Like so many times before, I started to be fooled by her. I started to believe that maybe she wasn't as sick as she looked. I was horribly wrong.

Just as we were passing the broken swing sets at Parsons Park she stopped, then she screamed real loud and clutched underneath her stomach so hard that I thought she was gonna break a bone. I ran around to her. Her face was all twisted up with pain, and for just a second her eyes rolled way back in her head and all you could see was the whites. Then they came back to normal and big beads of sweat started to form on her face.

"Kambia!" I screamed. "What's wrong?"

She opened her mouth to say something, but another wave of pain hit her. Then she hollered again like she had got her foot run over by a lawn mower, and fell to her knees.

"Oh, my God! You're really sick! You have to go home! You need a doctor or something!"

"No," she said through really heavy breaths, like her breath was having a hard time coming in and out of her mouth. "No, Shayla, please," she begged, struggling to get up. "Don't make me. Just walk with me to school. Everything will be fine when we get there, you'll see."

"No, it won't! Kambia, something is bad wrong with you," I cried, trying to help her to her feet. "I don't know what, but something is really wrong. You can't go to school like this. You have to get some help."

"No, I don't," she said, trying to steady her body. "I told you, Shayla, I'm fine. I just need to go to school," she begged again. She took a couple of shaky steps forward, but screamed and fell to her knees on the hard pavement again with a loud *smack*. I tried to get her up again, but her body was like a solid block of concrete when I tugged on it. She had lost the ability to help me pull her up.

"Oh, God! Oh, God!" I said.

She groaned loudly, then her eyes rolled back in her head for a second time and returned back to normal.

"I gotta go get somebody!" I yelled. "I gotta go get your mom!"

"No! No! No, Shayla," she said. Huge trickles of sweat started to drip down her face and onto her dirty dress collar. "Don't, Shayla, please!" she said, grabbing hold of the tail of my dress. "Please, please don't! Why can't we just go?" she whispered between gasps of air. "Why can't we just go?"

"Kambia, you're really sick," I said, mopping the sweat off her face with the palm of my hand. "You can't go anywhere. We have to get your mom. Why are you holding your stomach?" I asked. "Is there something hurting you in there?"

She shook her head weakly. "No," she whispered. "I told you. I'm just fine." Her eyes focused on my green cotton dress for a minute. "Do you know where cotton comes from, Shayla?" she asked, yanking my dress tail. "Do you know how they make it? I do," she said. "I can tell you where it comes from. Far away, near the South Pole—"

"Stop it, Kambia! Stop it! I don't want to hear a stupid story!"

She broke into sobs, real gut-wrenching wails, not the hunger cries that babies make.

"I just wanna go to school," she wailed. "I wanna go to home-room." She tugged on my dress as hard as she could, momentarily causing me to lose my balance as well, then she pulled herself to her feet and tried to take a couple more steps, but the minute she did, another bullet of pain shot through her. She screamed and doubled over.

"I'm gonna get your mom!" I said, starting to take off, but she grabbed my arm.

"Please don't, Shayla! Oh, God, please! Please! Don't!"

"Kambia, what's wrong with you? Just tell me what's wrong."

"I can't!" she wailed. "I can't, Shayla! You don't understand! The wolves will get me! They told me not to tell! They'll hurt me really, really bad! I can't, Shayla, please. I just wanna go to school!"

"I'll keep the wolves away, Kambia," I said. "I promise I will. I'll tell your mom, too, and she'll make them stop." The tears started to well up in the corners of my eyes. "You have to go home, Kambia," I said. "You just have to." I pried her hand off my arm and stepped backward, but she reached for me again.

That's when I noticed it. Blood! It was running all down her bony legs. Thick streams of it were pouring over the sides of her worn-out Nikes onto the black pavement.

"Oh, God! Kambia, you're bleeding! There's blood all over you! I gotta go get your mom! I gotta tell her that you're bleeding real bad!"

"No!" she said, shaking her head real fast. "No! I don't want her, Shayla. I don't want her. Please don't go get her!" she begged. "She's not my mom. She's not! Don't go get her, Shayla! Don't go get her. She's not my mom. She'll bring them with her! They'll hurt me again!"

"Okay, okay, I won't," I said soothingly, reaching out and patting her arm. "But I have to get somebody. I'll get somebody that we both can trust, I promise."

"No!" she cried. "No, you promised me, Shayla! You promised me. If you do, I won't be your friend anymore! I swear I'll never be your friend again!"

"Kambia—," I said, but I didn't finish my sentence, because all of a sudden her face went completely blank. Her eyes rolled back once more, but this time they didn't return to normal. They started to blink rapidly, then they closed and she crumpled to the pavement like a puppet without strings. "Kambia! Kambia!" I yelled, shaking her. She only groaned. I backed away and ran off down the street.

It was only three blocks to the tabernacle where Tia was staying. Tia would know what to do, and Kambia would let Tia help her. Tia wasn't an adult, just close to one. Everybody liked Tia. Everybody trusted her.

Teary-eyed and out of breath, I reached the back entrance of the church in less than two minutes. I ran up the concrete walkway and began banging on a small, unpainted door that Tia usually let me into each afternoon when I came to visit. She pulled it open after the third bang. She was dressed in the same short-short yellow skirt that she had worn at least three times since I found her, but her long hair wasn't braided. She had pulled it back into a really tight ponytail that turned her slanted eyes into tiny slits. They went all wide again when she saw me.

"What are you doing here this time of the morning, girl?" she asked. "Why ain't you in school? What's wrong?"

"It's . . . It's . . . Kambia," I stuttered, between breaths, sounding a lot like Doo-witty. "Tia, something's bad wrong with her. She's in the street bleeding all over everything. You have to come quick," I said, dropping tears everywhere. "She's really sick."

"Did you tell her mama?" Tia asked. "Why didn't you go get her mom?"

"She won't let me," I said. "She doesn't like grown-ups. You have to come. She's only a few blocks down the street," I added, pointing in the direction that I had come from. "You have to come help me. I don't have anybody else."

"Shayla, I can't go out," Tia said quickly, looking around nervously. "You know that I can't. Nobody knows that I'm here. I can't go. Everybody will know where I'm at. I just can't," she said, shaking her head. "Go tell her mother."

"She won't let her help her. Please, Tia," I said, starting to sob something fierce. "Please, something is really wrong with her."

Tia ran her hand up over her forehead, finally letting it fall over her hair. Responsibility and confusion tugged at the opposite sides of her face, and you could tell that her brain was turning and churning with decision.

"All right," she said after a few seconds. She grabbed me and shook me by the shoulders. "Stop crying," she said. "You stop crying and go upstairs to my bedroom and call nine-one-one and tell them what's going on. You tell them to hurry," she said, running off down the street toward Kambia. "You tell them to get here now."

I did exactly what Tia told me to do. I ran upstairs to the room that she was staying in, dialed 9-1-1 on her phone, explained the situation to the emergency people, then ran off down the street after her, sure that things would be better now that she was there.

But things weren't better. I arrived back to the place where I left Kambia to find her lying on her back in the street with Tia bending over her. She was even whiter than she was when I left her, deathly white, and there was still blood streaming over the sides of her legs, even though Tia was trying real hard to stop it from flowing by pressing Kambia's dingy dress up against her thighs. I ran over to them and grabbed Kambia's cold hand. It was limp and loose with no grip at all.

"Kambia," I said, pulling her hand hard. "Get up! Get up!" She didn't respond, and at that moment I was sure that she never would again. There was nothing at all in her eyes, no life, no fear, no sadness, nothing. It was as though she had finally taken off for a fantasy land that she wouldn't return from.

By the time the ambulance drivers showed up ten minutes later, we were surrounded by a crowd of drowsy, curious people in ratty bathrobes who had dragged out of their beds and gathered around us. With sad, worried faces they watched as Kambia was loaded into the big white ambulance, but when one of the drivers, a huge blond guy with bulging muscles and sharp blue eyes, started to ask questions, they simply shrugged their shoulders and walked away, not willing to put anything on the line for a child that wasn't their own.

So the drivers were left to get their information out of me and

Tia. Since Tia didn't know anything, all she could do was cry and say how she had tried to help, and that left only me. But all I could tell the men was that I was the one who had called the ambulance, and that the girl who they had just loaded into their ambulance was named Kambia, and she was my best friend. I could tell by their faces that there was a whole lot more that they wanted to know, but Kambia was too sick for them to spend time on silly questions. They let me and Tia hop in the back of the ambulance with Kambia, then they closed the door, and before I knew it we were speeding off down the street with flashing red lights and an ear-splitting siren.

Kambia stayed unconscious all the way to the hospital. She didn't respond even once when me and Tia called her name, or when the ambulance people shone funny penlight-type instruments in her eyes.

When we got to the hospital, the men unloaded Kambia and rushed her through a set of double doors. They stopped long enough to say something to a pair of plump nurses in crisp pink uniforms, then the whole group disappeared through another set of double doors down a long corridor of linoleum triangles.

Not knowing what else to do, Tia and I flopped down in a couple of worn-looking velvet seats next to the second set of doors. I started rubbing the tears out of my eyes with the back of my hand. Standing across from us, a smart-looking redhead wearing a classy business suit and carrying a leather briefcase did the same. I guessed she was crying over her own loved one. After a few moments she got up from the velvet chair and started pacing in her high-heeled pumps. I folded my arms across my chest and watched her moving back and forth in front of the bare hospitals walls, like a duck in a shooting gallery. As she passed an oversized potted rubber plant sitting in the center of the hall, I wondered if she honestly thought that she could walk away all of the fear.

"What's wrong with her, Tia Chia?" I asked, turning to Tia. "What's wrong with Kambia?"

"I don't know," she said. "But Grandma always says that in time of trouble you think about the best and not the worst, because the worst don't need no help at all to happen, but the best needs all the help that it can get." She reached into the pocket of her yellow skirt, pulled out a quarter, and handed it to me with bloodied hands.

"Go call Mama," she said. "I guess I done worked out all that I ever will work out in the past hour," she said. I didn't know what she meant by her words, but I got up and ran to find a phone.

While Tia found a bathroom and washed up, I called Mama and told her where I was and what had happened to Kambia. I didn't tell her about Tia. There was no way that I could bring myself to say the words over the phone. Besides, Tia was right. What was between her and Mama was between her and Mama. They had started the whole mess together. They were going to have to end it that way. All I could do was fill my mind with good thoughts and hope that some of the goodness would find a way into whatever was going to make Kambia better. So I did what Mama told me to do after the plastic dolphin died. I cleared the bad out of my head and replaced it with the good, the times that I had spent with Tia the previous week, and some of the fun times that Kambia and I had had together.

While Tia and I waited, a short nurse with a mushroom haircut and really full lips came over and asked us the same questions that the drivers had asked us; again we answered in exactly the same way. Tia only knew what I had told her, and all I knew was that the girl in the emergency room was named Kambia, and she was my friend. The nurse went away with a scowl on her face, thinking that we were lying, but we weren't. What we told her was exactly the truth. We just didn't add any more to it, and I really hoped that when Mama showed up she wouldn't either.

Mama and Grandma didn't look at all happy when they made it to the hospital an hour later. They came with worry walking all over their dark faces, and annoyance flickering in their eyes. They weren't dressed too good either. Mama wasn't wearing her blue work uniform. She had on a crumpled jean skirt and a short-sleeved T-shirt that looked like she just pulled it out of the clothes hamper. Grandma looked only slightly better. Her daisy-flowered blouse was starched and crisp, but she could have used more than a few licks of an iron on the hem of her rayon skirt.

"Shayla, what in the world is going on here?" Mama cried, walking up briskly, holding her arms out to me for a hug. "What have you got yourself into, little girl? What in the name of Jesus done happened to that child Kambia?"

I ran over to her and hugged her, burying my face in her warm breast. She bent down to say something to me, but that's when her eyes must have fallen on Tia, because she suddenly let me go, as if I had shocked her. Her hands flew up to her face. Then she let out the loudest scream that I had ever heard in my life, even louder than Kambia's screams, even louder than the screams that she and Tia had made during their first fight. It was so loud that the business lady in the tan suit stopped pacing, so loud that the nurse with the mushroom haircut came running back over to us to see what was going on.

"What's the matter? Can I get something for you?" she asked. Mama didn't say anything. She just started shaking her head real slowly like she couldn't believe what she was seeing, like her eyes were trying to fool her brain. I moved out of the way, and Tia walked up to her.

"Lord, Jesus!" Grandma Augustine cried when she saw Tia's smiling face. "Lord! Lord! Praise God! Praise Jesus!"

"It's me, Mama," Tia said. "It's me." She threw her arms around Mama and hugged her, but Mama still didn't stop shaking her head, shaking it like she thought that Tia was an impostor. Slowly, very slowly, she lowered her gaze, and you could see her brown eyes going over Tia's hair, over her face, over everything, and just remembering, like I had done with Tia. Finally, after a minute or two, she got a real satisfied look on her face and a rainbow started to appear, not the kind that shows up after a storm with all the bright colors, the kind that comes from your heart. It's just that hot-chocolate warm that you get on a cold day, the one that makes everything feel just fine on the inside. That's what showed up on Mama's face, the look that would let everybody know that the hole Tia had put in her heart had finally been plugged up. She hugged Tia real tight, rocking her from side to side in her arms, and calling her name over and over.

Mama hugged Tia longer than I'll bet that any mother has ever hugged a daughter. She held her until her arms got tired and Tia got dizzy from swaying back and forth. Then she started kissing her, over and over, on her forehead, on her cheek, everywhere on a face that a mother could kiss a daughter. I would have been embarrassed, but Tia wasn't. She just closed her eyes and let Mama shower her with all those mother hugs and kisses. She let her shower her with them, like Mama's kisses and hugs were worth gold. Then after Mama let her go, Grandma Augustine grabbed her and added some Grandma hugs and kisses to Mama's.

In just a few minutes Tia got enough hugs and kisses for a hundred Tias.

"Lord, Jesus, praise God!" Grandma Augustine said between smacks.

"Amen to that," Mama said, patting Tia's back.

After Grandma and Mama were all kissed out, they let Tia go, and the four of us just stood staring at each other, not having even the slightest idea what we were supposed to say to one another. Overcome, Mama walked over to my empty chair and sat down. She started to let the tears run out of her eyes for only the second time in her life. But these weren't pain tears, these were tears of joy, and when Tia saw them, she sat down beside her and dropped a few more of her own.

"Mama, I'm really sorry," she said between sobs.

Tia and Mama cried until the tears refused to keep coming. When they were all dried out, they both agreed that there was so much that they had to talk about, but that their talk had to wait until later. None of us wanted to do it, but we put everything else on hold but Kambia. She was the reason that we had all ended up in the same place. She was the reason that Tia had agreed to come out of hiding. Mama patted Tia on the cheek, then she and Grandma Augustine started back down the hall toward the nurses desk to see if they could find out anything. But they had only gone a couple feet up the corridor when they were cut off by a frowning, nicely built black policeman with a shaved head, smooth face, deep brown eyes like licorice gumdrops, and two huge, jagged scars on his right arm that made it look as if he had been in a fight or two. Mama and Grandma stopped dead in their tracks. The policeman walked up to them. Me and Tia ran over to see what was happening. As we did, a short, brunette female doctor with freckled skin came walking up and joined the cop.

"Are you the little girl Kambia's mother?" the doctor asked Mama with a serious voice.

"No," Mama said. "My daughter is a friend of hers. They go to school together. She lives next door to us."

"Oh," the doctor said. "I see. Do you happen to know her mother's name?" she asked. "We've been trying to get in touch with her for a while. Her little girl is very, very sick. We've had a social worker, a Miss Sayer, trying to get some information out of the little girl, but so far we've had no luck. We really need to find her mother."

"My daughter told me that that child was very ill," Mama said. She turned around and looked at me, with worry all over her face again. "Shayla, what did that girl's mama say that her full name was that time she stopped by the house? I don't quite recall."

"I don't either," Grandma said. "With the way she was acting and all. I don't remember her full name. I just remember her actions."

I shrugged my shoulders. "Me neither," I lied softly, then I lowered my head and stared at the floor.

"What did you say?" Mama asked. "Look at me, Shayla," she said. I raised my eyes up slowly.

"What did Kambia's mother tell you her name was?" she repeated. "I know you remember. You don't forget anything."

"I don't know, Mama," I lied again, and I looked at the floor again.

"Shayla," Mama said in a puzzled voice, "what's wrong with you, baby? Why you acting so peculiar?"

"I'm not," I lied once more. "I just don't remember. Is Kambia going to be all right?" I asked the doctor. "You're going to make her better again, aren't you?" She just reached out and patted me on the head, like I was a kitten or something. I wandered back to my chair and sat down.

"Shayla!" Mama yelled at me from across the hall. I didn't go back over to her. I couldn't answer her question. Kambia had asked me not to let her mother know what was going on with her, and it was a promise that I intended to keep. She had said that her mother was not her mother, and that her so-called mom would bring the wolves with her and they would hurt her some more. I didn't doubt her words. There wasn't a lot that I believed in. I still wasn't too sure about Grandma's God, life on other planets, or that when you really kissed a boy for the first time you could feel his lips on yours long after he had finished. I didn't quite believe in any of those things, but I did believe Kambia. I had already broken part of my word by getting her some help. I wouldn't break all of it. I wouldn't tell them any more about Kambia. She said that if I did, she would stop being my friend. I didn't want that to happen.

"Shayla, get back over here," Mama snapped.

I folded my arms across my chest. "I don't remember her mother's name," I repeated.

"Look, what is this all about?" Grandma Augustine asked, with fear and just a touch of anger in her voice. "If the child needs help, I'll sign any papers you got to get her some," she said. "Her mama can take it up with me later."

"Thank you, ma'am," the doctor said. "But it's not necessary. We've already set things in motion to work on the child. We don't need her mother's signature in an emergency like this."

"Then I don't understand," Mama said. "What is it that you want? What is the law doing here? What's going on with the child?"

The doctor glanced over at me, then back at them. "The policeman is just trying to get a few preliminary answers," she said cautiously. "He just needs to know who the girl is and where she goes to school, so that he can put things in motion. He can do it on his own, but it will be much easier, and take a lot less time, if he can get your daughter to help him out."

"What kind of things does he need to put in motion?" Grandma asked suspiciously. The doctor beckoned to Mama and Grandma Augustine.

"Can I talk to you ladies over here?" she said, walking a piece down the hall. "There's a situation that you need to be aware of." Mama and Grandma walked over to the lady doctor. The policeman followed. Tia came back and sat beside me.

"It'll be all right," she said. "Don't worry. It'll be just fine."

Mama and Grandma Augustine talked to the doctor and the officer for several minutes. As they talked, Mama and Grandma often threw their hands up to their faces and shook their heads while the officer scribbled down stuff on a small yellow notepad. Even though I couldn't hear their words, I knew that whatever they were rapping about couldn't be too good. I bit my lip and waited, trying real hard to keep good thoughts in my head, but terror was floating around me like fog from dry ice.

Finally, after I was sure that I couldn't hold one more nice image on my brain, Mama and Grandma came back over to us. I expected Mama to come and ask me again for Kambia's mom's name, but she didn't. She just walked over and beckoned for Tia to go for a walk with her, then the two of them went off down the hall, walking arm in arm and whispering. The businesswoman, who had been simply standing there listening to our conversations the whole time, resumed her pacing. Up and down the hallway she walked. I glanced over at the officer and the lady doctor, and tried to read their faces, until Grandma got in front of me and blocked my view.

"We need to talk, little girl," she said, lifting my chin with her hand, then she sat down beside me. Grandma reached over and grabbed my hand and started caressing it gently, running her callused palms over my smooth skin.

"Shayla," she said after a few seconds of rubbing, "do you remember what I told you about your word being who you are?"

"Yes, ma'am," I said. "You said that your word was your bond with people. You said that if people can't take you at your word, they can't count on you for anything."

"That's right," she said. "That's just what I told you. You *do* have a good memory. You remember everything real good."

"Yes, ma'am," I said.

"Now, let me tell you something else," she said, pressing down on my knuckles, as if she were trying to straighten out the bumps. "Sometimes the wrong thing to do is the right thing to do in some situations. A dinner roll ain't always a roll, sometimes all it takes is just a little cinnamon and sugar and some nuts to turn it into something entirely different."

"I'm not sure that I understand, Grandma," I said, wondering how she could be talking about food at a time like this.

"Do you remember that picture show that we watched on TV the other night?" she asked. "The one with the cop that knew how to do all that kung fu stuff with his legs."

"Yes, ma'am," I said. "That guy tried to kill him."

"That's right," she said. "That mean ole rough-looking guy with a bad attitude tried to do him in just as ugly as you please."

"I know, I know, Grandma," I snapped, growing impatient, as I usually did with one of her longer tales. "I know, I saw the whole thing. What does this have to do with anything?"

"Just let me finish," she said patiently. "Just hold on. I'll get to my point. Well, if you recall, that policeman had to kill that guy at the end of the movie instead of just arresting him, like he was supposed to. But Lord knows he really didn't want to do it. Do you remember why he did?"

"Yes," I answered. "Because the man told him that he was going to kill his whole family if he didn't. He told him that he was going to hunt him down for the rest of his life, and that he and his family would always have to be in fear. So the cop popped him. He wanted to keep his family safe."

"That's right again," Grandma said. "He did something bad, but at the time it was the right thing to do."

"What are you saying?" I asked, looking into her glossy brown eyes.

"Sometimes it's okay to change the rules, as long as they make things better and not worse. Do you understand me?"

I leaned forward in my chair, placed my chin in my hands, and thought about it. The sense of it started to rush into my head quickly, at least some of it.

"You're talking about the promise that I made to Tia," I said. "You're talking about the fact that I shoulda told Mama where she was and all."

"Yes," Grandma said. "Vera is Tia's mother. She had a right to know what was going on with her. She had a right to know that her child was alive. What you did was really wrong. You broke a bond with one person to make a bond with another. It doesn't work that way. When you do, both people lose. We all lose."

"I'm sorry," I said, realizing the truth in her words. "I didn't mean to hurt anybody."

"I know, baby," she said. "I know. Look at me, Shayla." I looked down at my lap instead. "Tia isn't the only thing that you messed up," she said softly in my ear. "You let your word get you into another mess as well."

"How so?" I asked.

"Come with me, baby," she said.

Grandma Augustine got up and hobbled over to the set of double doors that the ambulance drivers had taken Kambia through. I followed her quietly, anxious to know what was going on with Kambia, but terrified to find out. When Grandma Augustine pushed the door open, I briefly closed my eyes and hoped that when I opened them the hospital and everything would just go away, and Kambia and I would be back on the road walking to school.

When I opened my eyes, the hospital was still there and so was Kambia, or what I hoped was Kambia. I wasn't really sure. She didn't look very much like herself. She was lying underneath a flimsy ivory blanket on a narrow rectangular table in the center of a room filled with all kinds of strange, square, computer-like machines with flashing yellow lights and red buttons. Attached to each of her hands, with gauze tape, was a skinny yellow tube. The tubes traveled down the sides of her body and connected to two fat, balloonlike bags hanging on a metal post with wheels that reminded me of a huge hat rack. The bag on the left side of the pole was filled with a clear liquid that looked a lot to me like bottled water, but the other one was crimson red, and there was no doubt in my mind that it was blood. Kambia's eyes were closed real tight, and I could see no eyeballs softly fluttering beneath her lids. Her skin was still deathly white and lifeless, and I could barely make out the tiny rise and fall in her chest.

"What's wrong with her, Grandma?" I asked, afraid to go over and see for myself.

"They gave her some stuff to make her sleep," she answered. "They got to perform an operation on her."

"Why?" I asked, turning to her frantically.

She hesitated for a second, then cleared her throat. "What does she and you talk about?" she asked.

I shrugged my shoulders. "I don't know, Grandma," I lied. "Girl stuff."

"What kinda girl stuff?" she asked.

"I don't know, Grandma!" I snapped.

"Yes, you do," she said with a no-nonsense tone.

"I don't!" I snapped again. "I don't want to talk about it," I said, turning to leave. She grabbed me by the back of my dress.

"Shayla, this little friend of yours is hurt real bad," she said. "Look at me."

I turned back around.

"I know," I said. "Everybody keeps telling me that, but nobody tells me what's wrong with her. That's what I want to know, Grandma. I want to know what's wrong with her."

"You tell me," she said. "You tell me what you think is wrong with her."

"I already told you that I don't know," I said, looking over at Kambia. "I don't know anything."

"Shayla," she asked, "did Kambia ever tell you that somebody was doing something to her, hurting her?"

I didn't answer. I checked out Grandma's face. She seemed to have even more wrinkles than the new ones that I had spotted the day that we talked about death on the front porch. The small creases on her forehead and around her eyes had turned into deep trenches.

"Did she ever tell you that somebody was hurting her?" she asked again.

I shrugged my shoulders once more. "I . . . I . . . don't—"

"You do!" she said firmly. She snatched me by the arm and pulled me over to Kambia, dragging my sneakers across the linoleum with a loud *screech*.

"Look at her!" she said, even firmer. "Look at her! Baby, you got to tell what's going on with this child!"

I shook my head again and stared away from Kambia at the floor. Grandma Augustine pulled my head up.

"If you can't look at her, then you look at me," she said, staring into my eyes. "Baby, this child done put a big burden on you, one that you ain't got no business bearing alone. Now, you know that you can tell me anything. I would never do anything to hurt you. You're my baby. Grandma would never make you do anything bad. Just tell me what she told you. Honey, it's important that you break whatever promise that you made to this child."

My eyes slowly started to fill with tears again. In one day I had gone back on what I believed and cried more tears than any baby. Tia wasn't the only crier in the family. It looked like I was one too. I wiped my tears away with the back of my hand, letting Grandma's words play in my head, along with the ones that Kambia had said to me about her mom and about the wolves. Was Grandma Augustine right? Was it okay to break a bond or a promise if it was going to do something good for someone? But if I did break my word to Kambia and told Grandma the things that she had done and had told to me, wouldn't I be doing exactly what Grandma told me not to do, choosing one bond over another one, choosing Grandma's love and trust over Kambia's safety? Between Grandma and Kambia it should have been easy to make a choice. It was Grandma who fixed my breakfast on the mornings that Mama was too tired from work to get up. It was Grandma who caught the bus and brought my homework to school when I left it at home. How many cut fingers had she bandaged for me? How many clothes had she washed? The choice was clear, but not so clear, because Kambia was alone and hurt, and Grandma had all of us. When I looked down at Kambia, I saw someone small and frail, someone who needed me to take care of her, just like I needed Grandma to take care of me. I didn't know what was right to do. I couldn't even begin to weigh the situation out.

So I did what Kambia would have done, what I had seen her do several times. I placed myself in one of her stories. When I opened my mouth to speak again, I wasn't Shayla at all. I was one of Kambia's Story Bees about to whisper a tale in the ear of someone that I trusted. Grandma Augustine had never let me down. She wouldn't let anything that I said cause Kambia more pain.

"Okay, I'll tell you," I said softly, reaching over to stroke Kambia's arm. It felt cold and clammy. "I'll tell you everything."

"Okay," Grandma said. "Okay, that's good. You're doing the right thing. You're doing what me and your mama should have done. We let what might happen keep us from seeing what *was* happening. We never should have done that. We never should have stopped worrying about that child." She grabbed me and pulled me to her bosom. The familiar minty smell of her arthritis medicine made me feel warm and safe.

"I'm going outside, baby," said Grandma, gently patting me on the back. "You come out in a little bit. They gone be giving her a little more sleeping medicine in a while so that they can take her down to the operating room soon."

"Okay," I said. She let me go and I watched her hobble from the room for a minute, then I looked back at Kambia. When I did, I found her olive eyes staring back at me. They were bloodshot, hazy, and desperate. I reached over and started to caress her forehead.

"How do you feel?" I asked. She swallowed real hard for a second, like she had something in her mouth, then spoke.

"Don't, Shayla," she said weakly. "You promised. You told me that you wouldn't tell."

"I know I did," I said, brushing back a lock of her red blond hair. "But, Kambia, you're really messed up. We gotta tell what happened."

"No, you promised," she said, reaching up and grasping my hand. "You said that you wouldn't."

"I have to, Kambia," I said, then I leaned over and kissed her on the forehead. "You'll see, it'll be all right. My grandma is a good person. She won't let anything happen to you. I promise. You'll see, it'll be just fine." I gently took her hand off of mine and started for the door.

"You're not my friend," she called after me weakly.

"Yes, I am," I called back in a pained voice. "I'm your best friend."

I walked outside to find Grandma Augustine standing with the police officer. The officer had a frosty can of Coke in his hand, and he offered it to me as soon as he saw the pained look on my face.

"I haven't opened it yet," he said in a deep voice. "Would you like it?"

"She said that there were wolves hiding in her house," I blurted out. Both the officer and Grandma Augustine stared at me oddly, but I went on. "She said that there were wolves hiding in her walls, and that they made her do things that she didn't want to do," I said. "They did things to her down below that hurt her really bad. I saw some bruises on her once. Her thighs were all purple and red." The tears started to gush from my eyes. "She said that they told her that if she told anyone they would hurt her even worse. They told her that there was no way that she could get away from them."

"Did her mother know?" the officer asked, his face etched with concern. He handed the Coke to Grandma and took a small yellow notebook and a pen out of his shirt pocket.

"I'm not sure that she's her mom," I said as he started to scribble down my words. "She was yelling something in the street about her not really being her mother. Anyway, her name is Jasmine Joiner, and Kambia says that she knew what was going on. She told me that if her mom came to the hospital she would bring the wolves with her, and she would let them hurt her again."

"Lord Jesus," Grandma said, shaking her head. "Lord Jesus. What has my baby been holding in," she cried, reaching over to pat me on the back again.

I told the officer and Grandma everything I knew about Kambia, about the dangerous game that she had played that day on the cliff, her magic purple bracelet, the Lie Catcher, and how we had buried her underwear. I told them every single thing I could think of, everything that Kambia had trusted me enough to tell me, everything that I had promised Kambia I would keep to myself.

Then it was my time to listen. I listened while Grandma told me that it wasn't wolves that were hurting Kambia, but some of her so-called mother's so-called boyfriends. They were doing things to Kambia that people their age had no business doing to a twelve-year-old girl, making her do womanly things. During the talk Grandma Augustine used words like *raped* and *molested*. They were words that neither Grandma nor Mama had used before with me, words that they only whispered to each other when they were with a group of their female friends. Grandma said that one of Kambia's mom's boyfriends had done something especially bad to Kambia that morning. She said that Kambia was all tore up inside and that's where all the blood had come from. She said that the doctors were going to work real hard to stop it, and do everything that they could to make Kambia all better again.

After she finished telling me everything, the policeman explained to me why it was never okay to keep the kind of secret that I had kept for Kambia. "If somebody is being touched in a way that they don't like, you should always tell it to a responsible grown-up," he said. "That's the only way to make it stop." Then, before he left, he thanked me for being brave enough to tell the truth about Kambia, and he told Grandma that once Kambia got through her surgery, they would try and send her somewhere where nobody would ever hurt her again, as far away from Jasmine Joiner as they possibly could.

I watched the police officer hurrying off down the corridor in his smartly pressed uniform. It was all my fault. Maybe if I had told on Kambia earlier, someone could have taken her someplace safe before she got so hurt. But then I would have never got to really know her, and she would have never become my friend. I hoped that she still would be after this.

"Let's pray," Grandma whispered to me softly. "Prayer is the greatest healer. When there ain't nothing else, there's Jesus. He can take care of all of your physical and internal wounds."

I wasn't sure that I believed Grandma. I wasn't sure that Jesus should have allowed us all to get such terrible wounds in the first place, but I bowed my head and tried to pray with her. I tried real hard to recite the few prayers that I knew.

Chapter 10

*T*ia is back home and back in school. It was a rocky homecoming, with neither she nor Mama wanting to let go of her end of the rope, but finally, after several bad arguments, Tia pulled Mama over to her side of the pond. Mama agreed to let her come back home as long as she could follow one rule. Mama told her what it was the other morning at breakfast. I poked my head in the doorway to listen.

"Tia, like I told you before," Mama said, putting grape jam on her extra-crispy toast with a plastic knife. A huge glob of the purple spread slid off the bread and landed in the middle of her plate. She scooped it up carefully and reapplied it. "Like I told you, you my baby, a part of my own flesh, but I can't have no women-children in this house. Now, I can respect you, but you have to respect me as well. I don't want you and Doo-witty bringing no sex foolishness in my home," she said with a slightly raised voice. Tia rolled her slanted eyes.

"Mama, I thought we already been over this," Tia said in a voice slightly higher than Mama's. "I'm a big girl. Why can't you see that I don't need to be breast-fed no more?"

"I can see that, child," Mama said, shaking her head slowly. "Lord knows that I can see that." Mama sighed and set the bread down. She wiped her huge hands on a paper napkin next to her plate and reached for Tia. Tia's face went all tense, and her head jerked back a little, like it always did when she thought that she had done something to make Mama smack her a good one.

But Mama just gently pushed a cluster of Tia's long braids out of her face and started to caress her cheek softly. Tia's face went all smooth again. "I know I can't turn back nothing, Tia," Mama said in a much calmer tone. "I can't make you be the daughter that I had before, the one that I thought would have waited at least a few more years before she gave everything she had to a man." She shook her head again. "Tia, I didn't want to see myself remade in you. I didn't want you to do the things that I did. I wanted you to have your own world—not mine. I never wanted you to have to live the life that I lived."

"Mama, I know how you feel," Tia said quietly, clasping her small hand on Mama's wide arm. "But I'm not you. My world is my own, Mama, I'm responsible for what I do. If I mess up, it will be on me. It won't be your fault."

"It will. Baby, everything that you will ever do will have to do with me," Mama said. Her dark eyes looked deep and hard into Tia's, as if they could cut clean through Tia's eyeballs. It was yet another look that Grandma would have been proud of. It even made me shudder a bit. I placed my back against the door frame and waited to see what would come next. "Tia, we already talked about some things, and I know you know what I mean. I found them rubbers in your drawer. I know that you at least trying to be careful, and that's good. I don't want or need no babies in my house, Miss Tia. Now, I'm firm on that. You way too young for that kind of nonsense. Baby, I'm not gone let you mess up your life. I'm not gone let you lose everything."

"I won't. I'm not, Mama. I'm always extra careful. I been to the doctor and everything." She reached across the table and snatched a big, juicy orange out of the glass fruit bowl. She began peeling it with her slender fingers, dropping the peels in the center of our checkered tablecloth. "I know what I'm doing, Mama. Everything is fine with me and Doo-witty. We both make sure that everything is all right. I really do know how to take care of myself," she said.

"I'm not sure you do," Mama said, letting go of Tia's face and turning back to her toast. "I'm not sure that you do. But that Doo-witty does seem like a pretty good guy, I have to admit. I really did judge him wrong." She took a bite of her toast, chewed it, and swallowed quickly. "I don't know. I guess it ain't no sense in pulling those weeds again. It ain't much more to say on the subject. I was wrong about that young man." She cleared her throat. "The point is, there are some things that I just won't allow in my house. If you and Doo-witty are grown enough to do what you doing, you grown enough to make sure that you don't do it under my roof. I won't have that over Shayla," she said, pointing at me in the doorway.

"It's okay, Mama," I said softly.

"No, it's not," she said. "I'm sorry, baby, but you don't know what you talking about." She then pointed her finger at Tia. "I won't have no more crap being thrown your sister's way. She done had too much of sex mess in her life already, with that child Kambia and her mama. I won't have any more of that kind of stuff put on her. It's my only rule. I won't stick my nose into what you do outside, but I'm the only woman in my house. You can only be a girl here. Just a girl, nothing else."

"Then that's what I'll be," Tia said, splitting her orange open. Tiny drops of juice squirted into the air. "That's what I'll be," she repeated.

After Mama and Tia finished their talk, Tia told me that she didn't too much care for Mama's rule. Mama still wasn't treating her that much different from the day that she left. She had heard that same rule on that day as well, Mama just hadn't explained her reasons for it, but it was okay. She could hang out with Doo-witty in other places. Besides, it had been hard as rock candy to get Mama even to see that there was something about Doo-witty that she could love. It had taken two very special things to convince Mama of that.

One of the very special things, of course, was Doo-witty's paintings. The first day of their arguments Tia took Mama and Grandma Augustine over to the church to see them. Tia said that when she showed them the first painting in the main sanctuary, they didn't even believe her when she told them that Doo-witty had done it, even after she showed them his name scribbled at the bottom of it. Neither one of them wanted to admit to what they were seeing. Grandma Augustine told her that the signature was so small that she could barely make it out, and Mama told her that she had probably done it herself. It made Tia so mad that she could have spit hot sauce, but she continued on up the stairs and showed them the ceiling painting of her.

"Look, y'all," she said, pointing up at the ceiling. "Doo-witty did this one, too. Look, it's me."

"Glory be, that's my grandbaby!" Grandma yelled when she saw it, throwing her hands up in the air. "Glory be! Glory be!" She turned and grinned at Tia. "They say the Lord give everybody something unique, a special gift," she said. "But who would have known that Doo-witty's would have been this big." She shook her head. "The Lord sho do work in strange ways," she said. "He sho do work in strange ways. Don't he, Vera?" she asked Mama. "Vera, don't the Lord work in mysterious ways?"

Tia said that Mama nodded, but she was too overcome to say anything herself. She just stood there staring up at the painting with her mouth open so wide a cat could have crawled in it. She couldn't deny it anymore. Like Grandma, she knew that only somebody who cared about Tia as much as we did could have captured all that she was and put it up for the whole world to see.

"Vera, ain't it wonderful?" Grandma kept asking her over and over, but Mama just downright couldn't respond. In fact, Mama didn't say anything at all the whole time that she was there, because the minute it looked like she had finally found her words, Sister Ashada and Doo-witty came in with the second thing that convinced Mama.

"Daughter, I have something very special to tell you," Sister Ashada said as Doo-witty ran over to Tia. He grabbed her and gave her a really big hug. Tia squealed with delight.

"I've got some very good news," Sister Ashada said to Tia. "Dwight has done something great."

"What is it?" Tia asked excitedly.

"What is it?" Grandma chimed in.

"I . . . I got . . . got in," Doo-witty said. "T-T-Tia, I got into a college."

"What? What are you talking about?" Tia asked. She said that for a moment she thought that Sister Ashada and Doo-witty were just playing with her head, but when she saw the happiness dancing in Doo-witty's eyes, she knew that they were telling the truth.

"Something really good, daughter," Sister Ashada answered. "The college that I teach religious courses at has agreed to let Dwight in as an art student."

"Oh, my God!" Tia squealed, throwing her arms around Doo-witty. "I can't believe it. Doo-witty I'm so proud of you."

"So am I," Sister Ashada said, grinning. "I told them all about him and showed them his work. They were really impressed. They know that he will need a lot of help with his studies, and adjusting to campus life, but they think that he has a great talent, so they are willing to work hard with him, as long as he will work hard with them."

"Oh, he will. I know he will," Tia squealed. Doo-witty nodded.

"Lord, Lord! What a world. What a world," Grandma cried.

"There's more," Sister Ashada said. "It's a small private college, and they don't have much funding, but they have agreed to pay for Dwight's entire schooling if he will create a couple of murals for them as well."

"Glory be!" Grandma cried. "Glory be!"

"I-I'm going to . . . to college, Tia," Doo-witty said. "I-I'm going to a real school, just like my . . . my mama wanted."

When he said that, Tia said that she kissed Doo-witty right then and there on the lips in front of Mama, and then Grandma Augustine walked over and kissed him on the cheek as well.

"I was wrong about you," she said. "Lord knows I sure did make a mistake. Ain't that right, Vera?" she said to Mama. "You and me made one big mistake. Vera, say something!" she pleaded, but Mama still couldn't get nothing out. She was too outdone even to utter a tiny sentence, so she just came back to the house and tried to make up her mind about Tia and Doo-witty's relationship, figuring in all the new stuff that she had just heard and seen. She chewed on it for several days until she finally came up with her "one rule" answer. It was more like a twig than an olive branch, to Tia. But to Mama it was an entire tree. Mama went all out to make things right. She even went with Tia and Doo-witty the day that Doo-witty showed Frog his paintings and told her about being accepted to college. She wanted Frog to know that she wasn't going to fight Tia and Doo-witty's relationship anymore, and that she was really sorry that she had misjudged her son.

"Oh, my baby, my baby!" Mama said Frog had screamed when

she saw the paintings. "I knew that there was something special about my baby!" she yelled at Mama, hugging Doo-witty to her huge breasts. "I knew that God had blessed my child. I could always see it right in my baby's face. I could see it even when nobody else could."

"That's true," Mama said to her. "None of us saw what you saw, except my daughter. I'm really proud of her. I'm glad she had too much sense to treat Doo-witty like a fool. Look, Miss Earlene," she said, while putting her arms around Tia's waist, "I already told Tia that I don't like her going out with someone so much older than she is."

"I understand what you mean," Frog said, still clutching Doo-witty.

"I figured you did," Mama said. "Anyway, the way I see it, Doo-witty ain't so bad. He's a good man, and he's good to her. I trust him with her. He took good care of her when *she* was refusing to come home."

"He told me that," Frog said. "He told me everything."

"I guessed he would," Mama said.

"So did I," Tia said. "He doesn't like keeping anything from you."

"Look, Miss Earlene," Mama continued, hugging Tia to her side, "I can't make this young lady be a girl again, and I'm sure not ready for her to be a woman. It's not what I want at all. But I told her that I would leave her alone when it comes to her relationship with your son, and that I would try and let her mistakes be her own. I just hope that you can do the same with Doo-witty."

"I'll do the same, Ms. Dubois," Frog said, finally letting go of Doo-witty. "I'll let Doo-witty find his own way. He done proved himself to me a hundred times over!" she yelled, grabbing him again and kissing him all over the face. "He done proved that I really did see all the things that y'all said I couldn't see."

"That's true," Mama said, smiling at Doo-witty. "This whole neighborhood couldn't see when it came to your son."

When Mama said that the neighborhood couldn't see, she was really telling the truth. Everybody is pure dumbstruck over Doo-witty. The news has been swarming through the Bottom like mosquitoes, pricking everyone with awe and confusion. Who would have thought, dumb ole Doo-witty, not really that dumb at all? Who would have believed it? The men down at Austin's Car Wash, where Doo-witty used to work, certainly couldn't. "Who knew that Doo-witty had enough talent in him to fill up the bayou?" they said when they heard the news, their chocolate brown hands drenched in foamy soap suds, their kinky hair covered up with dirty head scarves. "Imagine that," they said, wringing out their filthy wash rags. "Imagine that."

"You ain't got to imagine it," Frog yells at them each afternoon as she passes by on her way to Lulu's Bakery for her regular slice of three-layer coconut cake. "The paintings is right up there in the church. Didn't I say that my baby was something special? Didn't I say that he could do most anything if somebody ever gave him a chance?"

"You right!" the men yell back. "We thought that boy was a fool, now we done found out he a king."

"You ain't said nothing but the truth," Frog says to them. "Y'all ought to be ashamed of making fun of my boy. Everybody ought to be ashamed of making my boy feel like a dunce."

Grandma Augustine and Mama are none too happy about the way that Frog has been treating people after they apologize. She returns each "I'm sorry" with an "I told you so." They think that she should be a bit more humble. They say that she should forget about the past and just be happy that all of her hopes for Doo-witty have come true. "But sometimes you get what you get," Mama says. "You have to take the bad with the good." The good is the people admitting that they were wrong and apologizing to Frog. The bad is her making them feel sorry that they did it.

"That's just the way it is sometimes," Grandma says. "Sometimes you ask for a brisket and you get just as much fat as you do meat, but you don't just throw the whole thing away. You trim off the bad and keep the good. It's better than nothing at all. You take what you can out of a situation."

I kept Grandma's and Mama's words in my head when I went to see Kambia at the hospital this afternoon. "Sometimes you get what you get. You take what you can out of a situation. You have to take the bad with the good."

In Kambia's case those sayings couldn't be truer. Kambia's situation has certainly been both good and bad, and she's lucky to get what she got.

The bad part of Kambia's situation is the fact that the police still haven't been able to track down the lady that was pretending to be her mother. The woman who called herself Jasmine Joiner disappeared the day Kambia got really sick.

"She could be anywhere," a really friendly police lady with a long, blond ponytail and really full lips told me and Grandma when we went down to ask about Kambia's case. "It's pretty clear that the woman who she was living with had some idea what had happened with the little girl the day she was taken to the hospital, and took off. Maybe somebody who witnessed the ambulance clued her in, or maybe she just got a bad feeling. At any rate, it looks like she might be gone for good."

"What can you do then?" both me and Grandma asked. "How can you help Kambia?"

"I don't know," she said. "Without a real birth certificate or some kind of record on the child it's anybody's guess who she might be. We can place her picture in the papers or on TV, but that will just bring around a lot of reporters. They'll ask her tons of personal questions and probably scare her even more, and neither Child Welfare nor us wants that," she said. She clasped her hands over mine and looked at me intensely. "Both the other officer who handled this case and Kambia's social worker told me that you are closer to her than anyone else," she said. "She trusts you. You're going to have to try to get her to tell you as much about herself as she can. Her social worker and I have talked, and we both think that this is the best way to go. You have to get her to understand that the best way for us to help her is for her to tell us where she came from."

"You can do that, can't you, baby?" Grandma asked me.

"I don't know, Grandma," I said, shrugging my shoulders. "It sounds like a good idea, but Kambia doesn't like to talk much about stuff like that. I don't know if I can get her to tell me anything."

"You just give it your best, baby," Grandma said. "Ain't nobody asking for any more."

"Okay, Grandma, I'll see what I can find out," I said.

I went to see Kambia right after school on Tuesday, like I had done each day since she had gone to the hospital, the same way that I went to see Tia when she was staying at the church. The first few times that I went to the hospital either Tia or Grandma went with me. But after a while Grandma's legs started to hurt too much from standing at the bus stop, and Tia wanted to spend more time with Doo-witty, so they both decided that I was old enough to make the trip alone. They said that they would visit Kambia on the weekends instead, until she gets released. I hope that will be soon, but I'm not sure.

Kambia is still pretty much hooked up to a lot of junk. She came through her operation really good, but the doctors say that she is still too skinny to leave the hospital. They say that she needs to gain a lot more weight before she can go anywhere. They are giving her vitamins, proteins, and other medicine stuff to help her get stronger.

I don't really know what to expect when I go to Kambia's room each afternoon. She's obviously still my friend, but I'm not sure if she's no longer mad at me for telling on her. She never brings it up, and sometimes she is really chatty when I go to see her. She tells me two or three stories and talks some about school. But at other times she won't say anything at all. She just lies there, staring up at the small television on the wall stand across from her bed, watching reruns of *I Love Lucy*, but she doesn't laugh at the jokes or anything, and she just blinks her eyes real hard when the commercials come on, as if she knows that the show isn't on anymore and doesn't really care. Once I tried waving my hands in front of the screen to see if she would yell at me to move, but all she did was roll over in her bed and face the wall.

Kambia's room was empty when I opened the door. A short male nurse told me that she was down the hall in the children's playroom looking at some old copies of *Highlights* magazine, so I hurried down there.

I expected to find several sickly-looking kids with clear, liquid-filled IV bags, like those attached to Kambia's hands, playing games on the large circular table in the center of the floor. It's where most of the kids who are well enough spend their time each afternoon, playing with colorful oversized puzzles, Play-Doh, coloring books, or LEGOs. They spend at least an hour each afternoon and morning sharing toys, talking about their favorite TV shows, and making friends with other kids who are going through some of the same things that they are going through.

But I didn't find any kids when I walked into the pine-scented room. All I saw was Kambia sitting in a wheelchair by a huge glass mirror. She was dressed in the blue terry-cloth robe that Grandma had bought her and given to her the last time she came for a visit, and her hair was braided into neat spaghetti-string braids that Tia had done this past Sunday morning before Grandma dragged both of us off to church.

I hurried over to Kambia, past a friendly-looking, cinnamon-haired nurse whose Grandma-like figure reminded me of the talking syrup bottle on the Mrs. Butterworth's commercials. As I tiptoed across the plush brown carpet she smiled at me, then continued picking up handfuls of discarded toys and placing them in a huge red plastic toy chest with the words CHILDREN'S WARD printed on the side in bold yellow, graffiti-like letters that looked as if they had been spray-painted on by one of the kids. I walked over to Kambia and stood behind her chair. It was good to see her out of her room. I guess she was feeling better than I'd thought.

"Ten," I said, looking over her shoulder at a find-the-missing-objects puzzle in her *Highlights* magazine. "There are ten birds," I said, counting the tiny heads of a flock of blackbirds sticking out of the branches of a big orange tree overflowing with tangy-looking oranges.

"No, twelve," she said, tapping a patch of dense green grass at the bottom of the paper. "There are twelve. There's two hiding in here."

I looked down and spotted the birds' yellow beaks sticking out between the blades of grass. "Oh, yeah," I said. "Twelve."

She hunched her shoulders and tossed the magazine on the windowsill. "It's for little kids," she said. "They didn't have any other kind, so I picked it up. I used to read it when I was little."

"Me, too," I said. "My school's library used to carry it." I sat down on the carpet beside her wheelchair. She reached down and tugged the ends of my short, freshly greased hair.

"Your hair is growing," she said. "Pretty soon you're gonna have real long braids just like your sister, Tia."

"Nah," I said. "It may grow an inch or two, but it'll never look like Tia's. Her hair is super-long."

"You never know," she said.

"You never know," I repeated.

I folded my hands in my lap and tried to think of good ways to get Kambia to spill the beans that the police wanted to know, ways that she wouldn't catch on to too quickly, but deep down I knew that there weren't any. Kambia was sharp as a porcupine quill when it came to word games and stories. It would only take her a second or two to figure out what I was doing. So I just unfolded my hands again, dove right in, and started to ask her personal questions.

"Do you have any sisters?" I blurted out.

"Yes," she said quickly. "You."

"No," I said, blushing a little. "I mean a real sister."

"What's a real sister?" she asked, focusing her green eyes on me. They were bright and lively again, totally free of sickness and fear.

"A real sister is, you know, somebody that you were born with."

"I wasn't born with anybody, Shayla," she said. "There was just me."

"That's not what I meant," I said, rubbing my hands over my

plump thighs, which were sticking out from my paisley shorts like two fat loaves of pumpernickel bread. "I meant somebody that is in your family."

"I don't have a family, Shayla," she said. "Except you. You're my family."

I sighed again, not wanting to hurt her feelings.

What Kambia said was true. She was like family to me, and I was glad that she had finally realized it. But Grandma Augustine says that *true* family is made from blood; you can have different daddies like me and Tia, but you still have to have blood. Kambia wasn't my blood.

"That's right. I am your family, Kambia," I said. "But it's just because we care about each other a lot. That's why we're a family, but it's not like a real one. The people that you live with, and look like, are your family. Family is blood. Do you know what I mean?"

She shrugged her shoulders again. "A nurse told me that when I was in the operating room they had to give me somebody else's blood," she said. "She told me that to make me all better they had to give me some nice lady's blood that had the same type of blood as me. Now she and I have the same blood. Does that make me and her family?"

"I don't . . . I'm . . . I'm not sure," I said, caught up in my own word web. "I guess not." Confused, I looked around for something else to do. I spotted a collage of pictures lying on the edge of the table and hurried over and picked it up. I brought it back and sat down beside her.

The collage was made up of several photos from a teen magazine. There were photos of pretty blond and brunette girls, with pimple-free skin and milky white teeth, glued together to form a huge circle in the center of a piece of hard cardboard. I ran my fingers over the slick magazine material.

"It's neat, isn't it?" I asked Kambia. She leaned over to take a peek.

"Shayla," she said, after she had looked it over a bit, "I bet you don't know who took the first photographs."

"Yes, I do," I said defensively. "Some guy in 1836 or something, I think. I saw a special on it."

"No, he was the second person," she said. "There was somebody before him. In fact, there were lots of folks before him."

"Who?" I asked.

"They were called the Grape People."

"What?" I said, giggling.

"That's right," she said. "They were called the Grape People because they had huge, round heads and they lived deep in a valley in a tiny, tiny village where nothing grew all year long but grapes. Red grapes, green grapes, purple grapes—that's all there was, was grapes. The people ate them for breakfast, dinner, lunch, and even midnight snacks, because that's all they had to eat."

"Man," I said. "I think I would have had to skip a few meals." She rolled her eyes at me.

"Anyway," she said, "there was something very odd about the people. Their memory didn't work too good. They couldn't remember anything from one day to the next. They would forget what the grapevines looked like, what the huge trucks that carried the grapes to market looked like, each other's faces, everything."

"They only had what our biology teacher calls 'short-term memory,'" I blurted again. "They could have used some of your Memory Beetles."

"I guess so," she said. "Only there wasn't any beetles around, because there was nothing in the village for them to eat. Memory Beetles can't just live on memories. They have to have other things, too, you know, real food. But they simply can't stand grapes."

"How come?" I asked.

"The skin gets stuck to the roof of their mouths."

"Oh, Tia doesn't like the skin either. In fact, she doesn't like grapes at all. She's allergic to them," I said.

"Well, since the people couldn't remember things too good, they had to come up with a way to tell what stuff was from day to day."

"So they invented photographs," I said.

"And cameras, too. Each day, bright and early, the people would get up and take as many pictures as they could of all that they saw—birds, cars, dogs, cats, the sun, whatever they wanted to remember. They would put the pictures on the mantel over their fireplace each night, and the next morning when they went outside, they would take them with them and say, 'Oh, I remember that,' or, 'I know what that is.'"

"It was a pretty good idea," I said.

"Not really," she said. "Because even though the Grape People could remember what things looked like with the pictures, they couldn't remember what they were called."

"Why didn't they just write the names on the bottom of the pictures?" I asked.

"They didn't know how to spell," she said. "They could say names, but they couldn't spell them. So there was no way to write them down."

"So what did they do?" I asked, leaning in close to hear the answer.

"They called the things that they saw something different each time they saw 'em. For instance, one day the sky would be a great, big blue ocean, another day it would be a group of angry gray monsters, and still another day, especially in the evening, it might be fat ladies in tangerine dresses. It was always something different to the people. But in real life it never changed. It didn't matter what name the people called it by—because of the way it looked the day that they saw it, or because of something new that they learned about it—it was still just the sky. Day after day after day after day. It was still just the same ole sky, the one that greeted them each morning when they stepped outside."

"Oh, that's really interesting," I said, imagining all of the names that I could call the sky—maybe a bowl of blue Jell-O on nice days, or a big jar of orange marmalade on even nicer evenings, right before the sun went down. I took a pencil out of my shorts pocket and started to write the names down in the empty spaces surrounding the collage.

"Shayla," Kambia said, watching me scribble, "I'm glad you made the wolves go away. I hope they never come back." I dropped the pencil and looked at her. Her face was happy and sincere.

"They won't," I said. "They'll never hurt you again. They went away for good with your mom. They won't ever come back to hurt you. The police will make sure that they stay away." I remembered the questions I was supposed to be asking. "Kambia—," I said, reaching over to pat her hand, but just as I did, the frizzy-haired nurse came walking over.

"Kambia, it's time to go back," she said. "You have to get a shower, and the doctor is going to come and take a look at you." She smiled at me again. "She'll be busy for about forty minutes or so. You can come down to her room and see her after that."

"Yes, ma'am," I answered politely. "I'll see ya in a bit," I added, waving good-bye to Kambia.

I watched the nurse wheel Kambia out of the doorway, then I turned back to scribbling down names for the sky. I thought of what Kambia had said about it and the Grape People. It didn't matter what they called it, it was still just the sky. Even though the people saw something new in it each morning, it wasn't new at all. I stopped scribbling and began tapping on the cardboard with the pencil. What was Kambia saying to me this time? There was always something hidden away in her stories. She never, ever told me a tale that didn't have some meaning to it.

"Different, but really the same." I started to write this phrase over and over on the cardboard. Suddenly it struck me—it was clear as springwater. It didn't matter. It really didn't matter at all, about Kambia, that is. Nothing about her mattered. It didn't make any difference if I found out that Kambia wasn't really her name, that she had a sister or two, that she had a mother and father who owned a pet shop in a big mall in another city, or that she liked to read the end of her Linda James mystery stories before the beginning—she would still be Kambia. Nothing could change that. She would still be the same red-haired little girl that I met that day on the street, the one that I kept secrets for, shared stories with, and hung out with at school. I could learn all kinds of new things about her, for the police or the Child Welfare people or whoever, but she would still just be Kambia, my friend, my sister but with different blood.

I started scribbling down names again. When I went to see Kambia, I wouldn't ask her any more about herself. I would let all those other people find out about her the best way that they could. I already knew what I needed to know. She was my friend. As far as I was concerned there was no more to know. Maybe they would never find out who she really was, but I already knew.

After Kambia took her shower and got her checkup, I went down to her room and we chatted some about Tia and school. After that, I watched *Lucy* with her, and started saying my good-byes for the day. But before I could get the farewells out, Kambia's social worker, Miss Sayer, a petite, smart woman with a pleasant personality, showed up in a bland beige suit that made her peaches-and-cream complexion look more cream than peaches. She also wore a serious look that would have put one of Grandma Augustine's severe faces to shame. I thought that she was going to call me outside and ask me what I had learned, but looks can fool you. She only wanted to give Kambia some good news.

"Hello, Kambia," she said, walking briskly into the room. "The nurses tell me that you've been up and about most of the day. I trust that means you are feeling much better."

Kambia nodded, but she didn't look up. "I feel okay, I guess," she said. "One of the nurses took me down to the playroom."

"That's good," Miss Sayer said. "I'm sure that you're tired of being in this room."

"It's okay when Shayla is around," Kambia said. "She's my best friend."

"I know she is," Miss Sayer said, smiling at me. "She's always coming to play with you. Hello, Shayla," she said.

"Hello, ma'am," I said.

Miss Sayer walked over to Kambia's bedside, where I was sitting, and I got up so that she could take my place on the crisp blue sheets. She eased down on the bed gently and took Kambia's free hand.

"Kambia," she said. "Remember that I told you that you couldn't go back to your old place?"

Kambia shrugged her shoulders. "I remember," she said.

"Well, I have something nice to tell you about the new place where you're going to live. A really fine couple have agreed to take you in."

"Who?" I asked, but Kambia just kept pushing the buttons on the remote control, like it was actually Miss Sayer that she was trying to turn off, even though she had told me once or twice that she really liked her.

"They're an older couple," Miss Sayer said, turning to me, then she looked back at Kambia.

"They're an older couple," she repeated. "They absolutely love children, but their children have all grown up."

"Oh, really," I said, with just a bit of disappointment in my voice. I couldn't imagine folks like that having much time for Kambia.

"It's all right," Miss Sayer said quickly, rubbing Kambia's hand. "I've met them. They are extremely friendly, patient, and kind. Kambia, I told them all about you," she said. "I told them why you are in the hospital, and about your old home—and, honey, they really want you to come and stay," she said in a soothing voice that hardly seemed that it could come out of such a serious face. It was warm and earnest. I immediately felt relieved.

"Kambia, you'll like them," she continued. "The mother is a retired schoolteacher, and the father has worked as a manager at a movie theater for nearly thirty years. And you know what else? They live only a few blocks from here, so you'll still be able to see your friend."

"Where do they live?" I blurted out.

"On Pear," she said.

"I know where that's at!" I yelled. "It's down by the old Negro Union tracks. Kambia, we really can still be together!" I said.

"Isn't it nice?" Miss Sayer said to Kambia. "You and your friend can still have fun." She looked at me again. "I wanted to make sure of that," she said.

"Thank you! Thank you, ma'am!" I squealed. I was truly excited. Kambia being too far away for me to visit was the one thing that I worried about the most; now the worry was over. Kambia would be just down the road. It was great news, the best we could have got, but Kambia didn't seem to feel the same way.

"Shayla, I don't feel so good," she said to me. "I'm really, really tired. I want to get some sleep."

"Oh, Kambia, you're not really that tired, are you?" Miss Sayer asked with a nervous giggle. "Your new family is waiting outside," she said. "I was hoping that you could meet them this afternoon."

"I'm very, very tired," Kambia whined. "I just want to sleep."

Miss Sayer looked at me and sighed. Confused, I shrugged my shoulders.

"Okay, perhaps another day, then," she said to Kambia in a voice that sounded as if she had just got rotten fruit thrown at her. She let go of Kambia's hand and touched Kambia's cheek lightly, then she walked toward the door, but I stopped her before she could go out.

"She's just a little tired," I said, speaking for Kambia. "Just come back in a little while. I'm sure she'll want to meet them then."

Miss Sayer walked over and patted me on the head. "You're a really good friend to her. Kambia, I'll be back in a bit," she said, and went through the door. I walked over and sat back down on the hospital bed beside Kambia.

"What's wrong, Kambia?" I asked. "Don't you think that this is great news? Isn't it wonderful? They found a nice home for you with really good people."

She shrugged her shoulders and leaned over and placed the black remote next to a clear plastic water pitcher sitting on a small nightstand next to the bed. "You're really good people," she said, yanking a pale green blanket up to her chest.

"I know," I said, "but so are they, and they live real close. We can see each other every day. I bet we'll even be able to go to school together. I'm sure that you'll be in the same school zone."

"It won't be the same," she said. She pushed a red button in the center of one of the iron bed rails. The bed made a whirring noise and slowly pulled itself forward until she was sitting straight up. "You won't be next door. You're my family, Shayla. I want to be with you," she said, teary eyed.

"You will be," I said. "I'll be over all of the time. Besides, don't you want a good family?"

"How do I know that they're good?" she asked. "How do I know that the wolves won't be hiding in their house, too?"

I sighed and looked at her face. It was scrunched up something fierce. Worry and fear were crawling all over each other, like lobsters in a tank.

"They won't," I said, taking her hands in mine. "The wolves will never hurt you again. You'll be safe there."

"How do you know?" she asked, staring deeply into my eyes.

"Because out of all the little girls in the world, they chose you," I said with a big grin. "They knew that you were someone special they could love, someone that they wanted to keep safe forever and ever."

"Really?" she asked.

"Really."

Her face softened again, her mouth turned up into a smile.

What I had said to her was the corniest thing I had ever said to anyone. It was a line that I had heard on TV a few months back, in one of those sappy family-type specials. At the time I had laughed out loud when I heard it, but it didn't seem so funny now. I felt with all my heart and soul that Kambia was going to a good home, and that the people who had chosen her truly believed that she could bring something special to their life. They had agreed to take her in, knowing how messed up she was; not many folks would do that for a girl Kambia's age. Not many folks would be willing take a child like her in.

No, there would be no more hurt coming Kambia's way. I was sure of it. I would make sure of it. I really did intend to stick my head in her door every chance that I got. Her wolves *would* be trapped and put to sleep forever.

"Okay," she said. "Okay, Shayla, I know that everything will be fine if you're around."

"It will," I said. "Nothing will ever hurt you again."

"Will you be with me the day that I get out of the hospital?" she asked.

"I'll be with you on that day and every day after that," I said.

"I know you will, Shayla. I know you will. I'm real, real glad that you're my friend."

"Me, too," I said. "I'm real glad too."

I waited at the hospital until Miss Sayer came back with Kambia's new parents. They were just as she described them, elderly and patient. They were really neat. They brought Kambia all sorts of presents—three pretty brown-skinned dolls with frilly lace dresses, a tape player and tapes, some nice new clothes to wear home from the hospital, and a hand-carved wooden music box that played "Mary Had a Little Lamb" when you opened the top. I thought that some of the gifts were a bit babyish, but Kambia loved them all. She beamed when the presents were given to her, and did something that I would never have expected her to do. She hugged both of her new parents, and they hugged her back, deep and hard, as if she really were that special girl that they had been looking for.

Then they all started to talk, all three of them. Kambia actually pulled herself away from her stories and talked to them in plain talk, about me, about school, about a fat gray squirrel that had been running up and down a large oak tree outside of her window for the past two days, about her favorite Linda James mystery novel, everything—and they listened. With eyes filled with love and amusement they listened to Kambia's voice, to a voice that I know had been stolen from Kambia, like everything else, long before I met her that crazy day on my way to school. It was a tiny little bunny hop, her talking normally, just a small little jump, the first of many that she would need to leap from her story world into the real one.

I left the hospital feeling like sweet watermelon on the inside. The only thing that could have made me feel better was bags of blueberry muffins falling from the sky. Kambia would be safe, and just down the road. A mist of happiness was covering the whole world.

When I got home, I stopped long enough to pick a few late-blooming roses from the bush where Tia's bra used to lie, then scurried up the steps. I was going to press the pink petals between the unused pages of my blue notebook and let them dry. After they dried, I would take them out and sprinkle them all over the front porch like I had seen Grandma Augustine do on several occasions. Rose petals, especially dried ones, sprinkled on the doorstep were supposed to keep all kinds of evils from getting back into your house after something really mean and nasty had got into it. It was a belief that Grandma Augustine got from her Great-Great-Uncle

Urzel, who owned a barbershop but liked to work a little roots on the side. I usually didn't hold too much stock in Grandma's beliefs, but things were going so well, I didn't want to mess them up.

I shoved the rose petals in my shorts pocket and ran up the steps. I unlocked the front door with my key, expecting to find Mama, Tia, and Grandma Augustine plopped down on the sofa watching *Oprah* on the small black-and-white TV, but they weren't. Mama was there, but not Tia and Grandma, and the only sound in the room was the sound of the large nail file that she was raking over her short, jagged nails.

I went over to the sofa and plopped down beside her, thinking that Mama would ask me about Kambia. She just kept raking the file back and forth over her nails, dropping bits of nail sawdust all over the skirt of her navy blue uniform.

"What's up, Mama?" I asked. She stopped filing her left hand and switched to her right.

"Your daddy is leaving, Shayla," she said. "He's packing up now, getting together what little he come here with."

"Oh," I said with my usual fake daughter voice. "Where is he going?"

"Your daddy got a new life situation," she said. "He making some changes in his life."

"What kind of changes?" I asked. "What do you mean by 'a new life situation'?"

Mama stopped filing and looked up at me. I could see the sadness in her eyes long before they met mine, but it wasn't the same kind of sadness that she had had over Tia. It was more like a realization sadness, the kind of sadness that you get when you realize that things ain't going the way that you hoped they would.

"Your father is getting married," she said.

"What?" I asked. "To who?" I couldn't believe it. Mr. Anderson Fox, the unmarriageable, getting married. It had to be a joke. "Are you serious, Mama? What's her name?"

"I don't really know her name," Mama said. "Some young, pretty gal. I heard that she ain't been here for too long. He met her down at the pool hall. They say she got a good job at some restaurant on the north side of town. She a chef or something like that. She got her own place and everything." She started filing again. "Your daddy say she got a baby on the way," she said.

"A baby," I whispered.

"A baby."

I leaned back on the sofa, feeling the burlap scratch the back of my neck. I just couldn't believe it. Mr. Anderson Fox was actually going to tie the knot with some young chick who was going to have a new baby, a new Shayla. He was going to add yet another one to the list.

Like Grandma, I knew that Mama had been fooling herself about Mr. Anderson Fox. But of all the reasons that she could have given me for his leaving, I didn't see this one coming at all. Oh, deep down I was sure that it would probably be some fine chick and not my anger that would finally get Mr. Anderson Fox packing, but I never expected a marriage, or a baby. I didn't think that even Mr. Anderson Fox could be so cruel to Mama. I shook my head. So that's what he had been trying to hook up.

When he first moved in, I had foolishly thought that it was Mama. The joke was on me. I had been fooled by Mr. Anderson Fox, just like I had been with Doo-witty. There was something buried deep in both of them that I couldn't see. In Doo-witty it was something great, his talent, but in Mr. Anderson Fox it wasn't anything good at all. Behind that slick-as-okra grin was a craftiness even bigger than I had expected.

"I'm sorry, Mama," I said.

"I know, baby," she whispered. Then she placed the file on the coffee table, picked up a bottle of clear polish, and started to smooth it over her sawed-off nails.

"I'm going to my room," I said. "I got homework to do." I got up to leave, but she caught me by the back of my shorts.

"Go say good-bye to your father," she said. "He's in the kitchen getting a few things he left in the refrigerator. You go tell him so long."

"I don't have anything to say to him," I snapped.

"Yes, you do," she said softly. "He's your father. Don't let what's between me and him come between you and him. No matter how old you get, no matter how much you don't like it, he's gone always be the other part of what brought you into this world. He's gone always be your daddy."

"So what," I snapped again, feeling Mr. Anger return to my eyes for the first time in weeks. "So the heck what."

She pulled me by the shorts back onto the sofa. "Shayla, listen to me," she said, leaning in real close to my ear. "You listen to me, child. This is only another cow sitting in the road that I got to push out of the way to get by. I don't like this very much, but I'm all right. I got you and Grandma, and my baby Tia is back home. I'll get through this. It'll cut at me a bit, but I'll be just fine." I turned around and looked at her, but she looked down at her short nails, her head bent real low over them, like she was praying for them to get longer. "You go tell your father good-bye, and try to make peace with him. It's the right thing to do, for you—and me."

I got up from the sofa slowly and walked to the kitchen, dragging my feet like a man about to be hanged. I didn't want to make peace with Mr. Anderson Fox. I didn't want to make anything with him. I just wanted what I wanted the first time that he walked in the door. I wanted him to go away and leave us in peace.

When I entered the kitchen, I found Mr. Anderson Fox bent over in the refrigerator retrieving a package of smoked turkey luncheon meat, a half jar of pickles, and a barely used jar of mayo that I was absolutely sure Mama had bought, not him. He was dressed in what looked like a brand-new black pin-striped suit, and had on a sharp-looking pair of smooth leather shoes with a shiny silver-plated half-moon on each toe.

"You gonna make a sandwich?" I asked. He quickly raised up from the fridge and placed the food into a large brown grocery bag sitting on the counter. Then he turned to me with his big toothy grin.

"Hey, baby girl," he said. "I didn't hear you come in. Whatcha doing sneaking up on your papa?"

"I didn't sneak," I said coolly, seeing no reason for my fake daughter voice. "I just walked in the door."

"Oh, yeah, yeah, you right," he said, looking a bit shaken by my tone. "I just didn't hear you. Naw, I wasn't making a sandwich. I was just getting a few things together, that's all."

"Are you going to a church picnic or something?" I asked. "You're really dressed up."

"Naw," he said, looking at me closely with his searchlight eyes. "I'm . . . I'm moving on, baby girl. I done took up too much of your mama's time and space. I gotta find some other fridge to put my milk in. So I'm packing up and pushing forward. Y'all ain't gone have me in the way no more."

"Where you going?" I asked, noticing the tiny sweat-mist on his forehead. He wiped his face with the back of his hand, his searchlight eyes moving all over me, obviously still searching for that hole in me that he was sure he could crawl through.

"Oh, uh, I got a new place, not too far from here," he said after a few seconds of searching. "It's just a bus ride away. You know, if you catch the one that goes into Second Ward, underneath that bridge by the chemical plant. I'll be on that route. It ain't too far."

"You got an apartment?"

"Yeah, it's all right. Not much, but it'll do," he said, shifting his bag of groceries from one arm to the other.

"Oh, you must have got a new job," I said. "To pay your rent and all."

"I got a little something hooked up," he answered, then he looked down at his feet, but he wasn't thinking or anything like Mama sometimes did when she looked down at hers. He was looking down at them the way I had looked down at mine the day that I didn't want to answer the questions about Kambia's mom, the way I always did when I didn't want someone to see what I was really thinking. It was a babyish thing to do, not something that you would expect from a father. I sighed, then for some strange reason looked down at my feet as well, taking in the differences between my shabby sandals and Mr. Anderson Fox's sharp loafers with the fancy silver plates.

In those plates I saw Mr. Anderson Fox's reflection. I could clearly see in the shiny metal something that I had perhaps been ignoring since the first day that I met him: shame, and just a little care. Mr. Anderson Fox actually cared some about me, about my feelings—not a lot, just enough to make him hang his head instead of telling me the truth. He was trying to protect me, trying to keep me from knowing that he had chosen another woman over Mama, and another child over me.

I don't know why, but as I looked down at those expensive shoes of his underneath his fine tailored suit, I started to feel just a bit sorry for Mr. Anderson Fox. He had no idea how to be a good father. He didn't even know how to be a good man. He was useless as wheat flour with weevils, and probably would always be. He was starting a new life, but unlike Kambia's, it wouldn't be any better than the life that he already had. There was no way that you couldn't feel just a little sorry for someone like him. God only knows why, but I plucked out some of the pins that Mr. Anderson Fox had stuck in me over the years and tossed them away. I wouldn't hurt him like he had hurt me and Mama. I would let him leave in peace. That's the only way that I would get peace for myself.

"I hope you like your new place," I murmured in my false daughter voice. "I hope that it's all that you want it to be."

He cleared his throat and looked up. "Thanks, baby girl," he said quickly, heading for the doorway. "I figure that I'll make do with it." He bent down and picked up a small tan suitcase next to the door. "Well, ain't nothing to it but to do it," he said. "I guess it's time for me to be out, turn myself loose on the world."

I nodded. He adjusted his bag in his arms and left the kitchen.

I followed Mr. Anderson Fox through the living room, past Mama, who just continued to saw at her nails quietly, out through the front door, and out onto the porch step. When we got outside, there was a brand-new green Ford with heavily tinted windows parked in front of the house. Behind those heavily tinted windows was the new Mrs. Anderson Fox, the one that would shortly give birth to yet another Shayla, male or female, I didn't know which. I just prayed that by some miracle Mr. Anderson Fox would treat her better than he had treated all of the other Shaylas before her. I wanted so badly to follow Mr. Anderson Fox down the stairs and get a good look at his new bride, but I didn't really have to. I knew what she was like, naive and hopeful. She was a younger Mama.

So instead I stared out over the neighborhood, up at the orange smoke pouring out of the concrete smokestacks of the J&R chemical plant down the street. I watched it whirl and twirl high up into the sky, toward the bright sun, until I heard the slam of a car door and the sound of the engine starting. Then I looked back at the Ford and watched it speeding off down the street, stopping once for a group of tall, limber girls in short shorts, jumping and shouting cheers in the middle of the road. After the car was out of sight, I walked back to the doorway, took the undried rose petals out of my pocket, and tossed them all over the front porch. Goodness was sprinkling down on the porch like powdered sugar, and I wanted to make sure that it was the only thing that got tracked in the house.